Nicole 'Dell
RISKY BUSINESS
Interactive Fiction for Girls

BARBOUR
PUBLISHING

Published by Barbour Publishing, Inc., P.O. Box 719, Uhrichsville, Ohio 44683, www.barbourbooks.com

Our mission is to publish and distribute inspirational products offering exceptional value and biblical encouragement to the masses.

 Member of the
Evangelical Christian
Publishers Association

Printed in the United States of America.
Bethany Press International, Bloomington, MN 55438; March 2011; D10002724

MAGNA

DEDICATION

To my grandpa, Papaw. He was the best possible
earthly example of grace and unconditional love.
"Anything for my kids." He said it. . .he meant it. . .
he lived it. I love you, Papaw. See you soon.

Chapter 1

→

CLASS-ACT
WARDROBE

"Purple and yellow polyester gym clothes? This school needs a new wardrobe!" Molly looked at the locker room mirror in disgust as she pulled her shirt off. "They're so ugly, and we have to wear them every single day."

"Plus, it's so gross that they only let us take them home once a week to wash them." Jess wrinkled her nose and pinched it with the tips of her fingers. She dropped the sweaty gym uniform into her duffel bag, careful to touch as little of it as possible.

"I know." Sara gestured over her shoulder to an unkempt girl seated on the bench down the row. "*Some* people should wash their clothes a lot more often than that."

Molly looked at the girl—her clothes way too small and her hair obviously unwashed. *She has more pimples than I have freckles. But still, why does Sara have to be mean?* Molly turned away to swipe some gloss on her lips and changed the subject. "Forget about gym clothes for a sec. What about the rest of our clothes? You know, we're in high school now. I don't know about you, but I'm having trouble finding cool stuff in my closet. Everything is so junior high." Her voice trailed off in a whine as she tied her long blond hair back in a ponytail and fluffed her bangs with her fingertips.

Sara nodded as she ran a brush through her dark, silky hair. "I kn–"

"I'm having the same—" Jess said at the same time and then laughed.

Molly zipped her bag shut. "Okay. Well, I see we're all having the same problem then. We should do something about it."

"I've been thinking. . . . We need to get jobs." Jess slammed her locker closed and spun the combination lock.

"No way anyone would hire us. We're not old enough." Sara slipped into step with Molly and Jess as they walked out into the hallway and blended in with the student traffic.

"Besides, we're not trained for anything." Molly shrugged, dismissing the issue.

Jess jumped in front of them and turned in a half circle, walking backward. "Well, I've thought of all of that, and I have solutions." She grinned and put up her hand to stop the flood of protests. "Just hear me out a sec. Okay?"

Molly closed her mouth and nodded, then winked at Sara. Jess had taken charge. Something interesting would happen whether they wanted it to or not.

Sara scowled and shook her head, then she sighed.

Jess grabbed their sleeves and pulled them to a stop. "Okay, we need new clothes, so what better place to work than a clothing store? On top of a paycheck, we'd also get a discount." She raised her eyebrows.

"Now that's a good point." Molly nodded.

"Hadn't thought of that, huh?" Jess teased. "Sure, we're not sixteen, which makes it more difficult to actually get the job. But we all get good grades and have an impeccable school record with lots of service activities and extracurricular things."

"I don't know if that's enough." Sara's eyes narrowed. "Lots of people have all that, plus they're older—some even with work experience."

"I made some calls," Jess continued, unfazed. "Here in Wisconsin, all we need in order to get a job at fifteen is a work permit. We'll need permission from our parents and a letter of recommendation from the school principal and a few teachers."

"But why would a business want to hire us?" Molly asked when Jess stopped for air. "I mean, Sara's right. They could get an older girl with more experience and a later curfew."

Jess paused at the door to her math class and turned to face the girls. "They can get someone older than us, sure. But why would they? We're not attached at the hip to a boyfriend, we have nowhere else to be, and we're highly trainable because we don't have any bad habits yet." She entered her classroom without another word.

Molly and Sara looked at each other and chuckled. They shook their heads as they walked away. They would probably be getting jobs—Jess would see to it.

"I do like the idea of a discount," Molly admitted. "More bang for the buck."

"I just hope we can work at the same place, at the same time." Sara brushed her hair out of her eyes. "I'd hate to have a job with no one I know to work with."

Molly snorted. "Oh no! I feel sorry for anyone who hires the three of us together!"

❀

"Let's make a list!" Molly jumped onto Sara's fluffy pink bed, crossed her legs, and poised her pen to write. "Where do we want to work?"

"Claire's—good jewelry." Sara touched the silver hearts dangling from her ears.

"Old Navy—great jeans," Jess added.

"What about a department store?" Molly tapped the tip of the pen on her chin. "I mean, think about it. Everything we could ever need would be in that one store."

"Yeah, but those stores are so big we might have to work in different areas."

"That's true, but a big store like that might be the only place that has three spots to fill at the same time," Jess countered.

"I've got it! Come here." Sara jumped up and scampered to her older sister's room with Molly and Jess close at her heels. She ran right to the overstuffed closet. "This." Sara pulled out a cute sweater. "These." She grabbed three great shirts and started to pile the things on the bed. "These!" Sara held up the coolest pair of jeans ever.

"I get it. Your sister has great clothes. So what?" Jess rolled her eyes.

"What do these clothes all have in common?" Sara looked from one to the other, waiting for an answer.

Molly stared at the clothes and tapped her lip with her finger. Then it hit her. "Magna." She grinned. "They're all from Magna."

"Right! That's where we need to work." Sara gave one confident nod.

Molly watched as smiles spread across their faces.

Perfect! Molly fingered the clothing. Magna, the most popular clothing store among the older girls, was the perfect place for them to get jobs. But now that they knew *where* to get jobs, they needed to figure out *how* to get jobs.

"Get out that trusty paper of yours, Molly." Jess turned on her heel and led the way back to Sara's room. "We need to plan. Let's make a list of what we need to do."

"We need to get our parents' permission— otherwise nothing else matters," Molly reminded them. "That might be a deal breaker for me."

"True. Put that at the top of the list," Sara said. "Then, we need letters of recommendation."

They brainstormed, schemed, and planned

for over two hours about how to get their dream jobs.

1. *Get a letter of permission from parents.*
2. *Get letters of recommendation from the principal and at least one teacher.*
3. *Figure out hours available to work.*
4. *Get a ride to the mall.*
5. *Pick up applications.*
6. *Fill out applications and turn in to the store manager.*
7. *Find a really cool outfit to wear to the interview.*
8. ~~*Find three other places to apply for jobs, just in case.*~~
9. *Find someone to teach us about interviewing.*
10. *Find out how much of a discount there is!*

"About number eight, I hope we're not sorry we decided not to look at other places." Molly shook her head. It couldn't be wise to limit their options so much.

"We can always make adjustments if things don't work out." Jess unfolded her long body and stretched her arms high above her head. She rolled a curl between her fingers.

"Yeah, I think we've got a good plan." Sara's

eyes brightened when the garage door opened. "In fact, I'll go talk to Mom as soon as you two are gone. A single mom of two teenage girls is never going to mind the idea of one of them getting a part-time job."

"What about you, Jess?" Molly chuckled. "Do you even have to ask your parents?"

"Of course I'll have to ask. But they won't care." Jess shrugged. "Mom and Dad don't say no to much."

"Well, I might have a problem." *No way they'll go for it.* Molly sighed. *I'll have to be very careful how I ask.* "We'll see. For now, though, we'd better go. My mom is probably waiting for us outside."

"This is a wonderful dinner, Kay. Will you please pass me the potatoes?" Molly's dad rubbed his trim stomach.

"You're awfully quiet tonight, Molly. Something wrong?" Mom peered intently at her.

Uh-oh. This isn't how I wanted to bring this up. She sat up a little straighter. "No, not at all." Molly smiled and took the bowl of potatoes to pass on to her dad. "I'm just thinking about something—nothing bad, though." *Oops. Looked like Mom wasn't buying it.*

Mom pressed a little harder. "Why don't you run whatever it is by me and your dad? I'm sure we can help."

Better tell her before she gets too worried and assumes the worst. Molly tried to sound confident. "Well, it's just that Sara, Jess, and I are thinking that we might want to get jobs. The thing is, we obviously need our parents' permission. I'm just thinking about the best way to go about getting that." She took a forkful of meat loaf and rolled it in her puddle of ketchup, hoping to look casual.

Mom pulled her head back like she'd been slapped. Her eyes open wide, she said, "Wow, this came out of nowhere. Hmm. Well, you're going to have to give us a little time to talk about this."

Molly's dad held up one finger.

Antsy, Molly poked at her food while she waited for him to finish the bite he'd just forked into his mouth.

For the next fifteen minutes he peppered her with questions about where she wanted to work, how much she wanted to work, how she'd schedule everything important in her life without letting school or church suffer, and most importantly he wanted to know why she wanted a job.

Molly squirmed. Her answer would sway their decision one way or another. She couldn't just say she wanted money for clothes. They'd never go for that. Oh, they might offer to buy her a new outfit, but that would be it. Somehow, without lying, she'd have to come up with the perfect answer.

"Well, there's more than one reason." Elbows on the dining room table, Molly ticked off the reasons on her fingers. "A job looks good on my transcripts. Working would be a really good experience for me. It will give me extra spending money for activities, clothes, and other stuff that comes up. I can help you guys with my expenses—"

"I'm not sure I'm liking the sound of this so far, Molly." Mom's worry wrinkles knit together between her brows. "Your dad and I have no problem paying for the things you need—and even a few wants every now and then. I don't know if I like the idea of you having a job now. You'll be working the rest of your life. Why start now?"

Don't sound whiny. "The thing is. . .I don't do much. I go to school and church, and I hang out with my friends. Why not hang out with my friends at a job? I have the time, and it's better to spend my time that way than to just shuffle around the mall aimlessly. . .isn't it?"

"In theory, yes." Her dad nodded. "It's not the working itself that's the problem. It's the commitment to the job and what that will require from you. Your mom and I are going to need to talk about this. We're not saying no. Just give us a chance to talk."

Molly opened her mouth to argue but had second thoughts. "Sure, Dad. Thanks for thinking about it." She stacked the dinner plates and headed off to the kitchen to wash them.

Several times she thought of ways to make her case stronger and turned to run back in to make her argument, but she refrained. Some things were better left alone.

A few hours later, Molly put her math book down and rubbed the creases from her forehead just as she heard a knock at her door. "Come on in."

The door opened, and Mom and Dad both entered her bedroom.

"Whoa. To what do I owe the pleasure of both of you coming to my room?" *Looks like it's a no.*

"Your mom and I have reached a decision, and we want to talk to you about it." Dad pulled up her desk chair and sat backward on the seat. His red tie draped over the backrest in front of him.

Mom sat down on the edge of the bed, bouncing Molly's book to the floor with a thud. No one bent to pick it up.

The suspense is killing me.

"Well, we don't really think it's going to be easy to find one, but if you're serious about wanting to—"

Molly's eyes grew wide and expectant, her heart double-timing.

"—we'll let you get a job. After all, the early bird catches the worm."

"Reeeally? Are you serious?" Molly slapped her legs and jumped off the bed. She ran to her dad and threw her arms around his neck. "Thanks, Dad!" She gave her mom a huge hug, too. "Thanks, Mom."

"Hold on, before you get too excited." Her mom's expression was very serious. "You have to agree to a few things first, Moll." *Splash!* Mom threw a bucket of cold water on the excitement.

"A few things? Like what?" Did she really want to know?

Mom looked at Molly. "Now, don't get all defensive. These are just some basics you should expect anyway." She looked at Dad as if asking him to take over.

"You're going to need to keep your grades

up. You'll have to stay as involved at church as you are now—no skipping youth group for work, and no working on Sundays at all so we can go to church together."

Molly cringed. "Youth group—I totally agree. But Sundays?" She tipped her head and stuck out her bottom lip.

"Just because you think it's boring to sit in church with us doesn't mean we're going to cave, Moll. We've had this talk before." Mom lifted her chin and crossed her arms.

Oops! Now's not the time to cause a problem. "No big deal. I didn't want to work on Sundays anyway—because of God, not church."

"God is everywhere, every moment. Sunday mornings, we're in church. Period." Dad continued after a slight pause. "You can only work two weeknights and one weekend shift. No more. And we get final approval on the type of job you get." He raised one eyebrow in a question mark and looked at Molly.

"That's it?" Molly breathed a sigh of relief. "No problem. I pretty much expected those rules anyway."

"Well, okay then." Mom smiled. "As long as we're clear on those things, you can go ahead and try to find a job somewhere like the mall, but I don't want you working at a restaurant."

She rose to leave the room, and Dad followed.

"Wish me luck," Molly called after them as they pulled the door shut. *I'm going to need it.*

Chapter 2

HELP WANTED

"Check your watches, girls. You have an hour and a half to collect applications. If you use your time wisely, you may even be able to fill them out and turn them in before I pick you up." Molly's mom inched the car up to the side of the curb in front of the main mall entrance to drop off Molly, Sara, and Jess after school on Tuesday—during the mall's slowest hours—so they could go job shopping.

"It won't take even that long, Mrs. Jacobs. We only want to apply at Magna. So we're going to go right there." Jess got out of the car first. "We should be able to fill out our applications and be back here to meet you in plenty of time."

"Really?" She looked surprised. "I hope you realize that by only applying at one place, you severely limit your chances of actually getting hired." She smiled and shook her head.

Sara and Molly climbed out of the car next, careful not to wrinkle their clothes or mess up their hair. They each took a moment to look in the side-view mirror. Jess took a quick peek at her clear complexion and no-fuss curly hairdo, and Sara smoothed her dark flyaways.

Molly tousled her straight blond bangs so they wouldn't look so blunt. One last glance— makeup was fine. All set. They turned and waved good-bye to her mom. There it was, that familiar longing. She knew what Mom was thinking: *My little girl is growing up too fast.* Molly smiled and blew her mom a kiss before she turned to catch up with the others.

Sara and Molly stalled at the makeup counter in Macy's while Jess checked out the running shoes. They wasted at least thirty minutes.

Enough's enough. Molly took control. "Okay. We're either going to do this or we're not. What are we so nervous about anyway? I mean, you guys, it's not like we're doing anything wrong. We're offering to work for them—not trying to steal clothes."

Sara and Jess nodded, their tense shoulders relaxing.

Molly looked in the mirror at the makeup counter and wiped at the edges of her lipstick. "We'll go together, walk right up to the manager, and one of us will do the talking. Ask for three applications—how hard could it be?"

"Okay, but who's going to do the talking? I don't think I can." Sara blanched.

"Oh, I'll do it if no one else will." Molly sighed. She spun toward the entrance to Magna and marched in.

Jess and Sara scrambled to catch up.

Passing the tables of folded screen-print T-shirts and hooded sweatshirts, racks of expensive jeans, and finally, toward the back, the clearance racks of shorts and flip-flops, Molly approached a woman with a scanner in her hands.

She looks important. Must be the manager. "Hi, I'm Molly Jacobs, and these are my friends Jess Stuart and Sara Thomkins. We'd like to know if you're hiring right now."

"Hi, Molly. I'm Donna." She nodded at Jess and Sara while she shook Molly's hand. "As a matter of fact, I do have some openings. I had several girls leave for college in the past couple of weeks. Let me get you girls some applications." She bent down to get the pad of applications from under the cash counter. The girls grinned at each other.

"Here you are. Just fill them out and bring them back when you can." She shook Molly's hand again and nodded at Jess and Sara.

Jess reached out her hand to shake Donna's. "Thanks so much for your time."

Sara shook Donna's hand and smiled but said nothing.

Be calm. They walked out of the store as casually as they could. As soon as they entered the mall commons and turned the corner, out of the view of Magna's front entrance, Molly turned to the other two, grabbed their forearms and squealed, her feet doing a little dance.

Jess collapsed against the brick wall that divided two stores, and Sara fanned her face as though she were hyperventilating. So relieved to have the hardest part behind them, they dissolved into nervous giggles that gave way to laughter.

The girls slumped in their bus seats for their ride home from school on Friday afternoon. "I can't believe she hasn't called yet." Molly looked out the window. Sara was glum beside her.

"I'm sure we won't get a call over the

weekend, because that's when the mall is the busiest," Jess added.

"My dad said we should call to check on our applications if we don't hear anything, so maybe we could do that on Monday." Molly stood up and held on to the seat in front of her when the bus stopped at the corner where she and Jess got off. Molly slipped on a wet step and held on to the door to avoid falling into the muddy puddle. Once she regained her footing and they were out of the way of the departing bus, they looked back to wave good-bye to Sara.

She mouthed through the rain-covered window, "Meet me online."

Molly and Jess nodded, pulled their hoods over their heads, and plodded through the cold, pouring rain. They hurried to their front doors, right across the street from each other, waved good-bye, and then disappeared into their homes. Molly stepped into her foyer and shook the rain off like a puppy. Small droplets hit the floor as she wriggled out of her hoodie.

"Hello?" The house seemed strangely quiet, like it had stood alone all day. *Where's Mom?* Molly went into their newly remodeled kitchen. On the shiny granite countertop lay a note that read: *Sorry, I forgot to mention that I had my book*

*club meeting and then a dentist appointment. I
should be home by 5, Dad by 6. I'll bring dinner. Be
good. Love you, Mom.*

Hmm. What to do? Sara's last words rang
in her head: "Meet me online." *Perfect!* Molly
foraged for a granola bar, a few cookies, and
a soda. Her mom's voice counting the carbs
echoed in her brain. She shook off the guilt,
grabbed her junk food and, to make Mom
happy, threw an apple on the pile. She scooted
the desk chair up to the idle computer in the
family room. Wiggling the mouse, she brought
the screen to life. Jess had already logged on.

Molly: *Hey Stranger! Long time, no see.*

Jess: *HA, right. Sara should be here in a few.*

PRINCESSSARA123 HAS SIGNED IN.

Molly: *Speak of the devil lol*

Jess: *Princess Sara, when are you going to
change your screen name?*

Sara: *I'm not! I've had this one for 5 yrs. It's
staying.*

Molly: *Why do I feel like we've had this
discussion before???*

Sara: *LOL*

Jess: *OK OK lol*

Molly: *Phone brb.*

Annoyed, Molly stepped away from her

computer to answer the phone on the end table next to the mahogany leather sofas. "Hello, Jacobs residence. Molly speaking." No way she'd keep saying that when she answered the phone after the job search ended.

"Hi there, Molly. It's Donna from Magna calling in reference to your job application."

Trying not to make any noise, Molly danced around for a moment. "Hi, Donna. It's great to hear from you. What can I do for you?" She glanced at the computer screen—her friends were just talking nonsense. She stepped over and grinned, her fingers poised above the keyboard. *This will get them going.*

Molly: *MAGNA*

Jess: *Huh?*

Sara: *You mean on the phone? What is she saying?*

Jess: *Is it for an interview? Ask if she's going to call us!*

Molly turned away from the screen so she wouldn't be distracted.

". . .group interview. There'll be approximately six to seven girls in that interview. It's pretty informal, just a way for me to sort through some applicants. Are you interested?"

"Oh, very much." *Woo-hoo!*

"Okay, great. Come to the store on Monday at three o'clock. I'd imagine it will take no longer than an hour. Do you have any other questions?"

Should she ask about Sara and Jess? Probably not. "I do have one question. How many positions are you looking to fill?"

"I have two openings right now. It could possibly be three, depending on hours and availability. But we'll figure all of that out later. So, I'll see you on Monday at three o'clock?"

"Definitely! Thank you so much for calling." Molly placed the phone back in its cradle and hurried back to her computer. She started typing before she even sat down.

Molly: *Interview Monday at 3.*

Jess: *No way! What about us?*

Molly: *I don't know, she didn't say. Fingers crossed.*

Sara: *That's so cool! What are you going to wear?*

Molly: *I don't know. . . . It's going to have to be good though.*

Jess: *Phone brb.*

Molly: *Wouldn't that be cool if Donna called all three of us!?*

Sara: *I'll bet that's her on the phone with Jess right now.*

Jess: *MAGNA*

Sara: *Watch, I'll be the only one who doesn't get an interview! It would be because I didn't say a word when I met Donna. What a dummy!*

Molly opened her soda and took a big drink. She drummed her fingernails on the desk and took a bite of a cookie. What was taking Jess so long?

Sara: *YAWN*

Jess: *I'm back. Interview Monday at 3. It's a group interview.*

Molly: *Oh, right. I forgot to mention that part.*

Sara: *Hang on, phone*

Molly: *Ho hum. . .waiting. . .lol*

Jess: *I know! Come on already!*

Sara: *Monday at 3 pm. . .me, too!*

Molly: *Okay. Planning to do, girls. My house tomorrow morning at ten?*

Jess: *Hey, maybe your dad can help us practice for the interview.*

Molly: *Maybe. Garage door, gotta go. Bye!*

Molly shut down the instant message program and gathered up the remains of her snack.

"Hi, Moll. I'm home."

Molly met her mom in the kitchen as she came through the garage door. Mom set her purse, keys, and a few grocery bags on the kitchen counter.

Grabbing the milk and eggs, Molly went to the refrigerator. "So, guess who called this afternoon?"

Her mom paused to think for a second. "Hmm, the president of the United States?"

"No! Way better than that, Mom."

"I'm going to guess, then, that the manager from Magna called to set up an interview." Her eyes twinkled.

"Yep! How'd you guess?"

"She actually called me this morning. She wanted to talk to me about you and your responsibility level and to find out if your dad and I were supportive of you taking on a job. She appeared to be very impressed with how you handled yourself when you first met."

"Really?" Maybe she'd get the job after all. But what if she were the only one who did? "I wonder if she called Mrs. Thomkins and Mrs. Stuart, too."

"I'm not sure. She didn't say." Mom hesitated. "Can I give you a small piece of advice, dear?" When Molly nodded, she continued. "Just be sure to be your own person in that interview. You're going there as an individual, looking to fill an individual spot on a team. If you go there as a unit of three girls who can't function without each other, she won't think you'll do well alone. Do you get what I'm saying?"

"Oh yeah, Mom. I've already thought of that." Molly stood on the tips of her toes to put the crackers up on the top shelf.

"Let me ask you this then. If you get hired, but your friends don't, will you still want the job?" She leaned back against the counter and crossed her arms across her chest.

"I think so. But it wouldn't be as fun." She shrugged one shoulder. *What if? Hmm.* "I mean, we're doing this together. But if that's what happens, I still want to do it."

"Just be sure you know what you're getting into, honey."

Palms sweating, the three girls, along with four others—obviously older than they—waited outside Donna's office for ten minutes before their meeting. Molly nervously checked her watch and chuckled when she saw three others do the same. Sliding her hands down her stylishly faded jeans, she hoped her palms would be dry when she needed to shake Donna's hand.

Molly studied the four older girls. *Could they be just as nervous as I am?*

At exactly three o'clock, the door to Donna's office opened and she stepped out with a huge smile, looking like a layered and accessorized Magna mannequin. She shook each girl's hand and called them by name.

Good memory.

Donna invited them to follow her back into a huge storeroom. Molly tipped her head all the way back so she could gaze up at the floor-to-ceiling shelves full of stacks of jeans and rows of shoeboxes. Along the sides, racks were stuffed full of shirts and dresses ready to make their debut on the sales floor.

Molly looked around in amazement at all the hard work that went into preparing the store for success. Afraid Donna would think she'd been daydreaming, Molly gathered her thoughts, took her seat with the other girls, and forced herself to pay attention.

Nervous and wanting the job more than ever, Molly flubbed the answers to several of Donna's first few questions. *Ugh.* Hopefully her sincerity made up for her dumb answers. She'd better get it together.

"What would you do if someone walked into the store, picked up a T-shirt, walked directly to you, and said, 'I want to buy this'?" Donna hugged her clipboard to her chest and looked at them expectantly.

Sara answered, "I'd ring her right up or find someone who could, if I wasn't trained to do that yet."

Jess took it a step further. "I'd offer her a fitting room."

Megan, one of the other girls, said, "I'd ask her if she had any coupons."

Donna tapped her lips with her pen and nodded along with each answer. She seemed to be waiting for something more.

Molly raised her hand about shoulder high and spoke up. "I'd say something like, 'Great choice! Come on, I'll help you find a necklace and earrings to go with that.'"

"Aha! That's what I'm looking for, girls." Donna beamed.

Finally a shining moment. Molly could hardly contain herself.

"We're a sales team here at Magna." Donna continued. "It's a fun place to be, but this company only exists because we sell to customers. Our business is built on selling complete looks, total wardrobes—not T-shirts. Does that make sense?"

Sara piped up, "But what if she only wants the T-shirt?"

"Ah." Donna pointed a finger. "See, that's the thing, Sara. Customers come into the store only wanting the T-shirt, but they leave our store grateful for the knowledgeable and helpful sales team who helped them discover what else they really needed."

After another half hour of open discussion, Donna said, "Girls, this has been a blast for me. I love eager young minds who want to learn and who are excited about this business. I hope you've gotten your questions answered. If you think of any others, feel free to call me here at the store anytime."

"Donna, if you don't mind me asking, when will you be making a decision?" Molly asked as they all stood to leave.

"Hmm, good question. I have a few more references to check and people to talk to. But I've got a pretty good idea of the direction I'm going to go." She looked at the schedule on top of the stack of papers she had in front of her. "I'll be in touch with each of you by Friday to let you know one way or another. Does that sound okay?"

"Mm-hmm." Sara nodded.

"Perfect." Jess grinned. "I'm looking forward to hearing from you."

Molly shook Donna's hand. "Sounds good, Donna. Thanks for your time and the opportunity."

Sara slapped herself on the forehead when they left the store. She put her head on Molly's shoulder as they walked along the storefronts in the mall. "I just know I totally blew it. Why couldn't I have at least shaken her hand? Not to mention my horrible answers." She shook her head and moaned. "Oh well. Nothing I can do about it now."

"You did fine!" Jess laughed. "Donna knows it was your first interview. Don't sweat it." She pointed out a cute top in a store window they were passing. "Although, Molly's got the job for sure."

"We'll see. I'm still hoping we all get offered a job."

"She'll never pick me. I can't even string two words together to make a sentence." Sara lifted her head and groaned again.

"What if only one of us gets hired?" Jess

looked from Molly to Sara.

Molly stopped walking and turned to face them. "Or none—maybe no one will get the job." *Which would be worse?*

Chapter 3

→

A RISING STAR

"Look, if Donna had wanted to hire me, she would have done so already." Molly shook her head and threw the ball across her yard. "Go get it, Rocco!"

Her Brittany spaniel sprinted across her yard, rust-colored curls waving like flags.

Molly turned to Jess and Sara, whose lifeless forms were slumped in deck chairs. "I mean, it's been ten days. She had already checked my references and even spoke to my mom before the interview. There was nothing left for her to do." She sighed. "At least with you two, she hadn't done any of that yet, which could at least explain what's taking her so long."

"Nice theory." Jess smirked. "But you can't spin the fact that she thought enough of you the first time she met you to do your reference checks even before the interview."

"And she still hasn't even called our parents." Rocco dropped the ball between Sara's feet. She picked it up and threw it.

"Well, it looks like it's not going to matter anyway. She hasn't contacted any of us." Molly lay back on the grass. "Rejection. Who knew it would sting so much?"

Jess sat up. "Maybe we should think about applying somewhere else."

"Maybe it's a sign that we shouldn't get jobs at all," Molly suggested.

The patio door slid open, and Mrs. Jacobs leaned her head out. "Molly, phone for you. Uh, you might want to come in here to take it."

Molly furrowed her eyebrows and threw the ball one more time, sending Rocco after it—a blur of fur darting across the grass—before she went to the house.

"Who is it, Mom?" Molly slid the door shut behind her.

Covering the receiver with her hand, Molly's mom whispered, "It's the manager from that store."

Molly wiped some doggy slobber on her jeans and then grabbed the phone. She took a deep breath and waited for her racing heart to calm down before answering. "Hello, this is Molly."

"Hi, Molly. It's Donna from Magna calling. I'm very pleased to be able to offer you a position with our store if you're still interested."

"I'm very interested! Thank you so much." Molly danced around and punched the air while trying to maintain her composure on the phone.

Donna skimmed the topics of hourly wage, start date, training, and a schedule. "We'll cover all of that in more detail during the training."

"That sounds great!" *What about Jess and Sara?*

"I'm really looking forward to having you start with us, Molly. Your training will begin on Monday. You'll be training alongside Amber. It's much easier to start you both at the same time. How does that sound?"

"Perfect. I can't wait." Molly grinned at her mom, who smiled and nodded. *No Jess and Sara, I guess.*

"Great. Do you have any other questions?"

"I don't think I have any. . . ."

Mom pointed at her clothes and raised her eyebrows.

"Oh Donna, just one question. What should I wear for training?"

"The first week it won't matter that much, because you won't be on the sales floor very often. Casual, jeans and a nice top, something like that. After that you'll need to wear Magna merchandise. We'll talk about all of that in your training."

"Great. I'm really excited. Thanks so much, Donna." Molly hung up the phone and grabbed her mom's hands and jumped up and down. "I can't believe it!"

"Congratulations, dear. Your dad is going to be so proud of you."

Uh-oh! Molly looked out the window. She stood rooted to the spot and stared at her friends playing with her dog in the backyard, knowing they'd be disappointed. *Bittersweet.*

Holding the door handle, Molly turned toward her mom and opened her mouth to ask her what she should do about Sara and Jess. But Molly already knew. She'd have to tell them right away. She shook her head and slid the door open. *Sigh.*

Sara and Jess compared cell phone pictures while Rocco barked for attention. Jess flipped her phone shut when she saw Molly's face. "What happened? You look like you just lost your best friend."

"I may have, I guess."

"What are you talking about? What happened?" Sara slipped her phone into her bag.

"That was Donna on the phone." Molly looked down at her hands and picked at an invisible hangnail, dreading what she had to tell them next.

When she didn't speak right away, Sara raised her eyebrows and shrugged. "What did she say?"

Still not looking up, Molly said, "She offered me a job."

"Hey, that's great!" Jess grinned.

"And that doesn't mean she's not going to call us, too, right?" Sara asked hopefully. She looked at Jess. "Hey, maybe we should get home in case she does."

Still smiling, Jess squinted at Molly. "No. Molly knows that Donna isn't going to hire us. Right, Moll?"

Molly tried to hold back the tears about to spill over to her cheeks. She slowly shook her head. "She isn't going to call you guys. Well, actually she probably already did leave a message for you to tell you that she isn't going to hire you."

"Why, though? Did she say why?" Sara looked like a little girl who'd just been told she wouldn't be going to the zoo.

"She didn't exactly say why, just that she hired me and Amber for evenings and weekends. I start on Monday." Molly bit her fingernail. "Are you guys mad?"

"Mad? Of course not," Jess said matter-of-factly. "In fact, I figured this is how it would go. Congratulations."

Molly shielded her eyes from the sun and peered at Jess closely, waiting for a glimmer of jealousy. She seemed to mean what she said, but how could Molly be sure?

"Yeah, congrats." Sara smiled, but the corners of her mouth quivered. She looked away, the disappointment evident in her dark eyes.

Molly slapped her jeans and got to her feet. "Look, I don't have to take the job. It wasn't my idea anyway, and it was something we wanted to do together. Why don't I just turn it down?"

Sara's eyes lit up for a second before they darkened again. "No. That wouldn't make any sense."

Jess shook her head. "No way! You're taking the job. After all, we only really need one of us to get the discount. Sara and I will just have to figure out other ways to make money so we can use it."

Molly laughed and exhaled deeply. "You're always thinking, Jess. But I'm sure there are rules about the discount. We'll have to wait and see."

Molly checked herself in the mirror at least a dozen times before she left her room. Then, passing the hall mirror on the way to the front door, she smoothed her hair and straightened her sweater one more time. She patted to make sure the back pockets of her jeans were buttoned down and decided that she looked as good as she could. . . . *Oops.* She scampered back up the stairs to her room. *Accessories.* A few minutes later, with a long necklace and matching dangling earrings, she finally felt ready to go.

Molly checked her watch at least a dozen times while she perused the racks of jeans at Magna. *Twenty minutes to go.* She decided to use the time to memorize the styles and cuts of the jeans.

I'll never figure it all out.

Donna stepped out of the back room and brightened when she saw Molly. "Hi, there. Doing some shopping?"

"Oh, I'm just nervous I won't remember all of the stuff I need to know about the clothes.

I'm just trying to get a head start."

"Good for you. You don't have to worry about that, though. I'm quite sure you'll catch on. There were lots of reasons I hired you, but the main reason was the look I saw in your eyes. I think you have an instinct for this. You're going to surprise yourself with how much you love it. Every once in a while I find someone who just gets it. I think that you're one of those people."

"Wow. Thanks, D–"

"Amber just got here. Let's go catch up with her and get started."

At Donna's lead, the girls followed her into the back room.

"Welcome to the Magna team, girls!" Donna sorted through a pile of papers she held and nodded her head toward the training table. Molly sat in the same chair she had used in the interview. Still scary, but in a different way.

Donna explained how to fill out the paperwork and told them to watch the two videos when they were finished. "We're also going to do some fun things like role-playing and maybe a game or two before we're done at nine o'clock tonight. Then, for your next training session, you'll be shadowing another sales associate on the sales floor." Her heels clicked on the concrete as she hurried out to help customers.

Molly put her pen down and cracked her knuckles. Amber finished just after Molly and stacked their papers together while Molly picked up the remote control to start the first video. It talked about the company, various media success stories, and had a segment celebrating Magna's rapid growth. The second one focused on theft or, as they called it, loss prevention. Finally, something interesting. *More money is lost to retail companies each year through employee theft than anything else? Shocking!*

Donna poked her head in just as the credits rolled. She clapped her hands together energetically and said, "Okay. I'm sure you're tired of sitting back here in this cold, dark storeroom. How about if we shake things up a bit?" She sat one hip on the edge of the table.

"I'm a customer. I just rushed in and said to you, the first sales person I saw, 'Help! I have a party to go to in three hours, and I have nothing to wear. I gained ten pounds, and nothing fits! I need something cute—fast!' Now, you both go out into the store and pick out the outfit that you would recommend to her. Anything goes. Use your creativity. You have fifteen minutes, go!" Donna glanced at her watch.

Molly and Amber scurried out to the sales floor and scattered in two different directions. Amber went toward the plus-size clothing, presumably because of the customer's weight gain. Molly went right for the jeans. Holding up the jeans to her own frame, she sensed that her customer had just gained enough to make her uncomfortable in her current wardrobe but hadn't quite crossed into the plus-size department.

Every outfit starts with a great pair of jeans. She held up several styles and read their descriptions. Molly settled on one that she thought would be more flattering to a curvier girl: It sat a bit higher on the waist and slightly fuller through the hips.

Jeans draped over one arm, she headed for the tops. There. A long-sleeved white T-shirt and a short-sleeved, black flyaway cardigan that would be flattering on any body shape. Having used only a few of her fifteen minutes, Molly went to the accessories tower and selected some red items to round out the look. She picked out some chunky jewelry and cute red and black high-heeled shoes.

Armed with her selections, she returned to the back room. *Ooh!* She had an idea. With six minutes remaining, Molly decided to put her outfit on one of the lonely, naked mannequins hiding in the corner. She tried to pull the clothes on over the mannequin's arms, but they just wouldn't stretch. Trying to free the sleeve, she knocked the arm and it came loose. She stared at the amputated arm in her hand. *Uh-oh! But wait. . .* Molly looked closer and realized that it was meant to come off. She easily took both arms off and slipped the tops on.

Squeak. The back room door opened, and then Molly heard the *click-clack* of Donna's high heels. It sounded like she was putting some boxes away in the shoe room which shared the wall Molly stood behind. She hurriedly finished accessorizing her mannequin with the jewelry she'd selected, hoping Donna wouldn't look until she finished. Molly hauled her mannequin to the other side of the room and pushed it behind a screen. She sat down at the training area with only seconds to spare.

Amber made it back to the training area just before she ran out of time. She stopped short when she saw Molly. "Oh. . .I. . .we. . . I was done a long time ago. I was just shopping."

"Great! Everyone's on time," Donna said from her office in her cheerful, upbeat way. She came out and took a seat at the table with them. "Let's see what you've found for our troubled customer. Amber, why don't you start?"

. "I wasn't sure of her size, but since weight gain had been mentioned, I went to the plus-size section and picked out these jeans and this sweater. I think both look stylish but offer her the comfort she needs and coverage for any troublesome spots." Amber blushed and quickly sat in her chair.

"Great, Amber. I really like how you thought of your customer's comfort as well as the fact that she'd want to camouflage any trouble areas. Good job. How about you, Molly?"

Molly stood up and moved her mannequin out to the center. Donna looked impressed, and Amber's jaw dropped. Pretending not to notice their surprise, Molly started right in. "Well, this is what I selected. I just put it all on this mannequin because I had a few extra minutes, and I thought it would be easier to see. First, I picked this cut of jeans because of the higher waist and roomier hips." She placed both hands on the mannequin's hips and then around her waist. "I went with a wider belt to give her waist more definition. I chose this flyaway cardigan because it skims the midsection without hugging in any of those unflattering places and nips in here, giving her shape." Molly gestured to the rib cage area and then continued.

"I went with a long-sleeved white tee for underneath. I chose this chunky red jewelry to bring some color into the outfit." She lifted the necklace. "Again, not knowing her exact size, I chose a long necklace because sometimes a chunkier, tighter choker can shorten the neck, but these long lines will make her seem taller."

Donna looked startled.

Knowing she had made an impact, Molly tried to hide her growing excitement. "I gave her a fun coordinating bag to carry and these killer high heels, which I'm going to have to buy for myself. Our customer is all ready for her party."

Donna stared openmouthed. "Molly, if I didn't know better, I'd think that you were a highly trained retail professional. You explained your choices like a seasoned trainer, definitely not like a trainee." Donna shook her head as she looked back to the mannequin.

Molly mumbled her thanks and looked

down, embarrassed. Had she gone too far?

Stepping back into the moment, Donna said, "Well, I don't have much to add, girls. You both made wise choices and had good reasons for what you picked. You also listened to your customer and focused on what she needed, not just on what you like. That's great." She paused for a moment before continuing, choosing her next words carefully.

"Again, though, Molly, you were focused on creating a whole look, not just on selling an item or two. Your customer would have left happy with either of these outfits. But she would have left feeling like a million bucks with Molly's. Can you see the difference?" She waited for them to nod in agreement. "Okay, great job, girls. That wraps up our training session for the evening. You can clock out like I showed you and take off for the evening."

"Thanks so much, Donna." Molly stood to leave but looked at the mannequin. Should she put the clothes away? *Well, if I don't do it, Donna will have to—probably shouldn't cause my new boss extra work.* Molly unbuttoned the top button of the sweater.

Halfway to the back room door, Amber

stopped in her tracks and looked back at Molly. She sighed heavily and then came back to get her clothes to put away. "I can see you're going to make this job a lot more work for me than it has to be—just to keep up with you."

Mmm. Hot chocolate. The smell greeted Molly as soon as she walked into the house. It hadn't even turned cold enough for a jacket yet, but anytime was a good time for her mom's special brew made with homemade fudge sauce and real cream. Molly selected one of the two steaming mugs waiting at the kitchen table and blew on the frothy foam.

"I want to hear all about your first day at work." Molly's mom picked up the other mug.

Settling into her familiar seat at the kitchen dinette, Molly let the steam envelop her face before taking a sip. *Hmm. Where to start?* She told her mom all about her night and everything that Donna had said to her from their first encounter before the training began to the story of the last training session with the mannequin. "Mom, I really wasn't trying to show Amber up. I just did what I thought would make Donna happy and what seemed logical to me. I'm afraid

I really made Amber mad, though. Do you think I went too far?"

Molly heard her dad's favorite chair squeak in the living room around the corner. Until then she hadn't realized that he'd been listening from the other room. "Sweetie, as someone who has had employees for years and years, let me give you a piece of insight." He walked into the kitchen and took a sip of hot cocoa from his wife's cup.

Molly looked up at her dad with wide eyes. If anyone knew about the subject of business, he did.

"Workers come and go. Employees are a dime a dozen. But associates, true business partners, are like gold. You were a partner in that business tonight. It sounds to me like the other girl is an employee like most good workers are. She'll probably do fine, but she'll never love it like it seems you do. Donna knows the difference." He squinted and rubbed his chin. "You know, though, it takes all kinds of people to have a successful business. Just like worker bees are necessary to the hive. But one thing you never want to do is hide your work ethic or passion, Moll, just to make a worker bee feel better about her job. Business is business."

Molly nodded. "You're right. I'm there to do a job and to do it well. It would be foolish to skip a good idea or act dumb just to fit in with the others. That's what you're saying, right?"

"That's exactly what I mean."

Mom jumped in. "But, Molly dear, maybe you can find other ways to make Amber and the rest of the girls feel special in their jobs, too. I mean, you don't want to climb to the top on the backs of other people. Just acknowledge their efforts now and then. If you have a question that they might know the answer to, humble yourself and ask them—give them a chance."

Dad nodded in agreement and squeezed his wife's shoulder.

"More great advice. What would I do without you guys?" Molly's chair skipped along the tile as she pushed it with the back of her legs and hugged them both. "Now, I have homework to do. I need to learn how to invest all of my vast riches so I can be a retail mogul one day."

Dad shook his head and chuckled as Molly turned to leave.

She barely got through the door before she

stopped in her tracks, darted back into the kitchen, grabbed her mug of hot chocolate, and then hurried up the stairs to her room.

I'm a lucky girl. . . . No, not lucky—blessed.

Chapter 4

TRUCE AND VICTORY

Molly groaned and covered her head with her comforter. Was she dreaming?

"Molly, you have a phone call!"

Ugh. Eight o'clock on Saturday morning? Who could be calling? What a long week—midterms, homework, extra shifts for training...

"Molly!" Her mom grew more insistent.

"I'm coming. I'm coming," Molly mumbled as she swung her legs over the side of the bed and padded down the stairs, rubbing her eyes.

"It's Donna," Mrs. Jacobs whispered, covering the receiver with her hand.

Molly cleared her throat and hoped she'd sound awake. "Hello, this is Molly."

"Molly? Oh, thank God!" Donna sounded frantic. "I'm sorry to bother you on your day off. But Heather, one of the girls you haven't met, just quit on me. She was supposed to work from ten to three today, and she just called to say that she isn't coming back. I'm really in a bind. I know that you've had a long week, but is there any way you could pick up Heather's shift today?"

Molly chewed her bottom lip. "Um. . .can you hold on for a second while I talk to my mom? In fact, how about if I give you a call back in just a few minutes. I need to work a few things out. Just a few minutes, okay?"

"Perfect! Thanks so much, Molly. I'll be waiting to hear from you—I'll need to know as soon as possible, though."

Molly plopped down on the couch and grabbed an afghan to pull over her body for just one more minute. Did she even want to work? But Donna would be mad if she said no. *Okay, I'm already up, have no homework, Donna's in a bind—but there's the swim party tonight. That's okay—I'll do both. Now to clear it with Mom.*

"Molls, I just don't want this to be a regular occurrence. Okay? Go ahead and do it because it doesn't interfere with anything else, and I'm available to give you a ride. But if you had homework or your youth group party was during the day, I'd say no. Understood?"

"Yep. I get it, Mom. I'm going to call Donna back, and then I've got to get ready."

Ahh. The shower perked her up. It would be her first real sales shift. Now she wouldn't have to hold herself back from helping customers like she had to do when she shadowed Amy. Molly dressed in a hurry. *This is going to be so cool!*

Right before she left, she e-mailed Sara and Jess—no way would she call them before ten o'clock on a Saturday morning—to let them know that they were still on for the pool party they planned to attend that afternoon. Molly wished they'd come with her to church sometimes. But at least they were going to the party, and they came to other fun things sometimes. They'd come around in time— Molly was sure of it.

"Thanks so much for helping me out today, Molly," Donna gushed as soon as she saw Molly walk into the store. "You obviously aren't trained to ring up customers, so it will be Amy and me behind the registers for the next couple of hours. That means you and Amber are out on the sales floor alone until Edie gets here at noon. Do you think you can handle it?" She flitted around trying to get the store opened.

"Everything will be fine." Molly clocked in. "I'm looking forward to getting out there with the customers." She rubbed her hands together. "Let me at 'em."

Donna laughed and opened the heavy gate. "Well, I'm here for anything you need. Please don't hesitate to ask me any–"

Molly cut Donna off midsentence when a customer walked in under the rising gate.

"Hi. Welcome to Magna. What are you shopping for today?" Molly got off to the right start. From the corner of her eye she saw Donna exhale deeply and relax her tense shoulders by rotating her head. She must have been worried.

Amber busied herself keeping the racks straightened, putting clothes away when customers left them in the fitting rooms, and helping customers when they sought her attention.

Donna took a break from ringing customers. "So Molly, what do you have going on right now?"

Molly looked around the store and pointed to the fitting rooms. "I have a mom and daughter in the first dressing room. The daughter wants to try on the white sweater on the mannequin in the window. So I'm about to go get that for her." She looked toward the front. "Let's see. That family over there is shopping for a gift for their cousin's birthday. See the two girls in back? The tall one is a bride-to-be, and she's looking for honeymoon clothes. I have fitting rooms started for all of them. . .gotta go." She walked away before Donna could ask anything else. *I hope that wasn't rude. Customers first.*

Molly pulled the mannequin out of the window display and took the sweater off. As she backed up, she almost tripped over a girl digging through a stack of T-shirts with her three friends standing beside her. "Oops! Sorry!" Molly's jaw dropped when she realized who it was. She stood face-to-face with the three most popular girls in her grade and one very popular junior.

"I. . .um. . .I. . . Can I. . . ," she stammered and stuttered. *Get it together, Molly.* She had a job to do. "I have a customer in the fitting room who's waiting for this." She held up the white sweater that she had retrieved from the window display. "I'll take it to her and then be right back to help you find what you need. Okay?"

"Great! Thanks, Molly." Kim, the junior,

spoke for all of them.

Molly stepped away for just a moment, but the four girls left before she got back. *Phew.* Time passed quickly and three o'clock came much faster than she expected.

Donna peered over her shoulder at the clock-in screen and said, "Your break's not listed. You must have forgotten to sign out for it. I'll take care of that for you. What time did you. . . Wait a second. Did you even get a break at all today?" Donna looked horrified.

"Oh, it's no big deal." Molly waved her hand. "I was enjoying myself and didn't even notice. I know it's my responsibility to make sure I get one. I'll remember next time."

"Okay. Let's not make it a habit, though. I can't have you burning out on me." Donna walked Molly toward the front of the store. "You were amazing today. I think you're the best hiring decision I've ever made. You really seem to enjoy yourself with the customers, and you stay so organized, even in the face of pressure. Just keep up the good work!" She started to walk away but had one more thing to add. "But don't be a hero, okay? Speak up."

Molly grinned. "Thank you so much, Donna. I promise to take care of myself."

"All right. Now get on out of here. I heard you have a pool party to go to!"

"Cannonbaaaall!" *SPLASH!*

"Oh no! It's one of those kinds of parties, huh?" Jess laughed as they climbed out of the car with their beach towels and bags.

"I guess so. But that's okay. It'll be worth it when you taste Pastor Mike's burgers," Molly promised and pushed the car door closed. "He does something amazing with them. He adds oatmeal and eggs, I think. Oh, and lots of garlic salt. I'm already starving, just thinking about them!"

"I'm just thirsty right now. Do you think they have diet soda?" Sara wondered.

Thwack! SPLASH!

"What on earth are they doing back there?" Molly laughed as they went through the gate into the backyard. One of the church members had offered the youth group the use of their heated pool one last time before the Wisconsin autumn set in. "I sure hope the owners are out of town." They went around the corner through the walkway of shrubs and turned to look at the pool.

Thwack! SPLASH!

Molly's head snapped back as a wall of water slammed into her. All the boys, the dry girls on the other side of the pool, and Jess and Sara just laughed. Molly gritted her teeth and felt like she could hit someone.

"This is a new outfit, and I fixed my hair. I wasn't even planning to get it wet, but now everything's drenched." Why was she whining? She begged herself to stop but just couldn't.

"Oh, it'll be okay. You look just fine," Jess said, wringing out her towel.

"It is a pool party after all, Molls— everyone's wet. Come on, smile." Sara grinned. She lowered her voice to a whisper, still smiling. "You don't want people to think you're a poor sport."

Molly took a deep breath and blew the air slowly from her lungs. "You're right. I'll lighten up." She stripped off her soaked cover-up, revealing her new one-piece suit, and then gestured to Jess and Sara. "Hey, cute suits, you guys."

"Thanks. Mine's new. I can't ever wear a one-piece." Jess tugged on the waistband of the bottoms of her red-and-white-striped two-piece. "They don't make them long enough."

Sara wore a purple tankini with swim shorts.

"You know why I wear these." She patted her hips.

Molly and Jess looked at each other and rolled their eyes. Changing the subject, Molly said, "Okay. Come on, girls. Since we're already wet, let's show these boys what a real cannonball is." She winked and tied her hair back in a ponytail.

"You don't mean. . . ?" Jess looked horrified.

"Oh, yes I do. Come on!"

Making eye contact with no one, the three girls walked expressionless to the diving board. All eyes were on them—something was up. They looked at each other—still no expression—and stepped up onto the board. Sara went first. She took off in a run and jumped as hard as she could.

Thwack! Immediately she tucked into a cannonball pose and landed with all her might on the surface of the water. *Splash!*

The instant Sara's feet lifted from the board, Jess had taken off running across it. She took advantage of the spring in the board from the momentum of Sara's jump. It flung her even higher and harder than Sara, and she caused an even bigger splash.

Thwack! SPLASH!

Molly did the exact same thing immediately

following Jess's jump.

THWACK! SPLASH!!!

When all three of them surfaced, the whole group erupted into cheers. "You win, you win! We give—truce?" A drenched Pastor Mike shouted from his perch on a deck chair.

When the roar settled into a soft buzz, he called out, "I think it's time for some burgers. What do you think?"

Thirty minutes later they were all seated around the pool deck. Some were on deck chairs, some sat right on the concrete. A few of them were a little ways off in the grass. Everyone had a plate with a thick burger and a big helping of Mrs. Beck's mustard potato salad.

With the students' mouths too full of food to talk, Pastor Mike took the opportunity. "Hey, gang, did you see what happened when Sara, Jess, and Molly jumped into the pool like they did?"

"You call that jumping?" one of the boys called out from the back. Everyone laughed.

"Good point. But whatever you want to call it, did you see what happened when they did it? First Sara went. Her cannonball caused a pretty reasonable splash, but when Jess followed right in her footsteps, the splash, the water displacement, and the level of bystander soakage was much, much higher."

"Tell me about it!" Brad Beck rolled his eyes and laughed.

"Molly went next. The momentum of her jump was fueled by the two who went before her. She couldn't have pulled back the power of that jump even if she wanted to. If she had decided at the last moment that she didn't want to do it, she wouldn't have been able to do a thing about it. She was committed to her choice whether she liked it or not."

Molly glanced around her. All eyes were on Pastor Mike.

"A lot of life is very much like that. When one person leads the way and others follow directly in the path of those footsteps, misdeeds or wrongdoings become easier and easier while the effects of them grow deeper and much further reaching, causing much more damage every step of the way. By the time it was Molly's turn to jump, she got the credit—or, depending on how you look at it, the blame—for the biggest splash."

"We'll go with blame." Brad jumped in again.

"I just want to challenge you all not to let yourselves get pulled along in the wake of other kids' splashes this school year. Be aware of the momentum of other people's actions so that you don't just get pulled along in their wake to go further and faster than you'd intended."

Molly looked around the group—some of them were still paying attention to their pastor; others had become completely disinterested, like Jess. She turned off her attention when anything reminded her of church. *I've got to pray for her. Sara, too, of course, but Jess most of all.*

Molly snapped her attention back to the pastor. ". . .have any prayer requests or concerns? If not, we'll close in prayer, and you can get back to your swimming."

"I have something to say, Pastor Mike, if that's okay." Brad stood up.

"Sure, Brad." Pastor Mike seemed eager—probably glad to have someone participate in the discussion.

"I just want to offer a cannonball truce and name the girls the winners."

Pastor Mike rolled his eyes and threw his hands up in the air, laughing.

Brad picked up his white towel and waved it in the air. "I think we ought to give it a rest, or there won't be any water left in the pool. What do you say, Moll?" Everyone laughed and waited for Molly's response.

Molly stood and took a bow. "We accept the truce and the victory."

Chapter 5

WHAT ARE "FRIENDS" FOR?

Molly felt someone behind her as she put her books in her locker the first thing Monday morning. Her books slipped from the stack at the bottom of her locker to the tile floor. She struggled to set order to her things before they were spread across the hallway. Finally she could turn around. Expecting to see Sara and Jess, Molly jumped when she saw Kim—the popular junior who had been in the store on Saturday—and her three friends, Pam, Marcy, and Jade. Surprised, Molly waited for someone to speak.

Kim put her arm across Molly's shoulders. "So, Molly, how are you today?"

"I'm great, Kim. What's up? I only have a minute or two before class." *Since when do they*

*like me? I'd better watch out for these girls—they're
up to no good.*

"Sure—us, too. We just wanted to talk to
you about something." She looked down at the
pointy red toe of her shoe—the same red shoes
Molly had used to outfit her mannequin on her
first day of training.

Molly's radar turned to high alert. Something
just didn't seem right. "Okay. . . ? What's up?"

"Well, you have the coolest job at the best
store. And I was thinking—well, I should say,
we were thinking—that you might like to share
your discount with us now and then. You see,
we both have something that the other wants,
and we can help each other get it."

Ah. So that's it. "Um. . .what exactly do you
have that I want?" *The nerve.*

Kim steered Molly down the hall with her
arm still draped over her shoulder. "Well, let's
face it. In this school, I have—*we* have—the
power to make or break someone's reputation.
With us on your side, you could be one of the
most popular girls. But with us against you,
high school as you know it would be over."

Molly stared at Kim with her mouth open.
What nerve to come right out and say that!
They never had anything to do with her before

71

this. *Ugh.* If she didn't do it, things could get really bad, but if she did, she'd be one of the popular girls. But at what price?

"I don't know, Kim. I mean, I could get into lots of trouble for that. I could lose my job."

"Oh Molly, you'll never get caught. We'll just try it once or twice. Okay?"

"You're going to have to let me think about it." Molly looked both ways down the hallway. "I've got to go now. Talk to you later."

Later that afternoon, at the lunch table with Sara and Jess, Molly just picked at her food. "What's wrong, Molly?" Sara furrowed her eyebrows.

"Hmm?" She looked up, elbow on the table, her head in her hands. "Oh, nothing," she replied and then shook her head. "That's not really true. Something is wrong. People are trying to get me to use my discount on clothes for them."

"Who?" Jess demanded. She sat up straighter and looked around.

"Oh, that doesn't matter. The point is that I don't want to be in that position, and I don't know what to do about it."

At that moment, Kim and company walked by, squeezing between students seated on the lunch table benches. As she sidled by Molly, Kim reached down and squeezed Molly's shoulder and gave her a quick wink.

"Never mind. I know who it is." Jess rolled her eyes in disgust. "It figures."

"So, what are you going to do about it?" Sara asked. "I mean, can you even do that?"

"It's really against the rules. I could lose my job. Not to mention, it's dishonest." Molly took a small bite.

"But I thought we were going to. . ." Jess looked confused.

"I know, Jess." Molly waved her hand. "Don't worry about it. I figured out a way to share with you guys that wouldn't actually be wrong."

Sara's eyes lit up, and she sat forward. "Really? How?"

Molly pulled apart her sandwich and scowled at it. She dropped it back onto her lunch tray. "The discount is given as a perk for employees but also to make sure that we can wear the clothes for work. So, I figure that as long as you guys use the discount on stuff I can also borrow and wear to work once in a while, it would be okay."

"Great idea. It's a win-win." Jess looked impressed.

"It's better than nothing. But that means no jeans for me." Sara put her uneaten cookie back in her bag.

"Maybe I could buy you a pair of jeans as a birthday gift or something, Sara. We're allowed to do that." Molly laughed. "It'll be okay. You can eat your cookie." She winked at Jess and then looked back at Sara. "Skipping one cookie isn't going to change your whole body type anyway."

"And Sara, for the last time. . . You're. Not. Fat." Jess softly pounded her fists on the table with each syllable.

"Oh, I know. I know. I'm just shaped differently." Sara rolled her eyes.

"What I wouldn't give for your waist— instead of looking like a little boy." Molly sighed and drank the last of her juice.

"So, back to the situation with Kim. What are you going to do?" Jess wadded up her trash and lobbed it into a nearby trash can.

"Well, I'm not going to share my discount." Molly looked up at the ceiling. "I wish there was a middle ground. A way to keep them happy but not break any rules." There had to be a way.

"I've got it!"

Sara jumped, startled at Molly's outburst.

"Got what?"

"I know just what to do to keep everyone happy but not get into any trouble." Molly waited for Sara and Jess to become interested.

"Well? Let's have it," Jess demanded.

"We have these things called Bounty Bucks. During the next ten days we're giving a ten-dollar Bounty Buck to customers for every fifty dollars they spend."

"Oh yeah, I've used those," Sara chimed in. "My sister and I saved them up. You get them at one visit, and then you go back at a later time to use them as free money."

"Exactly. Like a coupon," Molly explained. "What if I give Jess and her friends a bunch of those to use? It wouldn't be sharing my discount, and they're only coupons. It's not like it's free merchandise. I wonder if that would make them happy."

"Can you do that?" Jess sounded excited.

"I don't see why not. I'll just have to grab a handful of 'bucks.' They're out at the cash register for us to give out to customers."

"Perfect!" Jess and Sara agreed.

They all stepped over the bench to leave the lunchroom.

"So, when can we go shopping?" Jess asked.

"We'll have to do it like we're just out shopping—you know, trying on clothes but not buying. Then I'll have to go back and use my discount to buy the clothes you picked out. And remember, they have to be things I can wear, and I'll have to wear them to work at least once. Okay?"

"Okay. Sounds good." Sara nodded.

"So, when?" Jess asked again.

"Well, I work tonight and tomorrow. Youth group is on Wednesday, so how about Thursday after school?"

"Great. We can hang out at the mall for a while. I've been saving my allowance, and my grandma already sent my birthday money." Sara stopped at the door to her classroom, waved, and went in.

"Sounds great." Jess went into the room across the hall.

Molly continued down the hall alone toward her biology class.

Waiting just to the right of the door to Molly's class, leaning back with one foot up against the wall, stood Kim. She looked Molly up and down, lingering over Molly's new Magna outfit—jeans, high heels, and a khaki jacket. "Well, what's the verdict? You've had time to think about it. What's it going to be?"

"Kim, I feel like you're pushing me. Would you risk your job if you were me?"

Kim scowled and stared her down.

Whoops. Better talk fast. "But, actually, I have a better idea than sharing my discount. That was expressly forbidden in training. There's no way I can pretend that I didn't know. So, what about this. . ." Molly told Kim all about the Bounty Bucks plan.

At first Kim stared skeptically. "I don't see how. . ."

"Just let me finish explaining."

By the time Molly finished explaining, Kim looked like she understood. "So the ten-dollar Bounty Bucks are really just like gift certificates." She looked puzzled. "Hmm. That's way better than sharing the discount. How can you get away with that?"

"I don't think it's as bad as sharing my discount, because it was never mentioned as not being allowed," Molly explained. "The coupons are there for us to pass out. How would it be wrong?"

Kim snorted, shaking her head. "Okay, it's your call. So, you're going to get me some of those Bounty Buck things then?"

"Yeah. I work tonight, so unless something has changed at work I'll be able to get them tonight, and I'll give them to you tomorrow. But Kim, you have to promise that this is it. You won't bug me for other stuff from my work."

"Yeah, sure, whatever." Kim laughed as she sauntered away.

"Molly, I've got you on fitting rooms and cash register tonight. I really prefer to have you on the sales floor, because it's where you do best. But I do need you to learn how to work the cash wrap." Donna spoke fast. "Since it's supposed to be pretty slow tonight, I figured it would be a good time. Amy will be close by if you need her. I'm leaving for the day. So, any questions before I head out of here?" Donna, already buttoning her jacket, was clearly in a hurry.

"Nope, no questions. I'm good. Have a great night."

Amy looked annoyed as she approached with the clipboard in her hand. "Hey, Molly. How's it going? Okay, your sales goal is only five hundred dollars, because you'll be on register. You have a goal of two credit card sign-ups. Oh, and don't forget to hand out the Bounty Bucks to everyone who comes through the line. They get one for every fifty dollars they spend. Any questions?"

Molly shook her head quizzically at Amy's curt demeanor.

"Good. I'm going to take my dinner break. Amber will be here in about twenty minutes." She rolled her eyes. "So just hold down the fort while I'm gone. I'll just be in the back room. Come get me if someone needs to be rung up."

Molly looked around the empty store. *No one in sight—perfect.* She walked over to the cash register and grabbed the next week's schedule, pretending to look at it. She wasn't doing anything wrong. Was she? *If it's not wrong, why am I so nervous—and why do I have to hide it?* "It's just like coupons in the paper," she whispered. *Then why does it feel different?*

She put the schedule back and busied herself straightening the bags. Molly looked around the store one more time and then grabbed a thick stack of the coupons and put them in the cargo pocket of her khaki pants. *Snap.* She secured the pocket, just in case. She took a deep breath and exhaled, trying to settle her stomach. She would give the coupons to Kim and then never do anything like this again. It wasn't over yet, though. For the rest of her shift Molly battled her inner voice. *Don't do it. Don't do it. Too late.*

❀

"Here." Molly slapped the Bounty Bucks on the table in front of Kim where she sat at the lunch table with Pam, Marcy, and Jade. "There are five of them here for each of you. I don't ever want to hear of this again, though. Promise me you won't hold this over my head or ask me for more. I can't get more. Besides, the promotion ends in a few days, and that will be it anyway. Okay?" The four girls looked at Molly in surprise.

Molly wasn't sure if they were surprised that she actually got the coupons or if they were surprised by her tone. She hoped it was both—and that they took her seriously. It could get bad if they didn't.

"So, what exactly do we do with these?" Kim turned them over to read the instructions.

"You just take them to the store on one of these days," Molly explained, pointing to the dates printed on the coupon. "You can use them just like cash. They are redeemable for merchandise, even if you don't buy anything at all." *Oops.* The light dawned as Molly realized exactly how these were different than coupons.

"But think about it. If you walk in there with
five of these, since they are only given with
a fifty-dollar purchase, that's like saying you
had spent two hundred fifty dollars to earn the
coupons. There's no way you guys spent that
much. The manager would remember if you
had. So, when you use them, just use one or two
at a time and buy something else to go with it.
Okay?" *What have I done?*

"Okay. That makes sense," Kim said, and the
other girls nodded.

Kim motioned with her head for the other
three to leave with her. She patted Molly on
the shoulder. "Hey, thanks, Molly. You're a cool
kid."

Chapter 6

HANGING IN THE BALANCE

"This is only your third week of work, and you're already asking if you can skip church tonight?" Dad didn't like it at all. "This is where the rubber meets the road, Molly. It's time to put your money where your mouth is."

Molly rolled her eyes at her dad's incessant use of clichés. Usually she found it charming—cute, even. But when she was being lectured, she couldn't stand it.

"Hey, I don't appreciate you rolling your eyes at me. You're the one who promised to hold up your end of the bargain. But now you're testing the waters to see what you can get away with. Sorry, Moll. I'm going to hold you to your word. You're going to have to find out if it's even possible for you to handle so many irons in the fire."

She couldn't take even one more trite saying. "Okay, Dad. You're right. I'll be fine. I just thought it might be easier to have a catch-up night than to have to stay up late."

"I'll tell you when you can catch up—after school tomorrow instead of going shopping with the girls." Molly's mom teased her, knowing that the last thing she'd want to give up would be a trip to the mall with her friends. "No? Okay, well then I guess it's not all bad. Now, go get your things. It's time to leave for church."

After the short drive, Molly entered the gymnasium at church and immediately heard someone call her name. She looked across the crowded dodgeball game to locate the source of the voice. *Sara!* She had come without any prodding from Molly. *Weird.* Just as she pondered Sara's reasons for coming, *SMACK!* The ball slapped across the side of Molly's face. Her head snapped back, and her cheek flamed where the ball had struck.

For a second she was stunned and felt nothing. Then the sting set in, and it felt like a mild burn. Like a bee sting it continued to get worse until it felt like it was on fire. *Don't cry!* Trying not to look angry or start crying from the shock and the embarrassment—not to mention the pain—she hurried across the gym, past the openmouthed onlookers, to the kitchen. Sara followed her.

Sue, one of the youth leaders, jogged into the kitchen behind them. "You okay, hon?"

Molly nodded. Afraid she was going to lose her grip on her composure, she didn't trust herself to speak just yet.

In silence, Sue put together a makeshift ice pack. Molly hopped up onto the kitchen counter and held the ice on her cheek and sipped a soda that Sara had poured for her.

After a few minutes, Molly gained more control of her emotions. Sue looked right into her eyes and asked, "So, you okay?"

"Oh yeah, I'm fine. It's just that things are so physical all the time. I want to be a girl, and these boys are always splashing, throwing, shoving, pushing. . . It just gets tiring. I want to be treated like a girl, you know? And then when something like this happens, I have a hard time not getting really angry, and I wind up looking like a blubbering idiot. It's just not fair."

"No, it's not fair, Molly. Sorry to say, it's part of life, though. Boys are more physical, and they play that way—sometimes their whole lives." Sue laughed and shook her head. "Girls who are becoming women want different things. And, sometimes, that transition from being a girl to being a woman doesn't have a clear line dividing it, and the boys get mixed signals." She cocked her head and gave Molly a pointed look. "Like when you guys cannonballed the other day. From where I sat, it looked like you got pretty physical." She peered intently at both of them.

"Yeah, but only because we were slammed in the face with water the minute we got there. And that was another time I nearly lost my temper."

"Moll, you're changing. Your hormones are changing. It's going to take you some time to learn how to deal with the different thoughts and emotions you're having. The best advice I can give you is to just be honest." Sue hopped up to sit on the counter beside her. "When something happens, like when you got slammed in the face with water, instead of jumping in and fighting back, say something like, 'I really wish you'd treat me with respect, like a lady.'"

She lifted the ice pack to peek at Molly's cheek and pressed it back down. "You have to let them know what you want and not send mixed signals and then wonder why they haven't caught on. Do you know what I'm saying?"

Molly repositioned her ice pack. "I do. I hadn't thought of it that way before, though. I don't mean to send mixed signals—that's for sure. I'm going to have to try to remember that."

"You know, what you said really makes sense," Sara chimed in. "I guess we're the ones changing—not them, really. How are they to know things are different?"

"Honesty. Hmm. Worth a try." Molly smiled and jumped off the counter. "My face feels better now. Maybe we could go join the group?"

❀

"Take out a No. 2 pencil, and put all of your books and belongings under your desk. You'll have fifty minutes to complete this test. . . ," Molly's biology teacher's voice droned.

Molly stared with her mouth wide open, horrified that she'd forgotten about the test. Would it have mattered if she had remembered? When could she have studied? Molly surveyed the classroom. All the other students sat with their pencils poised, ready to begin the test. She fumbled in her bag to get what she needed. Saying a little prayer, she started to read.

Uh-oh. By the third question, Molly knew

she was in trouble. She'd never be able to just wing this test. It was all new information she could only have learned by studying—but she hadn't.

Even if she bombed the test, she could eventually bring her grade up, and she planned to talk to Donna about scheduling her either Monday or Tuesday, instead of both nights in a row. But, in the meantime, her parents would see this grade, and she'd been warned that if her grades slipped, her job would have to go. So Molly knew she'd better do some of her best guessing. She grimaced at the paper in her hands. *How do you guess when you don't even know what the words mean?*

Sure that she'd bombed her test, Molly slumped into the hallway. How had she let that happen? She dragged her way through the school and out the front door toward the waiting bus where Sara and Jess were probably already saving her a seat. At that thought she immediately brightened. *Time to go shopping!* She climbed aboard the bus and saw Jess and Sara in the middle. She maneuvered between the seats to get to the open seat beside Sara.

"Hey, you two! Ready to do some shopping?"

"Oh yeah. I can't wait." Sara grinned and

held up the money she'd been counting.

Jess held up a finger as she finished up a call on her cell phone. "Okay, I'll be home by seven . . . . Yes, Sara's mom is picking us up, and she'll drop me off. . . . Yes, I'll be careful. Why all the worry all of a sudden? . . . Okay, no big deal. See ya then."

"What was that about?" Molly asked.

"Oh, she goes in phases. You know how moms are. Well, come to think of it, you probably don't know. Your mom is always worried about you."

Molly laughed. "I don't know who's worse, my mom or my dad." She leaned her head back on her seat, sighing deeply. "I really need this diversion. I've had better days. . .but I'm leaving all of that at school. Let's go have some fun."

They were on a different bus than the one they usually rode—one that would drop them near the mall. They walked over to the mall and then called home to let everyone know they'd made it safely. They were even planning on eating dinner together at the mall—a first for them. But first—Magna.

"Molly!" Amy grinned as soon as she saw Molly come into the store.

Molly chuckled and shook her head. She never could figure out Amy's moods.

"Are you working with me tonight? I thought it was Amber on the schedule."

"Nope. Not me. This is just a shopping visit. Amy, I'm not sure if you met my friends when they were in before. This is Sara and Jess."

Both girls had learned from their hesitation last time and immediately reached out to shake Amy's hand and tell her that they were pleased to meet her.

"Hey Amy, is Donna here? I really need to talk to her."

"Yeah, but she's on the phone. I'll let her know you need to see her when she gets off."

The girls started their shopping. As usual they started in the denim section—jeans were the most important item, after all. At seventy-five dollars a pair, the choice was tough. But each of them hoped to find the perfect pair that day. Jess was long and very lean, so she had her pick of styles. Sara had slightly curvier hips but a very tiny waist which made things a bit more difficult. Plus, she was the shortest of them. Molly was average in every way—height and weight, right in the middle.

"Don't worry, girls. There's a perfect pair of jeans in these racks for each of us. I promise." Molly grinned and started digging.

They each took six or seven pairs to the fitting rooms. The girls were each trying to pull on a pair when they heard a knock on the door. They stopped giggling and said, "Who is it?" Which, for some reason, made them giggle even more.

"Sounds like you girls are having fun in there." Donna laughed. "It's just me, Donna. Did you want to talk to me, Molly?"

Molly hurried to button the pair of jeans she'd been trying on. "I'll be right out."

She opened the fitting room door just a crack and squeezed through it because Jess hadn't gotten her next pair of jeans on yet. "Hi Donna. Sorry, were we being too loud?"

"Oh, not at all, Molly. You girls have fun. You deserve it. Now, what can I do for you?" She had her purse in her hand and her jacket over her arm. It looked like Molly had caught her on her way out again.

"Oh, well, I won't keep you long. It's just that I wanted to talk to you about the schedule, if that's okay."

Donna nodded for Molly to continue.

"Well, the past couple of weeks I've been scheduled both Monday and Tuesday nights, and then I have church on Wednesday nights, which is really important to my family, and then usually I have exams on Thursdays." *Slow down, Molly.* She took a deep breath. "So, I'm having a tough time getting all of my studying done. Would it be possible to be scheduled only one of those nights, either Monday or Tuesday and then another night of the week, say Friday night?"

"You mean you want to work on Friday night instead of Tuesday night?" Donna laughed. "I hardly ever get a request like that. But, yeah, that works for me. I'm sure Amber would appreciate being freed up on Friday nights. So, will a schedule like Monday night, Friday night, and Saturday during the day work for you then?"

"That would be just perfect," Molly said. "Maybe once in a while I could work Thursday night instead of Friday or Saturday—once a month, maybe?"

"That sounds great, Molly. Thanks so much for being honest with me about it. I want to be helpful, but I can't if I don't know what you need." Donna smiled. "Now you get back to your fun. I've got to get to a dinner."

Molly squeezed back into the fitting room where Jess and Sara looked triumphant. They had each found the perfect pair of jeans. Since

Molly loved the ones she still had on, they called the jean search successful. *Time for tops.*

Sara and Jess each bought a couple of things full price, and Molly set a stack of clothes aside to buy later. In the meantime they wandered the mall.

Sara looked at her watch. "Hey you guys, I'm starving. Can we go eat?"

"Yeah, now that you mention it, I'm hungry, too." Jess rubbed her flat tummy.

"Sounds good to me." Molly agreed.

In the bustling food court they waited in line and got their food. They walked around for a minute or two trying to find a table. When they finally sat down, Molly saw Brad Beck from youth group. When he looked their way, she waved at him.

He wandered over.

"Hi, Brad." Sara spoke first.

"Hi, Sara. How are all of you tonight?" He looked at each of them.

"Oh, just doing some shopping." Molly wondered if she should invite him to join them, but she didn't want to annoy her friends.

"Care to join us?" Sara offered, scooting over on the bench seat so he could sit down if he wanted to.

"I'd love to." He looked around the food court, up and down the row of fast food offerings. "Let me go grab my dinner, and then I'll be back to join you."

Molly watched Sara watch him leave. She looked at Jess, who was also staring at Sara as she watched Brad. Jess and Molly raised their eyebrows and nodded knowingly. By unspoken agreement, they remained silent, waiting to see how long it took Sara to snap out of it. Her big blue eyes were locked on one tall figure all the way across the food court, and they were seeing nothing else.

After a minute or two, Sara jumped out of her daydream. Too late. She had more than given herself away.

"Okay, you've been holding out on us. What gives? What's with you and Brad? You like him, huh?" Molly peppered her.

"I have one question, Sara." Jess had a twinkle in her eye. "And your answer will tell me all I need to know." She paused for impact. "Did you and Brad set up this *chance* meeting ahead of time?"

Oooh. Molly sat forward in her chair. Good question. Not only would the answer tell them whether or not Brad knew that Sara liked him, but it would also tell them if Brad and Sara had spoken outside of church. Molly watched Sara's face as she struggled to think of an answer.

Sara rolled a french fry back and forth in a pile of salted ketchup and shoved it in her mouth. They were still staring at her, so she shrugged and pointed to her mouth and made exaggerated chewing motions.

Brad walked up with a tray of food that would feed an army. Tacos, a few burritos, a big plate of loaded nachos just dripping with cheese, and what looked like a gallon of soda.

The girls eyeballed his food. "Are you going to eat all of that?" Molly sounded horrified.

Brad patted his tummy. "I'm a growing boy."

"I guess!" Jess laughed.

Sara's cheeks were as red as her ketchup-laden french fries that she ate as fast as she could. But the sparkle in her eyes gave her away.

Chapter 7

PROMOTION
COMMOTION

"You've been here just over six weeks, Molly. I wanted to have a little meeting to talk about how things are going." Donna held up a finger and answered her ringing phone.

Molly fidgeted in her seat and picked at a fingernail. She'd been doing a good job, right? What if Donna didn't think so? What if she'd found out about the Bounty Bucks? Or that she had shopped for her friends?

"Okay, sorry about that. Where were we?" Donna hung up the phone and turned back to Molly.

"Well, let's see." Molly tapped her fingernail on her glossy lips and pretended to think for a moment, trying not to smile. "If I remember

95

correctly, you were about to tell me what a fantastic job I've been doing and how you're about to promote me to manager." She kept a straight face and waited.

"Ha, ha. Funny. But, you know, you're not too far from the truth. The thing is, you have been doing a really terrific job, Molly. Did you realize that since your very first sales shift, you have never, ever missed a goal of any kind? Ever." She squinted at Molly and shook her head as though she couldn't imagine such a thing. "That's amazing. You're a very driven employee, and I think you would do well with any job you decided to do. But, in this case, you have one more thing going for you. Passion." She nodded and pressed her fist to her heart. "I think you love what you're doing, and you're a real natural for this type of sales. Can I ask you, Molly, what is it about this job that inspires you?" Donna leaned forward.

"Hmm. I guess I hadn't really thought about it before." She thought for a moment. *Ah.* She had her answer. "You know what it is? It's the rush of knowing that people need my help, and I can help them. It's having a certain knack for a subject that's very important to women." She sat forward in her seat, excited just thinking about it. "And take, for example, the units-per-sale goal. We're supposed to sell an average of three items to each customer, right?"

Donna nodded, appearing to soak in every word.

"Well, some people think that's just greed on the part of the company, but I get the point. We're not to just sell three things—we're to put together a whole look. It takes at least three items to do that. So, the customer looks better and leaves happier. Magna is more successful, and I'm more successful. But aside from all of that, there's nothing like helping a frantic or depressed customer leave here with a big grin because she feels confident and beautiful."

Donna pondered Molly's words for a moment. "You know what, Molly? Since you've been with us, you've awakened something in me that I've let sleep for a while. I think I've become too business minded and have forgotten about some of those feelings. Since you've been here, I've felt a renewed passion for people, not just my passion for this business. I'm grateful to you for that, and I hope you manage to hang on to it." She looked reflective, so Molly sat quietly until Donna had gathered her thoughts.

"I have an offer for you, Molly." Donna

turned all business again. "I want to make you an AMIT, which is an assistant manager in training."

Molly opened her eyes wide. *She's got to be kidding!*

"You can't be an assistant manager until you're seventeen, and even then, I think you'd be the first in the company to be so young. But you can be a key holder at sixteen, which would be the next promotion after this one."

Donna reached down into her file drawer and pulled out some papers. "As an AMIT, you'll train for the assistant manager position so that you're ready when it's time. Over the eighteen months until you're seventeen, you'll learn everything about that job." She pointed to the job description. "You'll learn how to set goals for the sales associates, how to make the schedule, how to process freight, and everything else that goes with being a manager. Your schedule will stay the same, and you'll get a dollar-an-hour raise, plus your discount will go up to 45 percent off full-priced merchandise. What do you think?"

"Really? Wow!" Molly's jaw dropped. "I just can't believe that you'd take a chance like that with me. Of course I want to do it. I'm so excited!"

"Great. The promotion is effective immediately. Here's your new name tag and your new sign-in password for the computer. Congratulations!" Donna flashed Molly a huge grin and handed her a thick envelope.

"Thank you so much, Donna. You won't be sorry!" Molly hurried from the office so she could put on her new name tag. *Molly Jacobs, AMIT.* She ran to the restroom to look in the mirror. Turning to the left and then the right to catch her reflection from all sides, she couldn't tear herself away.

Oops. She checked her watch and realized that she was almost late for clocking in for her shift, so she shoved her things into her locker and smoothed her clothes. For the next hour, she tried to focus on her job, but every time she passed a mirror on the sales floor, she paused to look at herself, beaming with pride. Nothing could dampen her mood. Until *they* came in.

Molly had been struggling to get a cute new dress onto a mannequin when she heard activity behind her and looked to see if a customer had come in the store. Her heart sank to see Kim, Pam, Marcy, and Jade headed right for the expensive jeans. She'd have to help them and treat them like every other customer, or Donna and Amy would know something was up. Molly helped them into a fitting room, hoping they would take their time so Donna would be gone before it was time to ring them up. Trying to drag out the length of their stay, Molly kept bringing them new styles and different options after they had tried on everything they had picked out themselves. Good deflection disguised as great customer service.

Phew! Donna left before the girls had finished picking out what they wanted to buy. Still, Amy had to be the one who rang them up, because Magna had rules against associates ringing up their own friends or family members. *Not that they're my friends.* Molly poked her head into the stockroom. "Amy, there are some girls from my school here to buy some things. Do you want to ring them up, or should I?"

"I'll come do it. Thanks, Molly." She wiped her mouth with her napkin and stood up.

Kim and Pam were laughing about something while Amy scanned their items. Together their purchase totaled $104.42. Kim took a five-dollar bill out of her purse and handed it to Amy along with their ten Bounty Bucks. Marcy and Jade were next. Their purchase totaled $138.87, so Jade gave Amy ten

Bounty Bucks and two twenties.

Molly wanted to disappear. *Why did I do this?* It really hadn't felt wrong. . . . *Oh come on, even if I hadn't realized the truth of how wrong everything was at first, I could have ended it anytime since then. But now it's too late. Right? Should I do something? I'd get fired, probably.* She stayed busy filling the bag bins and taking the extra hangers to the back room while Amy seemed to go slower and slower. Finally it was over. The girls had their bags, and they were ready to leave. *This is my last chance to put a stop to it. . .but I can't.*

"Okay, bye you guys. See you tomorrow at school." Relieved, she watched Amy closely for the next few minutes. Did she suspect anything? Of course not. Why would she?

The evening passed quickly, and nothing was said about Kim and the girls. Amy seemed completely normal, and Molly could finally breathe easily. She could move on and not have any of that hanging over her head. *Think about your promotion, not all that other stuff,* she kept telling herself.

By the time Molly left work that evening, she hardly gave it another thought. She ran into the house after her dad drove her home and shouted up the stairs. "Mom? Can you come down here? I have news!"

"Huh? We drove all the way home together, and you said nothing about any news." Her dad was clearly confused.

"I know! It was so hard to contain myself, but I wanted to wait to tell you both together." Molly grinned.

"What's all the commotion?" Mom pulled the belt tighter on her robe as she entered the kitchen with a rolled-up magazine under her arm.

"Guess what!" Rather than waiting for them to guess, Molly just showed them her name tag.

"I'm guessing that means something good, but what does 'ANLT' mean?" Mr. Jacobs asked, holding the tag at arm's length and squinting.

Molly's mom took the name tag from him. "If you'd wear your glasses. . ." She sighed. "AMIT, it says AMIT," she scowled at her husband. "What does that mean, Molly?"

By the time Molly got done explaining the details of her promotion and all that Donna had said, her parents were grinning widely.

"I'm so proud of you, sweetie," Dad said.

Her mom gave her a hug. "Congratulations,

Moll. Those people sure think highly of you. Keep up the good work."

Ugh. They do think highly of me. Molly's stomach flipped as the image of Kim handing over the Bounty Bucks flashed through her mind. *Nope, not going to go there.* She shook her head to clear her thoughts. "Thanks, you guys. Now, I have some homework to do. I'm still working on bringing up that biology grade after that test I bombed."

"That sounds like a great plan—we'd hate to see you have to quit after such a great accomplishment. Off you go!" Her mom waved her magazine toward the stairs.

"A rolling stone gathers no moss!" Her dad called up the stairs.

Molly and her mom both groaned.

Molly slipped her corduroy jacket on over her lace-trimmed tank top and pulled on knee-high leather boots. *Wow. That's a long way from my usual T-shirt, jeans, and running shoes.* She ran some smoothing serum through her thick hair, hoping to tame the flyaways, and then swiped some gloss across her lips. She bent down to grab her book bag on the way out of her room.

Flanked by Sara and Jess, each wearing a screen-print tee and jeans, she walked into school a little while later. She felt like a million bucks. *Thud.* Her heart sank when she saw Kim and Jade leaning against the wall near the girls' restroom. They had on some of their new clothes and just stood there watching her. They didn't smile, nod, or say a single word. *Creepy. I'm going to have to keep my eye on them. If only I could go back.*

Jess must have seen her watching them. "Don't mind them. What could they do to you anyway?"

Molly groaned. "They could get me fired. They could threaten to get me fired so I would give them more stuff. They could get me into trouble here at school by spreading rumors. . . . Oh, there's a lot they could do."

"I wish we'd been a lot smarter and told you not to get mixed up with them," Jess lamented.

"Tell me about it. Too late now, though." Molly sighed. She was stuck.

"Yeah. They're trouble. Just steer clear of them. Maybe they'll leave you alone now." Sara brightened.

"Ever the optimist, Sara." Molly chuckled.

"Oh well. What's done is done. I can't worry about it. I'll have to deal with whatever else they do as it comes up. I'll just pray they stay far away."

Chapter 8

ALL FOR ONE

Oh, my bed. Approaching the church Sunday morning, Molly longed to be back home rolling around in her covers. Even the appearance of the church annoyed her unless she was going there for youth group. Stained glass windows on every side, deep mahogany wood floors and walls, beams on the ceiling, an organ with floor-to-ceiling pipes that the organist sure wasn't afraid to use, a choir of one hundred people in gold robes. The whole thing was all very regal and rich, which, to Molly, meant stodgy and impersonal. Least favorite to her were the long, entrapping, purple-velvet padded pews. She shuddered just thinking of sitting in one of those coffins.

She thought back over some of the churches

she had visited last summer when they did a local missions trip visiting various area churches to help them with service projects. Some of those churches were nowhere near as stately but were far more personal. She felt closer to God amid the casual spirits of the people who encouraged individuality and freedom of expression than amid hymns and repetitious prayers.

Molly looked at her mom and dad in their Sunday best—Mom in a dress with pantyhose on and Dad in a suit and tie. They thrived on the traditions and constantly argued that no contemporary song could even come close to the majesty of an old hymn. Perhaps they were right—if majestic music was what you were looking for. Maybe she didn't know what she was looking for, exactly.

Molly sidled into one of the pews with her parents beside her on the right. She tried to scoot all the way to the other end so she'd have an escape route, but another family had begun to file in on her left, each person like another nail hammering her into a velvet coffin. Fidgeting, Molly hoped she wouldn't have to excuse herself to go to the restroom.

Think about something else. *Count the hats.*

*One, two, three. . . Does that woman have feathers
and a veil on her hat?* Molly rolled her eyes.
Finally the organ started to play—its opening
notes so loud that everyone jumped.

Molly giggled.

Mom ground the heel of her shoe into
Molly's foot.

"Ouch!"

"Behave yourself," she hissed at Molly,
turning red as people looked at them.

"Sorry." Molly turned her attention to the
song leader. She opened her hymnbook even
though she knew the song by heart. "Blessed
assurance, Jesus is mine. . . ."

After the customary prayer, song, communion, prayer, song, offering, prayer, Pastor Marshall
took his place at the podium. "Before I get started
on my sermon, which will focus on. . ."

Sigh. Molly tried to contain her frustration.
*He's going to do something even before he preaches.
I'll be stuck in this pew all day. Now I really have
to go to the bathroom.* She looked down each side
of the pew. Her choices were to step over five
adults on one side or two adults, two kids, and a
lady with a walker on the other. *Stuck.*

". . .we have an announcement to make. I'm
going to let Pastor Mike tell you what's going

on." Molly sat up a little straighter and forgot about needing to go to the bathroom. Curious, she even put down her bulletin to listen.

The youth pastor looked out over the families and smiled at some of his young people. "Folks, this announcement is a long time coming, and we're so glad that it's finally here. Beginning next Sunday, in the fellowship hall, we're going to begin holding a teen worship service. We feel—" He was interrupted by cheers as his words sank in. After giving the youth some time to celebrate, he smiled and continued. "We feel that our youth need something a little different. They need to be reached in ways that speak to them where they are."

He made eye contact with several adults in the congregation. "Now, I know that many of you feel that they should be raised in the same traditions and with respect for the history of the church. I agree with you on one level, but we're not willing to sacrifice their church involvement and spiritual growth just so we can be sure they know the hymns the same way their parents do."

He held up his hands in front of him, asking everyone to hold on. "But even though there will be some changes, important things will continue. They'll just have a different flavor. There will be a time of contemporary worship rather than hymns. There will be communion time, but the music played and the format might be a bit different. There will be an offering, but it may be done as a contest or a game sometimes. The youth will be taught to tithe, but the teaching methods will be different."

I can't believe it. Molly looked around for some of her friends. She saw Sue sitting across the room. As a youth leader, Sue surely had something to do with making this happen. And across the aisle from Sue, Molly could see Brad's tall head next to. . . *Wait a second. . .Sara? It can't be.* Brad leaned forward to pick something up, and Molly got a clear view of Sara, who just happened to turn at that very second and lock eyes with Molly. They both grinned. *Wow! It's a good day.*

The senior pastor took the podium again. "I hope you can all see that we aren't separating like this because we can't cooperate. We're doing it as a celebration of the different needs in our body. We aren't doing it as a concession to the irreverence of youth. We're doing it out of the realization that we're missing out on meeting a huge need in this body." He looked out and made eye contact with several members. "Mark my words, in ninety days I'll be able to report that the Sunday morning attendance of our teens has doubled. We can't reach them if they aren't here. And even though some of them are technically here, they aren't being reached."

Oh boy. Some people aren't going to like this one bit.

"One thing I want to caution the young people on, though, is to hold fast to the teachings and traditions of those who've come before you. They're rich and meaningful. Someday you'll be grateful to know 'The Old Rugged Cross,' 'Amazing Grace,' and 'It Is Well with My Soul.' Don't forsake your roots for what is new and fleeting. In all things may we all be open to the leading of the Holy Spirit and willing to move where He leads."

The entire congregation broke out in spontaneous applause and got to their feet—every single person. Molly looked on in awe. Something was finally being changed for the better.

The pastor moved into his sermon for the day, but Molly couldn't stop thinking about the very first youth service that would take place in just one week. Now to figure out how to get Jess to come.

✾

"Hmm, I don't know. I guess I have mixed feelings about it." Molly's dad hesitated as he turned the key in the ignition.

"Well, I think it's fantastic." Mom nodded vigorously. "If you want my opinion, this should have been done a long time ago. The Wednesday night youth group is more about fun than Bible teaching. Sure, there are devotions and a little bit of teaching, but I think we've missed out on some real opportunities with our young people. They need to learn the Bible and be held to higher standards of living."

"Well, sure. But doesn't that happen on Sunday mornings?" Dad countered. "Pastor Marshall teaches the Bible."

Molly looked out the window, trying to disappear into the landscape.

"That's the whole point, John." Mom flipped her sun visor down hard. She took a deep breath. "They don't relate to the adult teaching. It doesn't reach them where they are in their lives."

"Well, that's only a problem because we as a society have taught them that it's all about them. We have to cater to young people instead of having them learn from us. Whatever

112

happened to 'children should be seen and not heard'?"

That's it. Molly whipped her head around. "Dad! Seriously? Let me ask you this. . . . When you train people at work, do you train them all the exact same way or do you figure out how to reach everyone differently and how each individual is best motivated according to what will achieve the most results?" Molly waited confidently.

"You know the answer to that, because I've explained it to you before, Moll." His knuckles were white on the steering wheel as he looked up at the roof of the car and collected his thoughts. "You know what? You're one smart cookie."

Molly wiggled her eyebrows and grinned with victory. She offered a concession by throwing him one of his beloved clichés. "Chip off the old block."

Chapter 9

→ ## SHALL WE DANCE?

Monday morning magic awaited Molly, Sara, and Jess when they entered the school. Festive posters lined the hallways, and the doors were brightly wrapped like Christmas packages with shiny paper and bows. Glittery stars and sparkly icicles hung from the drop ceilings in classrooms. Teachers had their bulletin boards and windows decorated with die-cut Christmas trees and ornaments. Holiday music softly played on the PA system.

"I think they're trying to get us in the holiday spirit, wouldn't you say?" Sara gestured down the hallway strung with blinking colored lights.

"I don't remember them getting this decked out before. Do you guys?" Molly turned in a full circle as she gazed at the decorations.

Before they could answer, the music stopped and the system squawked and squealed as someone got ready to speak into the microphone. "I think we're about to find out what's going on." Jess pointed up at the speaker on the wall.

Students collectively froze in place and looked up at the ceiling.

"Good morning, students," the principal's voice chirped. "On behalf of the faculty of Ford High School, we want to welcome you to Winter Wonderland! Enjoy the holiday decorations, and let them put you in the mood for our Winter Wonderland Dance Festival that's only two weeks away. I hope you're making your plans, getting your tickets, and shining up your shoes. It's going to be the best party this school has seen—ever! And I have the distinct privilege of announcing to you that there will be a live band. Does anyone know of a band called HiJinx?"

Cheers erupted throughout the school, and the principal had to wait a full minute before he could resume his speech.

"I'm so glad you're excited. We all are! I can't wait to see you there. It's going to be something to remember. Merry Christmas, everyone." The microphone squealed again as it switched back to the Christmas track.

"So, you guys going to the dance?" Molly asked Jess and Sara as they started toward their classes again.

"I'm going to go." Sara blushed.

"Oh, I'm sure you're going." Jess laughed. "You and Brad have been joined at the hip for weeks now."

"How about you, Jess? You going?" Sara asked.

"I. . .well. . .I. . .I'm not sure," Jess said evasively.

"Whoa! Are you holding out on us? What's the story?" Molly pulled Jess to a stop right in the middle of the hallway.

"It's just that I might—I said *might*—be going with Todd Stotter. We've. . .um. . .well. . . we've been talking a little." Jess blushed beet red.

"Really? Wow. I can't believe you didn't tell us about that." Molly was shocked, and Sara just stared. Jess with a guy? *I didn't see that coming.* She just seemed too independent and self-assured. Who'd have guessed?

Molly decided to be up front with her friends, too. "I'm going to ask someone to take me. Is that too weird?"

"Who? Who?" Sara jiggled impatiently from

one foot to the other.

"No, it's not weird at all. Good for you." Jess looked impressed. "Who is it?"

"His name is Matt. He's the brother of one of the girls I work with. He goes to St. Augustine. Christa said he doesn't have a girlfriend right now. He's a junior, though. He may not be interested, but he's super cute. So, I'm going to give it a shot." She shrugged.

"Wow. You've really changed." Sara looked impressed. "The old Molly would never have had the nerve to do that."

The bell rang to signal the start of first period, and the girls turned to go their separate ways. "When are you going to do it?" Jess called down the hallway.

"After school today." Molly yelled back. "Wish me luck."

Jess and Sara both gave her a thumbs-up. "We're coming over!" Jess shouted.

Molly just laughed and shook her head. *How did I know she would say that?*

After school they giggled their way into the Jacobs house. It seemed like Jess and Sara were as panicked about the phone call as Molly. "What are you two so uptight about? You don't have to talk to him!"

"We're just nervous for you," Sara said with grave sympathy. "I couldn't imagine doing what you're about to do."

"Well quit it! You're making it worse." Molly flopped back on her bed and covered her eyes with her hands.

"Is your mom home?" Jess asked wisely. She would have a problem with Molly calling a boy and asking him to take her to a dance.

"No, she's out at a book club meeting or something."

"Okay, so quit stalling. Let's get this thing over with." Jess held out the phone.

"Okay, okay." Looking at a scrap of paper she had wadded up in the front pocket of her jeans, Molly sat on the side of her bed with the cordless phone in her hand. She read the number a few times and wiped her sweaty palms on her jeans. Her lips moved rapidly as she rehearsed what she wanted to say.

It's now or never. Molly punched in the numbers in as fast as she could and then held the receiver to her ear. She took several deep breaths while it rang. "Hello. May I speak to Matt, please?" She nervously shook her hand and crossed her fingers while she waited.

"Hi, Matt. This is Molly. I work with

Christa at Magna. We've met a few—"

"Hi, Molly. How's it going?"

"Oh, you remember me? Great." She gave Jess and Sara a thumbs-up and then winced. *Why did I tell him I didn't expect to be remembered?*

They grinned and nodded.

"Well, the reason I'm calling is that my school has a big Christmas dance in a couple of weeks. HiJinx is the band that will be playing—can you believe that?"

"Yeah, I heard that at school today. Word travels fast." He laughed.

"It's going to be great. . . ." She hesitated, afraid to ask the big question. Jess nudged her thigh and gave her a nod of encouragement.

"Well, I was wondering if you'd like to go to that dance with me." There. It was over. She'd done her part. Now she just mentally begged him to say yes.

"That sounds like fun, Molly. I'd love to."

"Really? Awesome! I'm sure we'll have a fun time. Okay, I'll be in touch as soon as I have more details. It's the third Saturday this month—the nineteenth."

"I'll be looking forward to it. Oh, hey, let me know what color your dress will be, too. Okay?"

"Okay, Matt. Thanks. I'll talk to you later." She hung up the phone, collapsed on the bed, and heaved an exhausted sigh. Then she started to giggle. "I. . .can't. . .believe. . .I. . .did. . .that!" she sputtered out through her nervous laughter.

"I'm totally impressed." Jess smiled at Sara and nodded.

When Molly recovered, Sara said, "Now that we all have dates, we have to figure out what we're going to wear."

"Ugh, I know! Matt told me to let him know what color dress I chose—probably so he could get me a matching flower."

"Oh, that's really sweet!" Sara made a fist over her heart and swooned.

"Yeah, but I have no idea what I'm going to wear. I have a little money saved, but I've been spending so much on casual clothes for work that I don't have much. I could ask my mom and dad, but they'll put up a fight about spending a lot of money on a dress that I'll only wear once. It would be different if it were prom or something."

Jess shook her head. "Well, I can guarantee that my parents can't help me buy a dress, so I won't even bring it up to them. I'll have to borrow one from someone or wear something

I've got." She looked thoughtful. "Unless I can figure out a way to earn some money."

Molly's eyes brightened. "I have these two dresses from my cousins' weddings you could see if either of you can wear them. They don't, um, fit me on top anymore. And there's no room to let them out."

"Your dresses will be way too short on me, Moll." Jess walked to the mirror, held one of the dresses up to her shoulders, and shook her head.

"This one might work." Molly held up a dusty mint green dress with layers of organza that cascaded into a slight train in the back.

"I'll try it on. . .but. . ." Jess looked skeptical. She pulled it over her head and adjusted it on her tall frame.

Molly and Sara sputtered behind their laughter. It was way too short, and the torso looked all wrong on Jess. The color beautifully set off her sea green eyes, though. "We could have it altered," Molly offered.

"Thanks, Moll. But with all of these layers of fabric and the delicate beadwork, it would cost a fortune to alter this dress. I might as well buy a new one."

The second dress was iridescent burgundy with swirls of plum and rich ruby throughout.

It would be perfect for the Christmas dance and would look just right with Sara's long, wavy dark hair; pale, luminescent skin; and blue eyes.

"Oh, wow! That one is gorgeous. But, yeah, they're both mermaid-style which will never work over my saddlebags, even if I could get them on." Sara patted her hips and turned sideways to look in the full-length mirror on the back of Molly's door. She didn't even bother trying them on.

Molly went back to her closet and took out a half-gallon glass jar full of coins and dollar bills. She dumped it out on the bed. "Let's see how much money I have. I'll share it with you guys if it helps." They counted it all out across the bed in little piles of ten dollars each: $112.77. "It's not bad, but I'm going to have to keep out money for the dance tickets. I invited him, after all. That's twenty-five dollars a couple. I do have shoes I can wear, though."

"Oh, I do, too. I just remembered," Sara said. "I have those silver strappy heels that would work with just about any dress."

"Have an extra pair of size nines lying around anywhere?" Jess lifted her foot in the air.

"Okay, so, eighty-seven dollars needs to buy three dresses and a pair of shoes? Do you think

I'll have to pay for dinner, too?"

"He'll probably pay, but you should probably have money just in case. So, you should hang on to another twenty-five dollars." Jess moved fifty dollars off to the side. "That leaves sixty-two dollars for three dresses and a pair of shoes. It's not looking good, girls."

Molly fingered the little ribbon bows on her comforter and then paced the room a few times before sitting at her desk. Maybe they just shouldn't go.

Sara tapped her fingernails on the nightstand while Jess thumbed through the pages of a fashion magazine on the bed.

Finally Molly got tired of worrying about it. "Let's go get a snack."

At that same moment Jess put down her magazine and said, "I have an idea."

The snack could wait. "What, Jess?"

"Tell us!" Sara immediately stopped her tapping.

"Well," Jess sat up, dragging her words out. "You know how clothing stores loan out dresses for fashion shows?" She waited for an answer.

Sara just nodded, and Molly said, "Yeah, Magna does that all the time."

"Okay, now just hear me all the way out, okay?"

Both girls nodded.

"What if we 'borrow' "—Jess wiggled her fingers in the air like quotes—"some dresses from Magna, don't remove the tags or anything, wear them for the dance, and then return them right after it's over?"

Molly was immediately shaking her head in protest before Jess even finished speaking, Sara looked horrified, but Jess held up her hand. "Hold on, I'm not finished yet."

They both closed their mouths. Molly crossed her arms and cocked her head to one side. *I'm not liking this one bit.*

Jess continued, seemingly unfazed. "It wouldn't be stealing because we'd be returning the dresses right away, and you do work there, Molly. I mean, they loan out dresses to people all the time. How much more do you deserve it than perfect strangers to the company?"

"First of all, it most certainly would be stealing, Jess. We can't be sure that we would be able to return the dresses unharmed. Plus, if we got caught, it would be me who lost my job, not you guys. And, yes, they loan out dresses all the time but by their choice and for marketing reasons, not just so someone can wear a dress for free."

"Hold on, Moll. You know, it's not the worst idea I've ever heard." Sara sat up straight on the bed.

"You've got to be kidding me. You're actually considering this?"

Jess got more excited. "Yes, Sara. It's not a bad idea, is it? And it technically isn't stealing, is it?"

"No, it's really not. We'd have to be so careful with the dresses, though." Sara tapped her chin like she was seriously thinking it through.

I can't believe this.

"How would we get them out of the store?" Sara sat forward eagerly.

"We wouldn't!" Molly punctuated her point by getting to her feet so fast her desk chair almost toppled over. "You guys, this just won't work!"

"Okay, picture this." Jess tried another angle. "It's your shift. It's the Thursday night before the dance, and it's really slow in the store. Amy takes her dinner break, so you're alone in the store. With me so far?"

"I'm with you, but I don't want to be." Molly sighed.

"Okay, while Amy's gone, we come in and grab the dresses that we picked out ahead of

time. You'll have the security tags removed
already. We go into a fitting room and put them
in a big shopping bag that we carried in with
us. We come out of the fitting room and leave
the store before Amy comes back." Jess leaned
forward. "Then, after the dance, we come back
on Monday night while you're working and do
the same thing—only this time, when we leave,
we just leave the dresses hanging there for you
to put away before Amy gets back. It can't fail."

Jess, likely encouraged by Molly's softened
expression, continued. "Then, Moll, we'd all
have great dresses for our pictures and for our
dates. We all want to look special, don't we?"

"What would we tell our parents, though?
I mean, won't they wonder where we got our
dresses?" Sara wondered.

"Hmm, good point." Molly pointed her
finger at Sara.

"Well, we could just tell them that we
borrowed them," Jess suggested. "I mean, our
parents don't really talk to each other. You say
you borrowed from me, I'll say I borrowed from
Molly. . . . Get it?"

"Ah! That would work. But what if Molly's
boss sees pictures? And what about Christa?"

"Yeah! That's true. What if Christa brings

a picture to work?"

"Well, your boss won't know anything about us. I mean, lots of girls will have dresses from Magna. right? You'll just have to say you borrowed yours, Molly." Jess had all of the answers.

"I can't tell you guys how much guilt I suffered with after the situation with Kim." *But Kim wasn't my friend—Sara and Jess are.* "I don't know. I'm going to have to think about this. Not only could I lose my job, but it's wrong. There are a lot of lies involved. . . . But it sure would be nice to have a great dress." She shook her head. *Why am I considering this?* "I really do want to help you guys out, too. Oh, and I know just the dress for each of us." Molly sighed, not wanting to even consider it but also afraid of disappointing her friends—plus she truly did want a great dress. . . .and it wasn't really stealing . . . .or was it?

The time has come to make a decision. Think long and hard about what you would really do if you encountered the exact same circumstances Molly is facing. It's easy to say you'd make the right choice. But are you sure you could stand up to your friends and disappoint them? What if you truly believed you wouldn't get caught and that you'd replace the dresses before anyone found out? Would you consider doing it? Are you sure?

Once you make your decision, turn to the corresponding page to see how it turns out for Molly—and for you.

Turn to page 129 if Molly decides to say no to her friends by refusing to "borrow" the dresses.

Turn to page 159 if Molly decides that she wants a new dress for herself and her friends badly enough to "borrow" them from Magna.

The next three chapters tell the story of what happened to Molly when she decided to do what she knew was right.

Chapter 10

JUST SAY NO

Sara and Jess were chattering on and on. To Molly their voices sounded like the hum of a fan. Caught up in an internal argument, she wasn't listening to them. She rubbed the ribbon on her bedspread between her fingers while she contemplated her next move. What should she do? She didn't want to disappoint them. . .but she wanted to do the right thing. Still embroiled in her inner struggle, she slowly rose from her perch on the bed and went to the mirror over her dresser. She picked up her hairbrush and began to brush her long blond hair. When she finished, she twisted it and wound it into a knot and then clipped it with a tortoiseshell hair clip.

I want to help my friends—I could just take the dresses for them. . .okay, for us. But why does my stomach hurt whenever I think I might? It's wrong—that's why! Of course I can't do it. . .but I'd like a dress, too. We won't get caught. No! Don't be silly. You know you're not going to do it. . . .

Lord, forgive me for even thinking of it. Come to think of it, please forgive me for all of my sins along the way that led me to this point. Please help me be a better example from now on. Amen.

Jess's reflection looked at her curiously in the mirror. She watched Molly silently fix her hair. "Hey, what gives, Moll? What's wrong?"

Molly looked Jess in the eye, knowing what she had to say but not wanting to say it. *I have to tell her.* No matter what, she had to hear it now. "I can't do it."

"What do you mean? You want to do it a different way?"

"No, I mean I can't do it at all." Molly shook her head and looked away. "I'm not going to steal from work."

Sara stopped digging in the closet and whipped around to face Molly. "But it wouldn't be stealing at all. Nothing would happen. It's almost impossible for you to get caught."

"Maybe I wouldn't get caught, but I could. And it's wrong, not to mention illegal."

"You're saying you won't help us then?" Jess demanded.

"No, I'll help you in any way that I can. But I can't help you *this* way." She threw her hands up in the air. "Look, you guys are welcome to anything I've got. You can wear my dresses, you can use any money I have. . .anything. But I won't steal for you."

"Molly." Jess looked at her pointedly. "You've already shared your discount with us, which is against the rules. You've also stolen coupons to give to Kim and those girls. You've already done illegal things—things that would cost you your job if they got discovered."

"Are you threatening me?" Molly couldn't believe what she was hearing.

"No no. Not at all. I'm just reminding you that you're not completely innocent in this whole thing. You're already in too deep to back out now." Jess looked at her without blinking.

"No, I'm really not, Jess. No matter how you see my past actions, I'm going no further. I'm out." Molly stared her down.

"Well, we see how we rank in importance to you. We're just not popular like Kim and company. We don't have anything to offer you, so you're not going to—"

Molly interrupted her. "That's just ridiculous, and you know it, Jess."

But Jess continued as though Molly hadn't spoken. "Oh, and thanks for the tips about the fitting rooms not having cameras and when the best time to 'borrow' something would be," she snidely remarked and then smirked at Sara. "Come on, Sara. We have planning to do."

Jess and Sara silently gathered their things and left the room before Molly recovered from her shock.

Molly sank onto her bed—stunned, alone. She couldn't believe that they would threaten her, dangle trouble like that in front of her face, and then use her own words against her. She'd thought they were really her friends. *I guess I was wrong.* She lay back on her bed and grabbed her favorite pillow to squeeze. Her tears mingled on her cheeks like her thoughts jumbled in her mind. Why couldn't she just go back a couple of months and start over?

"Molly, dinner!" Mom called from downstairs.

Rubbing her eyes, Molly sat up, surprised. How long had she been sleeping? She glanced at the clock. *Two hours?* She rushed down the stairs for dinner, blinking her eyes as she went.

"Hey, sweetie." Her mom welcomed her and then looked a little closer. "Have you been up there napping? I assumed you were doing homework after the girls left."

"I guess I did doze off for a little while."
Best not to say how long she'd been out cold, or
her mom would think she was sick.

"Well, wake up, sleepyhead, it's time for
dinner." She smoothed Molly's hair.

"I'm so hungry, I could eat a horse." Dad
rubbed his belly as he entered the kitchen.

Molly rolled her eyes and chuckled. "Let's
feed the cliché king before he gets going with
those things."

Quiet during dinner, Molly was glad her
dad had a lot of things going on at work that he
wanted to talk about.

Finally, toward the end of the meal, the
clinking of the silverware amid the noticeable
silence must have become too much for Mom
to ignore. "Molly, what's going on with you
tonight?"

"Nothing. Really."

Her mom wasn't buying it. She raised her
eyebrows and just waited.

"Well, the girls and I just had a little argument. Nothing major. I'm sorry if I've been too
quiet. Maybe I'm still trying to wake up. I hope
I'm not getting sick." She tried to keep her parents' attention off the argument.

Mom walked around the table, pushed Molly's blond hair out of the way, and felt her forehead with the back of her hand. "You might be a little warm, actually. Maybe you should take something and go back to bed."

Phew. "Good idea, Mom. I'll help you clean up, and then I'll do that."

"Nope. I'll help her," Dad offered. "You skedaddle. We don't need you feeling under the weather with finals this week."

"Okay, then. Thanks, Dad. I'm going to get into bed and study until I fall asleep again. I love you guys."

She walked alone to her classes all the next day. Thankfully she didn't share any with Jess or Sara. *Weird. Just days ago I wished for the opposite.* Rather than eating lunch conspicuously alone, Molly sat in the library—she wasn't hungry anyway.

As she entered her last class, she saw her friends for the first time that day. They were at the end of the hall talking to Kim, of all people. *Why her? What could they be talking about?* When they saw her, all three of them started to laugh. *Oh boy.* What had she gotten herself into? And Jess and Sara? Who were they anyway? Not who Molly thought they were, that's for sure.

After a lonely bus ride, Molly looked ahead through the long parking lot to the mall. She still had a ways to walk. Shivering, she pulled the collar of her jacket up tighter around her neck. Maybe she really was getting sick. But, no, she knew that wasn't the problem. Her stomach did somersaults as she walked into Magna and headed for the counter.

"Donna, we need to talk."

Donna looked up from the cash register, where she counted out the bank deposit. She used her hip to slowly push the drawer closed until it clicked, keeping her eyes on Molly. "Okay." She had a question in her eyes. "Do you want to go to my office?"

Molly nodded, her eyes welling up with tears.

"What's going on, hon?" Donna sat on the edge of her desk and put her hand on Molly's shoulder.

Looking at everything in the room except Donna, Molly said, "I have to tell you something, and then you'll probably fire me." She couldn't hold back the tears any longer. Donna reached below her desk to find a tissue. Molly pressed it against her eyes but couldn't stop the flow.

Donna waited patiently for a minute. Finally

her need to know won out over her patient support. "What's going on, Molly?" Her tone had grown more serious.

Slumped in her seat, hardly looking at Donna at all, Molly spilled the story, leaving out nothing. She told Donna about sharing her discount—but made sure to mention that she did wear all the clothes to work at least twice. She told her about taking the coupons and giving them to her *friends*. She also told her about the scheme they had considered in which they *borrowed* dresses for the Christmas dance.

When she had finished pouring the facts of her story out onto the desk in buckets of tears, she said, "I'm sure I'm fired." She wiped her eyes and rubbed her temples as relief set in—the worst was behind her.

"I've really loved this job, and I really, really appreciate the opportunity." Molly had nothing left to say, so she collected her purse and jacket and stood to leave.

"Hold on a second, Molly. Slow down. Let's talk about this." Donna stood and paced the room for a minute.

Molly timidly sat back down on the edge of her seat, still clutching her purse and jacket in her sweaty fists.

Donna took a deep breath. "Here's the thing. I share my clothes with my friends, too. Even the ones I buy with my discount. You wore them all to work, so I'd say it's borderline acceptable, but the fact that you feel bad about it tells me that you understand the intent of the discount is to dress you, not your friends. I appreciate your honesty and your grasp of that situation."

"Also"—Donna twisted her auburn hair around her finger as she continued to ponder the details out loud—"the plan to borrow the clothes is what brought you here to my office. You didn't do it. Other girls would have convinced themselves to try it, that it wasn't really wrong if they brought them back, and that they wouldn't get caught. Or, at the most, they would have said no and then moved on. I'm not bothered that your friends tried to get you to do it, because your friends aren't my problem. I respect that you stood up to them and said no. I also respect that you're telling me about it when you didn't have to. So those two issues are done and over with as far as I'm concerned."

Molly could tell that Donna needed to sort through her thoughts, so she just sat quietly, squeezing the straps of her purse.

"The one thing that really bothers me is the coupon thing. I understand that you didn't quite grasp how it worked when you first took them. At first you thought they were like coupons in the newspaper, free to people for general use. Is that right?"

Molly nodded. It sounded ridiculous even to her, but it was the truth.

"Your so-called friends understood though, which was evident in their shock when you offered them the coupons. Then, once they had them, you felt kind of stuck, even after you figured out how the system worked and that it actually was stealing."

Molly nodded while Donna continued to work out all the details. She had it all figured out just right. One thing had led to another, and Molly just sank deeper and deeper into the mire. She thought back to the diving board analogy that Pastor Mike had made. After the first bounce, the momentum helped propel her along until the final bounce sank her.

"I'm not going to fire you. But I will have to write up what happened with the coupons and put that in your file." She peered deeply into Molly's eyes. "I hope you understand that

I'm obligated to protect the interests of the company, and if anything came up in the future, your file needs to reflect what happened. Can you understand that?" She waited. Molly wiped her eyes again, and then nodded. "I trust you, Molly—you're like a little sister to me. I must say, it's refreshing to see a young person with an actual conscience. It's rare."

"Donna, there's one more thing that you need to know. It's about what they're still planning to do. . .tomorrow night."

At home later that evening her parents sat on the sofa in front of the fireplace, and Molly sat on the floor with her back to the fire. Even with the hot flames at her back, she shivered from nervousness as she told them the exact same story that she had told Donna.

They listened without saying a word, their coffee growing cold in their hands. Mom spoke first. "Molly, it's hard for me to imagine that all of this was going on in your life and we were unaware. How is this possible? How could you let this happen? You risked your job after they put so much faith in you. You were dishonest and a bad example to your friends."

Dad jumped up from the sofa. "You

condoned, supported, and even helped people steal from your own place of business—in fact, *you* stole from a boss who has been so good to you. I mean, I'm very happy that you're telling us now, and I'm so glad that you didn't do it when push came to shove. But it did go much further than I'm comfortable with. I have to wonder if you're telling us now because you're repentant or if you're just afraid that your friends will get caught."

"But Dad. . ."

"Molly, this could have been a lot worse. I think you're aware of that." He held up a hand to silence her. "I think your mom and I are going to need a little time to talk about how we feel about all of this. Like she said, though, we're glad you put a stop to it when you did. And we're glad your boss is so forgiving. I find it hard to believe that she's overlooking the coupon thing, though."

Molly hung her head and slunk up the stairs to her room. She collapsed on her bed and buried her face into her pillow. She could understand why her parents felt like they did. If only she could get them to understand her situation and believe that she'd truly had a change of heart. *I just wish I could go back to the beginning and do everything differently. A few choices that didn't even seem so bad at the time have amounted to me losing my friends and my reputation with everyone.* Molly couldn't control the flood of tears that continued to press against the dam of her thoughts.

After a few minutes, Molly heard a soft knock at her door. Without getting up, she gave a muffled, "Come in."

The door creaked open, and Molly's parents stepped in hesitantly. "Moll, your mom and I are sorry for our reactions. We responded out of anger and didn't think it through first." Dad sat down on the bed beside her and touched her shoulder hesitantly.

Molly sat up quickly, drawing her legs under her.

"We shouldn't have given you such a hard time. We know that you're going to be faced with all kinds of temptations as you grow up. You'll make some great choices, and some not-so-good ones."

Molly looked down at her hands and picked at her fingernail.

Mom grabbed Molly's chin and forced her to look up. "But the most important thing in all of this is that you know that we love you and that you're free to come to us with all of your concerns, questions, mistakes, and whatever else you might face."

She let go of Molly's chin and walked to the window. "Sometimes, like tonight, we might have too hasty a reaction; that's where we're imperfect. We were just taken by surprise over the fact that all of this was going on and we weren't aware of it—I think that stung our parental pride a bit. But we realize more and more of that will happen as you get older and lead your own life. We're just so glad you felt that you could come to us and that you wanted to."

Me, too.

"Also," Dad interjected, "we're very proud of the decision you made in the face of intense pressure from your friends. Admittedly, there were some bad choices along the way, but eventually you arrived at a fork in the road, saw where you had turned onto the wrong path, and fixed it. The end result is what's important. You know what? Your mom and I don't care about your past. We only care about your future. It doesn't matter where you've been. It only matters where you're going. And it sure seems like you're back on the right path."

Chapter 11

BUSTED

"Thanks so much for coming in tonight. I'm so glad we were able to find exactly what you were looking for. Come again and ask for me. I'd love to help you next time, too." Molly walked around to the customer side of the cash register and tightened the handle of the bag from the sale she had just completed. She continued chatting with her well-dressed customer as she walked with her toward the front of the store. "I'm sure you're going to love. . ."

Jess and Sara walked into the store, clearly being careful not to look in Molly's direction. They wandered around the front of the store for a few minutes, never even glancing at her. They each picked up a few pairs of jeans and a couple of shirts on hangers, presumably to try on. Sara carried hers in her hand, and Jess laid hers across the handles of the extra-large shopping bag she had with her—exactly as they had planned.

Molly's heart sank—they were going through with it. They had arrived when Amy was on break, they had large bags with them, and they were collecting several items to take into the fitting rooms. The only difference in their plan was that she wasn't a part of it. They hadn't even spoken to her yet.

She knew she'd done the right thing by telling Donna about their plans. But now Molly wondered if she should warn them. *Oh my. What have I gotten myself into?*

"Oh, I'm sorry," Molly told the kind lady she stood beside. "I was distracted for just a second. I hope everything works out for you. Come back and see me, okay?"

After assuring Molly that she definitely would be back, the customer left. They were alone in the store.

Sara and Jess had their arms full of the things they were taking into the fitting room to try on, including the two dresses they were planning to "borrow" for the dance. Molly wondered if they actually still planned to return the dresses or if they had decided to keep them. She bit her bottom lip, trying to figure out a way to stop them from carrying out their plan. She even went to the fitting room door and knocked. "You two doing okay in there? What else can I find for you?" Molly hoped that the attention would dissuade them from their plans.

From the other side of the door, Molly heard giggling and the rustling of a paper sack. She shook her head, knowing exactly what they were doing. Neither Jess nor Sara answered her, so Molly shrugged her shoulders, resigned to the fact that the girls were choosing their own fate. Having done all she could, Molly went back toward the front so Donna could carry out her plan. She wanted to be as far away from the trouble as possible. Donna would catch the girls, and it would be all Molly's fault. She wished she had warned them in some way because she didn't want them to get into big trouble, but on the other hand, she knew she needed to support her boss and stand up for the right thing. *I think I'm going to throw up.*

Trying to stay out of the way, Molly busied herself at the front of the store straightening and restraightening racks and buttoning shirts. Suddenly Sara and Jess exited the fitting room with their packages under their arms. They hadn't even bothered to cover the things they were taking. Molly could see the dresses peeking right out of the tops of the bags. *What are they thinking?* Silently, Sara and Jess walked to the front of the store without touching anything.

This is my last chance to stop them. If they leave the store. . . Oh no, it's too late. Molly's heart sank as her two best friends stepped over the threshold into the worst trouble of their lives. Only they didn't know it yet. *Here we go.*

The back of the store erupted into a melee of people and commotion. The security guards busted out of the back room and ran out of the store to confront Sara and Jess as they were walking through the mall toward the exit.

Molly overheard the guards tell Jess that they had seen into their bags from the overhead security cameras and mirrors once they left the fitting rooms. Molly knew—she was the reason Jess and Sara got caught, but it sure helped to think it could have possibly been another reason. She hoped and prayed they would believe the guard and not blame her. But feeling their glares burning a hole in her back, Molly could tell they didn't believe him at all.

Molly remained uninvolved when the

security guards took the girls to the back room. She watched as they stepped through the door, and just as the door was about to click shut, Molly caught a glimpse of Sara's tearful eyes as she turned to look pleadingly at her one last time.

They were back there for over an hour before their parents arrived. Sara's mom got there first. She bristled through the store like she'd been called from an important meeting and couldn't be bothered with such an inconvenience. She threw open the stockroom door and said loudly, "What is the meaning of this?" Molly closed her eyes and sighed.

Jess's mom and dad arrived next. Mrs. Stuart cried with her head on her husband's shoulder—she looked so sad. Mr. Stuart was stone-faced and unemotional. Molly shook her head. She said a prayer that Jess's dad would soften and show her the love she needed.

The end of her shift neared. She had to start straightening the store to close it for the night when the unthinkable happened. Molly stooped down to arrange a stack of shirts on a shelf near the floor. She heard people come into store and assumed they were customers. She stood up immediately and turned to greet them. Stunned, she stared as two police officers strode right by her as if she weren't even there.

Horrified, she followed them at a distance to the back of the store and then gaped at them as they authoritatively went into the back room. *What are they doing here? Are Sara and Jess under arrest?*

The metal door felt like ice against Molly's ear, but she hoped to hear something through it. She couldn't stand there long, though, because customers came in and she had to help them find things and ring up purchases. Any other time, Molly would have loved her customers, but in her preoccupation, they just grated on her last nerve. *Who cares about your muffin top, lady? Buttons or a zipper? What's the difference? Just buy one!*

Donna came out just before closing time and approached Molly. Sensing her panic, Donna calmly put her arm around Molly's shoulders and squeezed gently. "Here's what's happening, Molly. Magna's policy is to prosecute shoplifters. So they'll be taken to the police station."

Molly stumbled and gripped the countertop with white knuckles to steady herself.

"Now Molly, don't get upset. They'll be fine.

They haven't done anything in the past—they'll get a slap on the wrist. But this is part of the process, and it will teach them a valuable lesson. Just be glad you weren't in on this." Donna started to walk away but turned around to add, "You know, they had other things in those bags that they were stealing, too. They weren't stopping with just the dresses."

"Really?" Molly slid down the wall to the floor where she put her head in her hands. "I had no idea. I wouldn't have thought they'd have it in them."

"If you'd have asked them a month ago, they probably wouldn't have thought so either."

The house shook with the force of the slammed front door when Molly thundered in after school on Monday.

"What on earth is going on?" Mom ran into the foyer where Molly stood with her back slumped against the door, shoulders heaving with heavy sobs. "What happened, Molly?" She frantically searched her daughter's eyes.

"I'm just so sick of it, Mom. They've completely turned on me!" Molly yelled at the air and punched her fists against the door.

"First of all, young lady, you need to calm

down. We'll deal with your problems but not until you can be reasonable. Take a minute to calm down, and then tell me who it is you're talking about." She waited patiently while Molly took some deep, cleansing breaths.

Breathe. Breathe. Breathe. Be calm. Molly clenched her teeth and forced herself to be steady. "They've all turned on me, Mom. Everyone hates me." Her anger had given way to resignation. "Sara and Jess won't speak to me, but they'll sure speak *about* me to anyone who'll listen. Everyone is calling me a rat. Oh, and my personal favorite is Fashion-Police-sta Bible-Thumper. Nice name, huh?"

"Oh dear. That must be really hurtful, honey."

"You have no idea, Mom. I can't take it." Molly took three more deep breaths to fight off the frustration that made her ball up her fists again. "And to make matters worse, Kim and her evil minions have spread the word about me giving them the coupons. So now I look even worse, and everyone is just being so mean!"

"Ah, sure. It's a hard lesson to learn but this is why we, as Christians, need to avoid even the appearance of wrongdoing. Your choices have hurt your credibility and your Christian witness. No one is perfect, and you're forgiven by God for any sin. But your friends might not show the same mercy. Unfortunately there are consequences to your actions even after forgiveness." Mom gently rubbed Molly's back. "People love when other people fall and especially now, because they probably think that you think you're above them."

"So what can I do about it?"

"Sweetie, I'm going to be perfectly frank with you. You just have to take it. I know you; you can handle it. You aren't the first person to stand up for something righteous, so you aren't the first person to be persecuted without mercy. I want you to think about Jesus. He went through betrayal by His friends to a level you'll never, ever experience. And did He show anger or bitterness?"

Molly shook her head, looking down at the floor. "No, He didn't."

"What did He do, Moll?"

"What do you mean?"

"What did Jesus do in the face of all that hate, ridicule, and even His own murder? What did He do while He hung on that cross?"

Ah. I get it. "He prayed for them. He prayed for His enemies."

"Now you get it. Have you done that, Molly?"

Mom didn't wait for an answer. "I think you might be so worried about vindicating yourself that you haven't thought much about what your friends are going through and how they're hurting. Also, you're still a little more worried about how you look in all of this than you are about standing up for what's right. I think you need to consider how you can redirect that passion of yours."

Molly slid to the floor, her back still against the door. She rubbed her eyes, exhausted from fighting her own battle.

"Would you like me to pray with you right now?"

Chapter 12

PASSION RENEWED

"You look beautiful, dear." Mom looked over Molly's shoulder into the oval mirror where she was applying the last of her makeup.

"Thanks, Mom." Molly put down her lipstick and paced the floor of her bedroom while she waited for Matt to pick her up for the dance. Dressed in a beautiful soft plum satin floor-length dress and cute strappy sandals, she had her hair twisted into a knot at the back of her head with a few wispy tendrils loose on the sides. She wore delicate, understated jewelry of little rhinestone flower earrings and a matching necklace.

She closed her bedroom door so she could look at her full-length image in the mirror on the back of the door. She turned to the right and to the left quickly, twirling her dress in dancing motions. Even she had to admit she looked beautiful in her borrowed dress. Molly smiled. In the end, Donna had been so impressed with Molly's choices she decided to loan her the dress she'd been eyeing for weeks. *I guess you can get much further in life by just asking for what you need rather than taking advantage of people in order to get what you want.* She pirouetted in front of the mirror.

The one dark cloud hovering over the evening was that she couldn't share it with her friends. Molly didn't know if they'd be at the dance, and even if they were, they wouldn't want to have anything to do with her. She'd been able to forgive them for everything once she started praying for them. But there was no hope for their friendship until they decided to forgive her, which didn't seem likely because they felt betrayed, too—in a convoluted way.

The doorbell instantly snapped Molly out of her thoughts and forced her back into the moment. Suddenly, at the thought of her first date being let into the foyer, the butterflies in her stomach started fluttering again. She gave herself one last inspection in the mirror and, satisfied with what she saw, crept across the carpeted hallway to the banister where she could look over the foyer. Dad opened the door to a tall, handsome young man who held a delicate wrist corsage in rich eggplant and red. It beautifully coordinated with her soft plum dress, and the rich hues offered her outfit a very wintery feel.

She didn't want to get caught spying, so she said from the second floor, "Hi, Matt."

He looked up and grinned when he saw her. "Hi, Molly." He watched her come down the stairs.

Molly hoped and prayed she wouldn't trip on her new high heels while everyone watched.

"You look great," Matt said when she got to the bottom. "Here, I brought this for you." He slipped the flowers onto her arm and smiled warmly.

"Okay, kids. Before you leave, I think your mom wants to take a picture."

Mom stood to the side, gripping her camera and wiping her eyes.

Molly shook her head and laughed. *Really, Mom!*

Having washed her hands at the sink in the bathroom, Molly flung some of the water droplets into the sink and then reached blindly for a paper towel from the dispenser on the wall while keeping her eyes on her reflection in the mirror. Then she squealed, startled. A second pair of eyes stared back at her from the mirror—and then a third. Jess and Sara had approached her from behind and were looking into the mirror, too. She turned quickly to face them, trembling at the confrontation.

But when she looked into their eyes, her fears melted away. Sara's eyelids were dams holding back the tears, and Jess pleaded for mercy with her big green eyes. Jess spoke first. "Molly, I'm so sorry. I can't believe what we put you through."

Molly gulped and took a deep breath so she wouldn't break down in sobs. Not able to speak, she locked eyes with Jess and nodded.

Sara reached out a hand. "I'm sorry, too, Moll. I would give anything to go back a couple of weeks and erase all of this from our lives. But we can't."

"No, we can't." Molly shook her head sadly. "But maybe we've learned enough from this that it was worth it. It could have been a lot worse."

"Yeah. . ." Jess's voice trailed off. "So, just like that? You don't hate us?"

"Of course I don't hate you. What kind of a friend would I be if I didn't let you learn from your mistakes and move on? This wasn't fun for me, sure. But I love you, and all it takes is an apology for me to let it go."

"No way it's that easy. How can you not hold it against us?"

Sara spoke softly. "Because Molly knows what it means to have really been forgiven. Right, Moll?"

Molly nodded, praying silently that she'd have the right words to say. "That's right, Sara. The Bible says that to whom much is given, much is required. I've been forgiven for my sins—past, present, and future. So I'm required to forgive others for theirs. That even means my enemies. How much more the people I love?"

"I want to know how that feels, Molly," Sara whispered.

"All it takes is asking Jesus to forgive you for your sins, and He will." Molly shrugged. "It *is* just that simple."

Jess shook her head. "I don't know about all of that. But I do know that I want to be more like you, Moll. Maybe I'll check out this church thing you've got going on, after all. But for now, let's dance."

The three friends locked arms and left the ladies' room together, united once again.

The next three chapters tell the story of what happened to Molly when she made the wrong decision and gave in to peer pressure by stealing clothes for her friends.

Chapter 10

WHAT THEY
DON'T KNOW
WON'T HURT THEM

Molly made a quick decision, like pulling off a bandage. She'd wind up getting talked into it anyway—Jess could be so persuasive. So she'd get on board now, try to have fun with it, and save them all some time and energy. *It's not like we're actually stealing. And we'll never get caught.*

"I'll do it." Molly paced the room. *What am I thinking? This is so wrong.* The inner voice that wanted to do the right thing screamed at her to stop. But she wasn't going to turn back now. She didn't want to disappoint her friends; plus she really wanted something special to wear for her date. "You guys just have to promise you'll be extra careful and the dresses will go back right away," she begged.

"We promise. We already told you that ten times." Jess jabbed her in the ribs.

"I know, I know. Oh! And you can't wear perfume. And if you use deodorant—which I hope you do—use the spray kind, not the stuff that leaves gunky white streaks on clothes."

Jess and Sara cracked up.

"You've got to relax a little bit, Moll." Jess patted her on the back.

"Yes, please. . .for all our sakes," Sara pleaded with her, still smiling.

"Okay, so let's go over the plan. You're working on Thursday, two days before the dance, right?" Jess confirmed.

"Right. I work five o'clock until close. Amy will take her dinner break between five and six, because that's when we're the slowest."

"Okay, so we'll come in at around five thirty just to make sure Donna is gone for the day and Amy's on break. Sound okay?"

"That's probably the best time. You'll bring the bags?"

"Yeah. I have a couple of great ones. We got them when we bought winter coats, so they're really big and have good handles." Sara popped the top on a can of soda.

"But what if we can't decide on a dress? I mean, we don't want to take up a whole bunch of time in there." Jess looked concerned. "I have a hard time with dresses sometimes."

"Can we go shopping on Wednesday night to get them all picked out?" Sara looked at Molly.

"It'll have to be Tuesday. I won't be able to go on Wednesday. I have church. . . ." *Church. How could she go to church one night and then steal from her workplace the next night? What am I doing? No. No. It isn't actually stealing. It's all going back to the store.*

Molly got to the mall on time on Thursday. But she just couldn't bring herself to go in. She paced outside the main mall entrance for ten minutes. *It's going to be okay. You're not going to get caught. It's no big deal—it's not even stealing.* Finally, at five minutes after five o'clock, Molly went in to work. For the first time in the history of her employment at Magna, she clocked in late. She'd have rather been anywhere that evening than at Magna.

"I'm so sorry I'm late, Donna. I got a little behind trying to get here."

"Well, you just see to it that it never happens

again." Donna eyes twinkled as she teased. "I have to run—dinner plans. Amy's in back. She had to answer the door for the delivery truck. She'll be right out. You guys have a good night." Donna hurried out the door, and Molly was alone in the store.

Nervously she wandered between the racks of clothing, avoiding the dresses like they were rigged with time bombs. She buttoned the front of a jacket, straightened the direction some hangers were facing, fixed the accessories on a couple of mannequins and waited, thankful there weren't any customers to distract her from her thoughts.

The back room door squeaked. "I'm going to take my break since I'm back here already. Do you need anything while my food's heating up?" Amy asked.

"No thanks. I'm fine. See you in about forty-five minutes." *So far, so good.*

Minutes after Amy disappeared and the back door swung shut, Jess and Sara walked into the store. Giggling loudly and bumping into things, Molly assumed they were trying to appear like normal, casual teenagers—but they were going too far. Molly glared at them, shushing them with her eyes—it wouldn't help if they attracted attention of any kind.

"Hi. What are you guys shopping for tonight?" Molly asked, still trying to be normal.

Sara giggled again, which garnered more glares from both Jess and Molly. "Shhh. Come on, you two," Molly hissed at them. "Keep it together, okay?"

Jess and Sara quickly grabbed a few items along with the three dresses they had chosen when they shopped together on Tuesday evening. They took everything into the fitting room and shut the door. From Molly's post on the outside, every noise sounded like it was amplified through the PA system at school. *Amy is going to come running at any moment.*

It's not worth it. They're just dresses. Molly rushed to the fitting room door to put a stop to the whole thing. But at that very second, the door creaked open and Jess and Sara came out carrying their bags—and Amy simultaneously stepped out of the back room from her break. It was almost over, and it was too late to do anything to stop it.

"We've decided not to buy anything." Jess pretended to be a discouraged shopper. "Can we just leave the things we tried on in the fitting room?"

"Of course. No problem." Molly lowered her voice to a whisper. "Don't forget she knows you guys. Don't try to pretend you don't know me."

They walked right past Amy with their bags of unpurchased merchandise. *Not stolen. Unpurchased. Borrowed.*

Molly noticed with horror that the tags of the dresses were peeking out of the tops of the bags. *Why weren't they more careful? Just keep moving.*

Amy smiled in recognition. "Hey, you guys. How's it going?"

Sara had already wandered away with their bags but turned to wave good-bye to Amy.

"Oh, we're fine. Just out doing some shopping." Jess acted nonchalant and hurried to catch up with Sara.

It was all over. They'd done it—no going back. Molly breathed a sigh of relief that they'd made it out of the store and that they'd all have great dresses to wear to the dance. *But at what cost?* She'd have to get it together. She was a part of this whether she liked it or not.

Amy and Molly stayed pretty busy with steady customers for the next hour. Molly started to relax, and her racing heart slowed to a normal pace. Sometimes she could last minutes without any pangs of guilt. She felt confident

they'd gotten away with the whole thing. . . .
Then it happened.

Molly stood at the cash register ringing
up a customer when she heard a commotion
at the front of the store. She looked up to see
Amy talking to two security guards but thought
nothing of it until she noticed Jess and Sara
standing right beside them. Her heart pounded
so hard she was sure her customer could hear
it thumping. Her hands got sweaty, and her
fingers were trembly and shaky. *Maybe they
won't tell them I was involved.* But they were
her friends, so Amy would probably draw her
own conclusions. *Ugh.* Amy would have to call
Donna. . .her parents. . .the police? The reality
of her trouble pummeled her consciousness.

Like in slow motion, the security guards
steered Amy, Jess, and Sara toward the back of
the store. Jess was stone-faced, but Sara softly
cried and hid her face in the collar of her fleece
jacket. Amy stopped by Molly's side and said
quietly, "I'm going to stay out here on the sales
floor; you go on ahead in the back. They've
already called Donna. She'll be here in a few
minutes." Amy held Molly's gaze for an extra
moment. There was sadness in her eyes.

Molly hesitated at the door to the back

room. Her fingers on the handle, she thought about the possibility of still getting out of this. Could it be that Jess and Sara hadn't mentioned her? Would Donna believe she wasn't involved? Could she possibly not stand with her friends and face it with them? Those thoughts swirled around and around in her mind but had no answers to cling to.

Out of the corner of her eye, Molly saw Donna enter the store. As she approached Amy, Molly hurried into the back room. She'd better find out what was happening before Donna questioned her.

Jess and Sara were seated in gray metal folding chairs at the training table where Molly had watched the videos about loss prevention and employee theft. She'd been so horrified that most theft was due to employee dishonesty. Now she was a part of that statistic.

The security guards sat silently on two stools, towering over the girls, glaring at them with their arms crossed on their chests and matching scowls on their faces. Sara was still crying and had wads of used tissues piled in front of her. Jess looked cocky—slumped in her chair, chin raised arrogantly, arms folded. Molly pulled up a chair and sat down beside Jess, whose face was a mirror image of the guards' scowls. No one spoke.

Molly didn't know what had been said about her yet. Could they read her presence there as an admission of guilt? She wondered if she should feign ignorance by asking what was wrong, playing dumb until she knew for sure. *What do I do?* It was too late, though. The door opened, and Donna hurried in, her face white. Her eyes flashed with anger behind the glistening of tears.

She looked at the guards with a question in her eyes but didn't speak.

The guard who seemed to do the most talking stood up from his stool. "We caught these two over by the food court." He gestured toward Sara and Jess. "They were in line to buy food, and I noticed the tags hanging off the clothes in their bags weren't from the stores printed on their bags. When I approached and questioned them, they acted really nervous. We went back to the security office, and I took a look. They had three dresses in there from your store along with some jewelry—"

Jewelry? Molly shot Sara and Jess a questioning look, but neither of them would look at her.

"—but no receipt. She said they had bought

them and were bringing them back to exchange but had lost the receipt." He pointed to Jess.

Donna sighed. "No, when I left this afternoon, we had yet to sell a single one of this style." She picked up the beaded powder blue satin dress. "It just came in the other day. I could show you how many came in the shipment, and my records will show that none of them have sold."

The security guard nodded, eyeing Jess. "Does your company have another store locally where she could have gotten it?"

"Well, no. But did she even claim that to be the story?" Donna's sadness faded, and the anger took over. "You see, these three are best friends. Molly is—was—my star sales associate and even a manager trainee. But, like I said, they're best friends. They probably worked together." She turned to Molly, pleading with her eyes for it to not be true. "Is that what happened, Molly? Is it?"

Oh, God. What have I done? Molly gasped for air as her sobs escaped. Her shoulders shook, and she couldn't catch her breath. *Please tell them I'm not involved,* she silently begged her friends. But even if they did, she didn't know if her conscience could handle sitting by while her friends took the fall. *Conscience. What a joke.* She almost laughed at the thought of it giving her a nudge after all this. Unable to speak, she just nodded.

"Okay, well, that's that. I'm going to have to call their parents. Girls, please write your parents' names and phone numbers on this slip of paper." The security guard handed Jess a pen and slid a slip of paper toward her. She ignored it. Sara took it and wrote the information for both of them and then handed it to Molly.

"What do you want to see happen here?" the guard asked Donna. "Do you want me to call the police? This is pretty serious. The value of the jewelry and the three dresses is over five hundred dollars judging by the price tags. Two of them would probably be charged with misdemeanor theft, and this one," he gestured to Molly, "would be charged as an accessory. Is that what you want me to do?"

Donna rubbed her eyes with the palms of her hands. Molly noticed she had scrubbed her makeup off and had changed into sweatpants. She must have been sleeping or resting quietly at home—not at all expecting something like this. "I don't think so. If it were anyone else. . . truly. But Molly is special. I have to fire her, clearly—but I'm sorry to do it."

The security guard nodded. "I had a feeling you'd say that. I tell you what, though; if I could, I'd charge just that one over there. She's got an attitude." He shook his head in disgust at Jess's behavior.

"Eh, she's a decent kid, too. She's just scared and trying to act tough." Donna turned and looked at the three girls. "I don't really know what to say to you three. Molly, it's as if you're my own little sister who did something stupid." She shook her head and looked at them for a long time. A single tear coursed down her cheek. "None of you can ever come in this store again, do you understand?"

The three of them nodded, and Molly stared at the ground.

Waiting for her parents to arrive was so hard for Molly. *They're going to kill me. No, worse— they'll be disappointed. Ugh.* What would have happened if Donna had called the police? Molly wanted to talk to her, to say something that would make it all go away, but she remained quiet, sure nothing she had to say would make a bit of difference.

Twenty minutes later—though it seemed like three hours—Sara's mom arrived first.

Minutes later Jess's parents appeared. They
talked with Donna and the security guard
who had stayed in the store to wait with them.
Molly's parents arrived a few minutes later. Mrs.
Jacobs sobbed and leaned on her husband for
support. She shook her head and whispered,
probably praying.

Chapter 11

YOU PLAY, YOU PAY

Out of work, grounded for life, a social outcast at church and school, a disappointment to her parents—Molly realized a little too late that everything she'd worked for could be lost in a moment, in one stupid decision. Back on her bed again, with Rocco stretched out beside her, was the only peaceful place to be in the days since the "incident." Molly hoped she'd be able to fall asleep so the time would pass more quickly.

Her hands linked behind her head, legs stretched out straight in front of her, she seethed. Yes, she *was* mad. Sara and Jess hadn't stuck to the plan. They were supposed to leave the mall right away, not go eat in the food court. And then, they didn't have to let the guard look in their bags. They could have walked right out at that time. The security guards had no power to detain them or search their property. She had told them all that when they were planning. But no, they got ultra-confident and did something stupid that cost them everything. *Ugh! It didn't have to happen this way.*

She jumped off the bed, too frustrated to rest, and paced back and forth across her room. She had nothing at all to do. Finals were over. They were on vacation from school. She wasn't allowed to speak on the phone or use the computer. She no longer had a job. *What do people do who have no life?*

Wandering to the nightstand, she remembered a book she had started a few months ago. She picked it up and opened it to where the bookmark held her page, but it didn't seem familiar at all. She turned back a few pages, trying to refresh her memory about the story. It was no use. She remembered nothing about the book and had no interest in what she read.

Several days blurred into each other until it was finally Christmas Eve. Molly hoped her parents would be able to put all this behind them to celebrate Christmas together, like a real family. That night there would be a big dinner at Molly's aunt's house. *I'll probably be the outcast.*

Molly helped her dad load gifts into the trunk of the car. "Dad, can I ask you a question?"

"Hmm?" He seemed distracted as he rearranged packages in the trunk so more would fit.

"What does everyone know? I mean, the family—Grandma, Aunt Pat, the kids—what do they know about me?"

"We haven't told anyone anything, Molly. It's too much of a shock to us still, and to be honest, your mom and I are too embarrassed. We have always prided ourselves on your ability to make good decisions. It's hard to admit to people how wrong we were." He shut the trunk and went into the house without another word.

Will this ever end? Will I ever be able to put it behind me?

Christmas passed without much fanfare. Molly looked over her room at the presents she'd received. She knew they were given to her reluctantly, bought during a time of celebration—before the bomb went off. She'd been given some cute clothes, some makeup, and a little television for her room she'd been begging for. It still sat in its unopened box, awaiting an unknown date when Molly's punishment was lifted. Somehow it seemed an inappropriate time to celebrate with gifts and new gadgets anyway.

A few days after Christmas, sitting quietly in the front seat on the way to her twice-yearly dentist appointment, Molly picked at invisible lint on her jeans and played with the seat belt strap, wishing something would break the deafening silence. Molly and her mom hardly talked anymore, and Mom's almost-readable thoughts screamed in the awkward silence.

Molly knew her mom was disturbed by the events of the past month just about every waking moment. Though she'd said everything and tried anything she could think of, Molly could do nothing to convince her parents she was truly sorry. She looked in the glove compartment, wishing with all her might to find a fun magazine or some other distraction in there.

Finally she couldn't take it anymore. She turned the radio on to their favorite Christian station. The last few bars of a song were fading as the host welcomed a guest, Penny Summerfield, author of *Handbook of Grace*.

"Hi, Penny. Welcome to the show. We're so glad to have you here with us today. We'd like to offer you a *Penny* for your thoughts." The radio host laughed hysterically at his own joke.

Penny laughed like she found it funny that he thought his joke was original. Molly imagined her saying, "Ha, ha, like I haven't heard that three times since breakfast." But, of course, she didn't.

"Tell us about your latest book, Penny."

"Sure, Phil, *Handbook of Grace* is just that. It's a handbook, a guide, if you will, to help you navigate the path of God's grace and see where it's at work in your life every step of the way. You see, sometimes people—Christians—don't realize that hardships and trials in life can be an act of God meant to steer them more solidly onto the path of His will for them. The road-blocks and speed bumps that He puts in the way are just measures of His grace as He helps guide the way."

Molly didn't think all that she'd been going through was an act of God. He didn't make her steal. *But could He have had something to do with me getting caught? No, that's pretty much all Sara and Jess's fault.*

"Phil," Penny continued, "sometimes we expect things to go our way all the time, and we get angry when they don't. We can get angry with God, with other people, even with ourselves. But, oftentimes, the hardship is God's answer to a mistake or a wrong turn that we've made. If we're walking outside of His will for us and He uses circumstances to kind of bump us back in line with His plan, why do we not rejoice in that and thank Him for His attentive concern for us? Rather, we get bitter, angry, and resentful of our own mistakes and others who were involved along the way."

"Those are some great points—" Phil started to say.

But she wasn't through. "God's grace is there. It's right before us. Yet we dance around it, step on it now and then, rub it into the ground, ignore it, and turn away from it sometimes. But when we do that, we blame everyone but ourselves. Rather than grabbing the grace of God and applying it to our lives, we shun it and then resent that it wasn't there when we're the ones who pushed it away."

"I hear what you're saying, Penny. But how, exactly, does one, as you said, 'grab the grace of God' and apply it to our lives?"

"Aha! That's the key question right there." She sounded excited about her subject.

"Well, I can't wait to hear the answer," Phil said emphatically. "Let's take a commercial break, and when we come back, I think we're in for a treat, folks."

Hmm. She's not so bad. Molly was surprised at her interest, but Penny's infectious excitement and the fact that the subject spoke right to Molly's own heart was too much for her to ignore. Mom leaned forward and turned up the radio just a bit and they sat in silence, listening to the commercials.

Molly considered what she'd just heard in light of the events of the past few weeks. Her anger was misplaced. She had no right to be angry with her friends or her boss—she only had herself to blame. She also had no right to resent her punishment or her parents' disappointment. *But I can't help it.*

"We're back with Penny Summerfield, author of *Handbook of Grace*. She's about to tell us how a person can grab hold of God's grace and apply it to his life. I can't wait to hear the answer to this. Penny?"

"Thank you, Phil. Well, I'm sorry to say, there's no formula. As you know, as a Christian yourself, God's grace is free and available to all people. But how do we 'apply' it as I mentioned? Well, grace is freeing, it's the gift of God that gives us the freedom to walk in righteousness. Because of God's grace, we don't have to pay the price for our own sins. Jesus already did that for us. So, we are invited to claim that payment and walk in the freedom not to sin."

"Wait, the freedom *not* to sin? That seems like a strange way to put it."

"Oh Phil, everyone is going to do wrong—we're fallen beings. But it's only the follower of Christ, through the power of the Holy Spirit, covered in the grace of God, who truly has the freedom and the power to say *no* to unrighteous behavior. We can say no whether it's blatant sin—unholy attitudes like jealousy, pride, selfishness, anger, resentment—or even just being passive and unresponsive to God's call. We have the freedom, through God's grace, to say *yes* to righteousness, *yes* to God's call, *yes* to sound choices and right attitudes of the heart."

Oh boy, I've really been blowing it. Molly sighed.

"Rather than using God's grace as a way out when we sin, let's apply God's grace in such a way that it helps us to say yes to His perfect plan."

"I like what you've had to say, Penny. I hope our listeners are thinking of ways to say yes to God's grace right now."

They pulled into the parking lot of the dentist's office. Mom turned off the car and grabbed her purse from the console between the seats. She looked at Molly and opened her mouth like she had something to say. But, instead, she closed it again and climbed out of the car, shaking her head. Molly took an extra moment to collect her thoughts before she got out.

I had it all wrong. Molly had been missing out on the fullness of a true and right relationship with God. In her mind, up until that point, it had been about staying out of trouble and being forgiven when she did something wrong, rather than running toward the righteousness she'd been called to. She'd been living a battle between the selfish part of her that demanded to be kept happy and the holy part of her that longed to be like Jesus. Which side would win?

Molly and God had some things to work out. She woke up a bit anxious to get to church, hoping she'd find her way back *home*. When she opened her eyes, though, she was immediately taken aback by the brightness that filled the room. It wasn't the yellow of daybreak sunshine. Instead it was a blinding whiteness. Molly jumped out of bed and ran to the window.

Blankets of snow covered everything. Cars were stuck in the street behind Molly's house, and the back door wouldn't be usable again until spring. And the snow still came down in big flakes that wafted down slowly but heavily unto the piles below.

Oh no. There would be no church, and even if services weren't canceled, they'd never make it out of the driveway to get there. What a bummer. Molly had really hoped church would be the answer to her innermost needs today. The new youth services had been so wonderful in the weeks since they'd started—she needed to be there.

The snow continued to fall as Molly looked out the window at the beauty that lay before her. *It's just like sin.* Jesus covered sin just like snow covers everything in sight. Suddenly it hit her. *God's not limited to a church building. I don't have to go there to find Him—He's within*

181

me. Maybe this snowstorm is part of His plan. The storm meant Molly had to find her own way back to God—probably just how He wanted it.

The time has come.

Chapter 12

THE TIME HAS COME

"Mom and Dad, I need your help."

They were enjoying the leisure of the surprise snowy morning at home by lingering over a cup of coffee at their cozy kitchen table. Mom had just taken a sip from her pink and white WORLD'S GREATEST MOM mug. She looked up with wide eyes, startled by Molly's emphatic statement. She slowly lowered her cup and swallowed with a loud gulp.

Dad nodded and gestured to an empty chair. "Well, take a seat. What can we help you with?"

"You guys, I've been thinking." Molly paused for a moment, sinking onto the kitchen chair, chewing her bottom lip while she chose her words carefully. "Mom, do you remember that radio show we listened to yesterday in the car?"

She waited for her mom to think back.

"Oh, do you mean that author who spoke about God's grace giving us the freedom to live a righteous life?"

"Yeah, that's the one. Well, I've been thinking a lot about some of the things she said and some other things. . . ." Molly took a deep breath. "I think I've had it all wrong."

Molly's parents both leaned forward. "We're listening," Dad said.

"The thing is, I've been angry. I've been mad that I got caught and mad at my friends for doing something dumb enough to get us caught. I've been angry with everyone but myself, when I really have no one to blame but me. Funny how that works, isn't it?"

Molly's mom and dad both nodded but didn't say a word.

"Well, I guess I'd forgotten that being a Christian doesn't just mean looking good to other people. It isn't just about doing as much as you can get away with without getting caught. It isn't about just skating by. It's letting God's grace change your life so that you don't even want to do those dumb things that were once a part of you. Do you know what I'm trying to say?"

Dad sat back in his chair and laced his fingers

behind his head. "If I hear you correctly, you're saying that you've been living like a Christian on the outside but hadn't really changed on the inside. So when push came to shove, you didn't have what it took to walk in God's grace and say no to sin. Is that what you're getting at?"

Molly slowly nodded. "Yes, that's exactly what I've been trying to work out in my mind but couldn't quite put it into the right words. Was it obvious to you that I've been living like that?"

Mom smiled. "Honey, you have to understand, we know you very well. We know you love to make people happy. You've always wanted to make your dad and me happy, so you've been a good girl. You've been involved in church. You've done what you're supposed to do. You want to make people at church happy, so you adopted their lifestyles and ways of doing things—you learned how to talk the talk."

Molly nodded along.

Mom took a sip of her coffee and then continued. "You wanted to make your boss happy, so you worked really hard and won her favor and even a promotion. And you wanted to make your friends happy. This time that didn't work out so well for you. But where in all of that do we see that you want to make Jesus happy?"

Molly thought hard about Mom's words. "Mom, Dad, I can't believe I have to say this, but I can honestly say I've never considered pleasing Jesus. Like you just spelled out, everything I've done has been motivated by my desire to satisfy someone else. Most of the times that has been in line with what God would want from me. But you're so right. When push came to shove, I wasn't thinking about Him at all, and it shows by what I did."

Molly shook her head and looked down at the table. *What do I do now?* Suddenly she looked up at them, helpless. "How do I change?"

"Sweetheart." Molly's mom laid her hand over her daughter's hand. "You've made the first step. You've acknowledged you can't do it on your own anymore and you want to live for Jesus, not for everyone else. Now we need to pray together and tell Him. Then your dad and I will help you figure out how to apply it to your life."

"It's like that lady on the radio said, Mom. Through the grace of God, we have the power and the freedom not to do wrong things to please everyone else. And He gives us the power to say yes to the good things. Right?"

"Exactly. You know, Molly. . ." Her mom hesitated. "I don't think your dad and I have really been great teachers of the love and grace of God."

"Yeah, we've been kind of caught up in the tradition, the religion of it all," Dad admitted. He stood up and walked to the window. "I think your new youth service is just what you needed. What we all needed, maybe."

Molly folded her arms across her chest and grinned.

"I think we're going to start seeing some changes around here."

Lingering outside the store, Molly wasn't sure she should go in. Donna said never to shop there again. But Molly had a different reason for being there. She needed to try to make things right with Donna. Taking a deep breath, Molly shouldered her bag of schoolbooks and walked up to the counter where Donna was doing paperwork.

"Donna?" Molly shifted from one foot to the other.

Donna spun around to see who had approached. She had an inviting smile on her face—she probably assumed it would be a customer—until she saw Molly. Her smile disappeared. "You're not supposed to be here. You're going to have to leave."

"I'm not here to shop. I just wanted to speak with you." Molly's nerve crumbled.

"You don't have anything to say that I want to hear, Molly." Donna looked up at the ceiling as she took a deep breath. She looked Molly right in the eye. "Please leave."

"Okay, I understand." Molly's lip quivered, and her eyes welled up with tears. "I just wanted you to know how sorry I am." She left the store in a hurry and climbed into the car where her mom waited to drive her home. As soon as the door shut, the tears came like a flood.

"She wouldn't listen. . .to. . .me. . .Mom." Molly gulped for air between her sobs.

"Not everyone has a forgiving nature, honey—and most people have limits. I guess Donna reached hers. You're not responsible for whether or not someone grants you forgiveness. Your only job is to seek it. You did the right thing. Now you can let it go and move on."

Molly nodded, but it wasn't enough. "It's hard to let go. I feel like I have so much more to say to Donna. I think I might write her a letter.

She can read it someday when she's ready to hear me out."

"I think that's a fantastic idea. In the meantime, be praying for her," Molly's mom suggested.

They turned the corner onto their street and saw two people trudging through the snow from their front porch. *Jess and Sara.* Judging by the footprints, they had come from Jess's house. Molly took a raggedy breath. *Please give me the words, God.*

Once the car stopped in the driveway, Molly hopped out and took a step toward the girls. Her mom went discreetly into the house through the garage.

"Hey." Molly looked away as the snow clung to her eyelashes. "I'm glad you guys are here. Want to come in?"

Sara spoke first. "Is it okay?"

"Does your mom hate us?" Jess asked.

"No, of course not. It's been a little rough around here. But we've worked through everything. I really want to talk to you guys." Molly impulsively reached out and tugged at their puffy coat sleeves. "Will you please come in?"

"Sure. I'm up for it."

"Me, too." Jess smiled.

They stripped off their snowy coats and gloves in the foyer. Molly said, "You go on up to my room. I'll be right there with some hot cocoa." She could already smell it coming from the kitchen. *Boy, Mom works fast.*

"Thanks, Mom." She took the tray of mugs and cookies. "Please pray for me—for us."

"You'd better believe I will, sweetheart."

Lord, please give me the right words. Help me make a difference.

"You know what?" Molly started right in as soon as she set the tray on the floor of her bedroom in front of Jess and Sara.

They looked at her with huge, imploring eyes and took a sip of their cocoa.

"I really, really don't want to talk about the details of what happened. There's no purpose in it. I want to put it behind us. But I do want to tell you that I'm so sorry."

Jess opened her mouth and raised her eyebrows in shock. "You want to say you're sorry to us? Why?"

"Because I let you guys down. I told you I was a Christian, but I didn't live it. That's not going to happen anymore."

"Well, we're both sorry for pulling you down. It was all just so wrong." Sara shook her head and shuddered at the memory. "I mean, I didn't like how it turned out. . .but I agree—I don't want to talk about that either."

"I really don't either." Jess shook her head.

"It was wrong. Now let's put it behind us. Okay?" Molly waited for an answer.

"Okay. On one condition." Jess's eyes sparkled.

"What?" Molly laughed—Jess was back to her old self, the schemer.

"I want us all to start going to church together—that youth service sounds cool."

"Deal!" Sara looked excited.

"Now that's the best idea you've ever had, Jess. It's a deal."

My Decision

I, *(include your name here)*, have read the story of Molly Jacobs and have learned from the choices that she made and the consequences that she faced. I promise to think before I act and, in all things, to choose God's will over mine. I promise, before God, to try my hardest to not let the desire for material things, the desire to please my friends, or the desire to be popular lead me to sin.

Please pray the following prayer:

Father God, I know that I don't know everything, and I can't possibly have everything under control. Please help me remember the lessons I've learned as I've read this book. Help me to honor my parents and serve You by making right choices and avoiding questionable situations. Please remind me of my desire to please You rather than everyone else. And if I find myself in a tight spot, please help me find a way out and give me the strength to take it. I know that You have everything under control, so I submit to Your will. Amen.

Congratulations on your decision! Please sign this contract signifying your commitment. Have someone you trust, like a parent or a pastor, witness your choice.

_____

Signed

_____

Witnessed by

MAKING WAVES

DEDICATION

To my oldest son, Erik, who is about to become an adult, but who has already proven himself to be a man. I'm so proud of you and how you've learned from the choices you've made in your life. As I write these books, I think of you and wonder how to get my characters to the same point of growth and maturity that I've had the priviledge of witnessing in you. I thank God for you every single day. I love you, son.

Chapter 1

A LONELY PORTRAIT

The picture had been shot only six weeks before; but the edges were already tattered, and fingerprints smudged the image. Kate peeled it from the scrapbook page for what seemed like the hundredth time. She leaned back to lie on the floor and raised the picture above her head in one fluid motion—the rotating ceiling fan made the picture wiggle.

Three generations of Walker women stared back at her from the photo. Her silver-haired grandma sat elegantly, unsmiling, in a high-backed brocade chair, and her mom stood just behind, grinning. Kate's sister, Julia, looked regal with her ivory-lace wedding dress fanned out around the group like a moat around a castle. She wore her brown, velvety hair swept up in an elegant clip, revealing her long, graceful neck. Kate sat at her mom's feet just outside the moat, her legs twisted to the side as she tried to remain graceful, careful not to touch the ethereal hem of her sister's garment.

Julia. She drove Kate crazy most of the time, but Kate didn't know how much she counted on her big sis until Julia had moved out. She didn't live too far away—about fifteen minutes by car—but far enough so they usually only saw each other on weekends when Julia had free time, which, for a young newlywed, was pretty rare.

Kate heaved herself up with a sigh and returned to her scrapbook. She flipped one page back to what she had been working on the day before. Her gaze locked on an image of herself with her best friend, Olivia. Pacific Ocean waves lapped the beach behind where they stood together, laughing at a private joke forever frozen in the photo.

Kate smiled because the picture showed just how little they had in common. Kate stood tall and slender, her shape almost boyish. She easily leaned her arm down across Olivia's much-lower shoulders. Olivia's bright blue eyes contrasted Kate's sea green. Olivia had a deep tan, but an equal coating of sunscreen and freckles covered

Kate from head to toe.

Kate wiped the tear from her cheek. Missing Julia hurt, but missing Olivia was a different story entirely. Forced to leave Oregon, where she'd lived all her life, Olivia had to move all the way to Chicago to chase her dad's promotion. It seemed so sophisticated—and so very, very far away.

Of course, they had promised to stay best friends forever. But Kate wasn't that naive. Only a sophomore, Olivia would meet other people, develop other interests, and move on with her life. Kate would just be stuck in Bethany, Oregon, with the same people she'd gone to school with since kindergarten. Everything stayed the same for Kate, except now she had to do it all alone.

Enough! Kate slammed the scrapbook closed. She really needed to stop the moping and do something with herself. Her mom wouldn't be home from her job for a few hours, so Kate decided to go for a swim. There wouldn't be many more opportunities as the summer drew to a close. The past few nights, Kate noticed that the night air held a hint of the approaching fall, which meant cooler water, too.

It's now or never. She pulled on her swimsuit.

grabbed a towel, and headed off on the half-mile walk to the nearby lakefront beach. A nice long swim would do her good. *Oops.* She ran back into her bedroom to grab a sweatshirt for the walk home.

The lifeguards waved to Kate. She nodded a greeting as she tied back her unruly hair then waded out into Lake Blue. She hesitated as the waves came in above knee level. She shivered at the first touch of the water on her thighs, already colder than a week ago. With resolve, she gave herself a silent *one, two, three, GO* and took the plunge.

Pulling through the small waves refreshed her. Each time she turned her head to the side to breathe, she felt cleansed. With her head underwater, she didn't notice that she had no one to talk to or that no one wanted to talk to her. It no longer seemed odd to be alone. She felt normal. Just God and her—everything was best that way. So she stayed underwater for as long as she could. She swam. And prayed. And swam. *Ahh, freedom.* The cares of life a distant memory, buried at the bottom of the sea.

She went out about a mile along the shore and then another mile back, and stood to wade into the beach. As her head popped above the

water and the fresh air hit her face, the world
once again seemed as huge as the mountains
in the distance, but she felt stronger. Nothing
had really changed about her circumstances, but
swimming always had that strengthening effect
on her. Kate just wished she could swim all the
time.

Wait a second. Why couldn't she swim all
year round? She could join the swim team. She
had probably logged around two hundred and
fifty hours in the water this summer alone. It
would sure be different swimming for a reason
other than pure pleasure. But maybe if she felt
like it had a purpose, Kate could love it as much
as the lake.

There was only one way to find out.

Kate toweled herself dry and slipped on her
flip-flops then trudged through the sand toward
the road. She hurried toward home, hoping
she'd have time to make a quick dinner to share
with Mom when she got home from work. She
kicked at the pebbles on the road and thought
of her mom. Four years ago, she had taken a
job after Kate's dad passed away. They needed
the money. She didn't like being gone so much,
and Kate knew she struggled with loneliness,
too. She could hear Mom crying in her bed

some nights. But now, it was time—they both desperately needed a change.

"Mom, I think I want to join the swim team at school. What do you think?"

"Really?" Mom dipped the corner of her grilled cheese sandwich into her tomato soup and took a bite, leaning over her plate so she wouldn't drip on her business suit. She looked out over their backyard, seemingly lost in thought.

Blinking rapidly as though to reset her thoughts, she blotted her lips with her napkin and said, "Well, I think a sport is a great thing; and you're a fantastic swimmer. I just don't want it to affect your grades or keep you from participating in other important things like the church musical—you do that every year." She got stern. "You promised me when you took a year off from choir that you'd still participate in the musical. When does swimming start?"

Tryouts are in two weeks. Practices would start the second week of September. And, Mom, you don't have to worry. I'll stay on top of everything." Kate tried to look convincing.

"Well, what kind of schedule are we talking about exactly?" Mom narrowed her eyes, the skepticism evident.

"Practice would be every day after school until five thirty. There's a sports bus I can catch, which would have me home around six fifteen. On Saturdays, there's either a meet or a practice. If, by some miracle, I make the varsity team, I'd also have a ninety-minute, before-school practice."

"Wow, Kate. That's quite a commitment. Are you sure this is something you want to do? After your swim schedule, church activities, and homework, you won't have time for anything else."

"What else is there, Mom?" Kate dropped her uneaten sandwich onto her plate. "If I don't go swimming, I just sit around here by myself all afternoon." She gestured at the house. "I don't even crack my books until well into the evening anyway. I might as well do something constructive and fun. Plus, maybe I'll meet some new people." She pleaded for understanding.

Mom closed her eyes for a moment and then, without opening them just yet, she reached out and touched the top of Kate's hand. She patted it, then looked at her and nodded slowly, gently squeezing. "I know it's been a rough four years for you, honey. You've had to deal with a lot of loss. Seems we can't catch a break since your father died."

After a moment or two, Mom shook her head as if to clear her thoughts. "You know what? I think it's a great idea. You should go for it. And there's no need to ride the sports bus home. I'll just swing by the school on my way home from work to pick you up."

Kate's mood instantly brightened. "That sounds great, Mom. Thanks! Now I just have to make the team."

"Swimmers, take your mark!" The coach shouted from the side of the pool, her whistle at her mouth, ready to blow.

Kate, already poised atop the starting block, leaned down and grabbed the edge just like she had been taught in the training session. Being careful not to fall in, she waited for the next cue.

"Get set."

She drew herself a little closer to the edge, arms bent, pulling forward on the block but pushing back with her feet, like a loaded spring.

"Go!" The whistle shrilled.

Kate sliced into the water with ease, then used her powerful kick to propel her as she angled her way toward the surface, careful not to come up too fast and break her speed. The instant her head broke the surface, she pulled her right arm from behind her and began to swim.

She swam with the same long, strong stroke she used in the lake, but the still water felt lighter and crisper. It was strange on her skin, but a welcome change. She felt as though she were flying through billowy clouds on a sunny day. Kate swam fast, and she knew it.

Reaching the end of the lane, she grabbed hold of the edge and turned herself around to go back. She'd have to learn how to do a flip turn, but the coach had said that she'd have plenty of time for that. The turn cost her a few precious seconds, but she still kept the lead. Nearing the end of the lap, she tucked her head under the water and gave a final thrust toward the touch pad that controlled the timer.

She finished her tryout, removed her swim cap and goggles, then hoisted herself onto the pool deck before the next swimmer arrived back at the starting block.

Coach Thompson walked over. "Great job, um, Kate, is it?" she asked, checking her clipboard and pulling a pencil from her short, curly brown hair. She was shorter than Kate, but her sturdy stature exuded strength and power.

"Yeah, Kate Walker." She wrapped a towel around her dripping body.

"Where've you been? Why didn't you swim last year? And how did you learn to swim like that?"

"I have always loved to swim, and I just do it for myself. I swim in the lake a lot. And I mean a *lot*." Kate shook her head to the side to release the water from her ear.

"I can tell." The coach nodded and smiled. "Come to practice on Monday. I want to play with some ideas before we make any decisions about team placement. Okay?"

"So, does that mean I'm not on the team yet?" Kate's shoulders dropped.

"Oh no! You have a place on the team. It's just where that I have to figure out. Your speed and raw skill is good enough for varsity. But your start and turns need work. So we'll just see if we can make enough of a dent in those to have you swim varsity. Deal?"

"Deal! I'll be here." Kate sailed away as quickly as she could on the slippery pool deck to the locker room. She couldn't wait to give her mom the exciting news.

Brittany and Pam, two juniors, had just finished rinsing off in the showers. Pam turned off the faucet and nodded toward the pool. "Nice swim today."

"Thanks." Kate's body clenched in anticipation of a conflict.

"I'm sure you'll be swimming varsity," Pam said with authority.

"You'll be Coach's new prodigy, I'm sure," Brittany agreed.

"Oh, I don't know about that. I won't get in anyone's way," Kate spoke quickly.

"No, Kate. From the way things look, we'll be in your way. Coach is going to have you flying before you know it. It's good to have you on the team." They both nodded and smiled warmly.

"Thanks a lot." Kate returned their smiles, relieved they were just being friendly.

While she finished up her shower, Kate heard her cell phone ring inside her gym bag. She tucked her towel around her body so she could dig for her phone. *Olivia!*

"Hey, Liv!"

"Hey, Katie-bug. How's everything?" Olivia sounded a little down.

"Well, I just got finished with swim-team tryouts, and I made the team. That's about all that's new here." Kate's voice trailed off. She wished Olivia could be there with her.

"Of course you did! You're an incredible

swimmer. I can't believe you never joined before this. Why didn't you, by the way?"

"Oh, I don't know. Life, I guess. It always seemed like too much time, and I thought I preferred swimming for myself. But I'm getting a big rush out of this team-competition thing. We'll see how it goes as the season moves on, though. But hey,"—she hesitated, not wanting to let her friend down—"is it okay if I call you back later tonight? Mom's picking me up in a few minutes and we're going out to eat. And," Kate laughed, "I'm standing here in nothing but a towel."

Olivia laughed. "Okay, we can't have that. Call me later."

Kate slid her phone closed and dropped it back into her bag. Sadly, she realized that she'd have less and less time for talking on the phone now. She shook her head to clear the negative thoughts. She took her long, damp curls into her hand, wound them together into a knot and secured the entire bundle with a clip, swiped on some lip gloss, and applied a touch of mascara to her light lashes. Satisfied, Kate grabbed her gym bag and her heavy school bag, jogged out to where her mom waited in her car, and slipped into the passenger seat.

"So, how'd you do? Did you qualify for a college scholarship yet?" Her eyes sparkled as the car door swung shut.

Kate buckled her seat belt and chuckled, hoping her mom was joking. "You never know, Mom. You never know. But for now, let's eat! I'm starving."

Chapter 2

NO "I" IN TEAM

Coach Thompson stood at the edge of the pool in her purple track suit and rubber shoes, dangerously close to falling in. She looked up from her clipboard and peered over her pink and purple reading glasses at the girls swim team seated poolside on the bleachers. "Hey, this is a pretty good-lookin' group." She smiled and nodded as she looked across the rows.

"Okay. It looks like we have a pretty big team this year, and I'm really excited about what I saw at tryouts." She rested the clipboard on her hip. "I think this is going to be an exciting swim season if you each do your part individually to achieve great team results. Just remember, even though you swim alone, you're part of a whole. There's no 'I' in team.

"New swimmers, I want you to go to the posting on the locker room door and find your lane assignment." She tipped her head toward the door. "Then, go ahead and get into your lanes and wait for further instructions. Returning swimmers, you know the drill. The workout is posted on the chalkboard—get to it and have fun!"

Thirty-six swimmers in racing suits, goggles in hand, climbed off the bleachers and went to peer at the list on the locker room door. Milling around with their shiny black swim caps on, they looked like a bunch of eight balls rolling around on a pool table. Kate tried to get her cap over her thick head of hair—no luck. She pulled and tugged on that tiny cap—still no luck. Just as she secured it over one side and moved to the other, it rolled up and her hair sprang free. She considered swimming without it just as she felt a tap on her shoulder.

"Need some help?" Pam offered.

Kate reddened as she saw that Pam's luxurious blond hair had been tucked under her cap without any apparent struggle. "Please." She was desperate.

"The trick is conditioner. You should get it wet first. Then condition it, put it in a ponytail, and wind it around the elastic band." Pam took off her own cap to show Kate. "Then, your cap should slip on pretty easily. Plus, if your hair's already wet and coated with conditioner, it won't get damaged by being in the chlorine for so many hours every day. But here,"—Pam pulled an elastic band from her wrist—"use this for today."

"Thanks!" Kate took the elastic. "I'm doing that conditioner trick tomorrow, for sure." *How cool of her to help.* She managed to get most of her hair tucked safely away and went to look for her name on the list.

"Kate," Coach Thompson called. "I almost forgot. Your name isn't there. I want to use this warm-up time to figure some things out with you, if you don't mind."

"Okay. . ." Kate looked back to the locker room door and the other swimmers. "What do you mean 'figure some things out'?"

"Hop on in here." Coach gestured to the empty lane reserved for warm-ups and cool-downs. Kate lowered her body into the water, trying to look like a pro by not showing any reaction to the temperature.

"I think it's pretty clear that you can swim. You're really fast, and you have a beautiful freestyle stroke. I'm sure that your speed is going to improve even more as you start real practices, and I can't wait to see what we can do with your times." Coach squatted near the pool's edge and lowered her voice. "But first, I want to see how fast you can pick up flip turns and starts so we can decide if you're ready to swim varsity."

Nervous excitement buzzed through Kate's veins. Kate could do it; she knew she could. She listened intently as her coach explained the mechanics of the flip turn, and then she pushed off the wall. Approaching the opposite side of the pool, she glided in with her arms at her side. She tucked her chin and rolled forward. About halfway through her flip, she unfolded her body, just like the coach had said. Placing her feet on the wall, she pushed off. Slightly off center, one foot slipped from the wall so it didn't have the power it could have, but she rotated to her stomach and continued to swim. *Not bad.*

After about fifteen minutes, Coach nodded. "Okay, that's enough. You're going to be great. Go ahead and swim with the varsity girls in lane five. Just keep working on your flip turns."

Kate hoisted herself out of the pool. "Thanks, Coach!" Could things get any more perfect? She joined her group and eased herself into the water, careful not to get in anyone's way.

Pam and Brittany, along with a few other juniors and seniors, filled the lane. Since Kate had no idea how things worked, she stood to the side and let them pass.

Brittany blew a dramatic sigh and exchanged knowing glances with a few other swimmers. "See that chalkboard over there?" She pointed to the back wall, rolling her eyes. "You look there to find out what our workout is. It tells you how much to swim, how to swim it, and anything else you need to know." She rushed through her explanation. "It also tells you the times. See the clock? If you're given a certain amount of time to swim and you get back here earlier, that's a break for you."

Kate repeated the instruction in her mind so she wouldn't have to ask again, determined not to earn another eye roll. "Okay, that makes sense. There are so many girls, though. How does that work?"

"Well, we all start out swimming in a line on the right side. If someone wants to pass you, they'll touch your foot or leg to let you know. Move over to the right as much as you can and let them pass. Also, watch for swimmers coming toward you on your left as they're on their way back. Got it?"

Kate nodded and put her goggles in place. *Ready or not, here I go.* She pushed off from the wall and glided through the water until she surfaced and started to swim. Within seconds, she could reach out to touch the feet of the swimmer ahead of her. She considered not passing, just to avoid making waves. But that wasn't why she joined the team. So she reached forward and touched her foot and then passed.

In just a few more seconds, she touched the foot of the next person and easily passed that swimmer, too. At the end of the lane, she did a flip turn just like Coach had taught her—not great, but it could have been worse. On the last length of the lap, Kate passed two more swimmers, which put her first in line.

Sandy Coble, one of the star seniors, said through labored breaths, "Kate, go easy, this is a three-hour practice. Don't wear yourself out in the first thirty minutes just trying to prove something."

"Good point. But so far I'm fine. Thanks." Kate knew they thought—or hoped—she'd tire out toward the end of practice. But, in truth, she'd barely exerted herself yet. By the time practice ended, without even trying to—or really even wanting to—Kate had proven that she was the fastest swimmer on the team. She sighed. They would all hate her.

"Kate?"

"Mm-hmm?" She turned to the coach as she toweled off her hair.

"Can I talk to you for a second?" Coach beckoned with her finger.

Oh, great. Kate followed the coach into her office.

"You surprised me today. When you came out like gangbusters and passed everyone, I thought for sure you'd be worn out by the time practice was half over. But it looks to me like you could keep going. Am I right?"

Kate nodded.

"My guess is that you held yourself back a little to try not to get everyone mad at you. Am I right?" Coach peered at her over the top of her glasses.

Kate simply nodded again, not sure what to say.

"Hmm. Just as I thought." She rolled her desk chair away and looked at the ceiling, lost in thought. After a moment, she abruptly turned to Kate. "Okay, that's going to have to stop. You do your best at every practice, no matter what. Okay?"

Kate nodded again. She wished she would just open her mouth to speak instead of standing there nodding like a dummy.

"If you're up for it," Coach continued, "I think we can push you all the way to a college scholarship. I've never seen such natural talent climb into that pool." She gestured with her thumb out the office door. "I think we can take you pretty far if you're up for the challenge. But you'll have to put in the effort and the time. Everything will matter—diet, sleep, practice, everything. What do you think? Can you handle it?"

"Oh, I definitely think I'm up for it!" A fire lit behind Kate's eyes. She had joked about a college scholarship but never considered it a possibility.

"All right then, you get on home, eat lots of protein. Be here tomorrow morning at 6 a.m. for our varsity workout."

Kate hurried from the coach's office toward the locker room. Her bare feet slipped a few feet on the pool deck then, reversing her direction, she slid into the door frame of the office. "Hey, Coach."

Coach Thompson looked up from her

paperwork and raised her eyebrows in a question mark.

"Thanks!" Kate spun on her heels and hurried away, not waiting for a reply. She couldn't wait to tell her mom about all of this. Oh, and she had to call Olivia and her sister. They'd be so excited!

Kate turned off her lights and set her pink alarm clock to wake her at five thirty the next morning. Her gym bag and school bag were already waiting by the door. She could just jump out of bed and go.

What a great day. But her excitement had been clouded by the one dark shadow over the day's events—Olivia's reaction.

"Now I'll never get to talk to you," Olivia had whined when she heard the news. "You're a completely different person now. I guess it's a good thing I moved away."

Olivia had sounded lonely, and Kate wondered if life in Chicago wasn't turning out to be as exciting as they thought it would be. Kate decided to pray for her friend. But before she got two words out, she fell fast asleep.

Yawn. After two weeks of early morning practices and not getting home until almost six thirty from evening practices, exhaustion weighed heavily on Kate. And on top of the schedule, Coach pushed her harder than the other swimmers because of her potential. As much as Kate loved swimming and enjoyed her celebrity status on the team, it took far more out of her than she'd anticipated.

"What's the matter, Kate?" Pam asked when she and Brittany arrived at the locker room after school on Wednesday.

Kate tugged at the straps of her swimsuit. "Oh, I'm just beat. Practice today and church tonight. Then homework. Then practice in the morning. It's just a long day. I'll live, though."

Pam snorted. "Skip church. That's an easy one."

I love church. "My mom makes me go." Kate busied herself in her locker. Why hadn't she been honest with Pam?

"Oh, I would hate that." Pam wrinkled her nose.

"It's not so bad." Changing the subject away from church and back to the point, Kate said, "Besides, it's only a tiny part of the reason why I'm so exhausted."

"Try a cup of coffee in the morning. It'll give you energy for practice."

"Ewww. I hate coffee." Kate wrinkled her nose.

"No one really likes it at first, silly." Pam laughed and pulled her suit on. "They just need it. You have to make it taste good."

"Yeah," Brittany jumped in. "I hated coffee at first. Then I figured out just how much milk and sugar to add, and now I can't live without it."

"Yeah, I guess I could try it." Kate shrugged.

Pam waved her hand. "Oh, just doctor it up. You'll get used to it sooner than you think."

"Mom, can you show me how to set the timer for the coffeepot?" Kate asked after church that evening.

"Coffee? Since when do you drink coffee?"

"It just sounds good for the morning before swim practice—warm, caffeine, energy. You know." Kate held up the can of ground coffee and the pack of filters.

"Well, first you make sure the clock is set correctly or it won't go off at the right time— every time we have a power surge, it resets the clock. . . . See?" She adjusted the clock to the right time. "Then you measure out two scoops of coffee—well, I use two scoops and that makes me half a pot. So we'll use four scoops and share it." Mom scooped the coffee into the filter. "Then you add a pot of water right here,"—she filled the water reservoir—"turn it on, and you're done."

"Thanks, Mom." Kate gave her a quick kiss. "I've got to run—studying to do."

After what seemed like only minutes had gone by, Kate lifted the heavy social studies textbook from her chest and rubbed her eyes, trying to focus on the clock. Three in the morning. She rolled over to the side of the bed, let her books slide to the floor, and turned off her light. She pulled her covers around her fully dressed body and immediately fell back to sleep.

Riiiiiing! Kate jolted awake to the sound of her alarm clock. She groaned. *Five thirty, already?* Like a zombie, she climbed out of bed and stumbled to the bathroom where she splashed cold water on her face. Not yet awake, she made her way to the kitchen where she fixed a steaming travel mug of coffee with lots of milk and sugar.

Kate blew away the steam and took a small sip. . .and then a second sip, finally understanding why people drank the stuff. It barely tasted okay, but its warmth comforted her tired and cold body and even the smell perked her up.

Later, in the locker room, Kate struggled into her cold suit which still dripped from the evening before, rubbed some conditioner into her dampened hair, and pulled on her swim cap. She took a final swig from her brew and felt ready to face the day.

"Wake up, silly! Can't you stay awake long enough to talk to your long-lost sister?" Julia's voice, a cavernous echo.

"Hmm?" Kate lurched upright. She'd crashed on the couch after practice got canceled, confused for just a minute. "Oh. Hey, Jules!" She rubbed the sleep from her eyes. "What are you doing here?"

"I'm taking you and Mom to dinner. Surprise!"

"Cool! Does Mom know?"

"Nope, not yet. But we're leaving as soon as she gets home, so hurry up and get ready. Wear something nice," Julia added as Kate took the stairs two at a time.

Kate stood at her closet door and considered her wardrobe, hoping to find something more interesting than her beloved Oregon State University sweatshirt or one of her many track suits. She settled on a pair of new dark-wash jeans and an emerald green sweater. She even styled her hair with a blow dryer to smooth her frizz into silky waves.

"This is such a nice treat—having my two girls all to myself like this," Kate's mom said as she dipped a chip into the salsa at their favorite authentic Mexican restaurant. "And we don't even need an occasion."

"Well, actually, I do have some news." Julia sat back in her chair and grinned.

Kate and her mom both put their napkins down and swallowed simultaneously. Kate took a swig of water before she asked, "You're not moving away, are you?"

"Nope. It's nothing bad." Julia clearly enjoyed keeping them in suspense.

"You're killing us. What's going on, Jules?" her mom demanded.

"Well. . ." She paused, letting their anticipation build. "I'm going to have a baby." She sat back and watched their reactions. In shock, no one spoke. "You're going to be a grandma." Julia looked at Mom, whose eyes were wide open as the news registered. "And you"— she pointed to Kate—"are going to be an aunt."

"Seriously?" Kate squealed in excitement.

"Oh, honey! That's wonderful!" Mom found her voice. She got up and ran around the table to hug her daughter. "I'm so excited!"

"Me, too, Mom. So is Kyle. It's a big surprise—we were going to wait a couple of years—but there's no better surprise than this." Julia twisted her napkin and then continued, her voice lowered almost to a whisper, "Boy or girl, I want to name the baby Casey. . .after Dad."

Mom gasped, overcome by emotion. "I th–think that's a beautiful idea."

Kate watched as Mom went through the stages of emotion that had been evident in her eyes many times since Dad died. Joy. Loneliness. Sadness. And then back to joy. When Mom could finally speak again, she said, "C–Casey. It's as it should be."

Chapter 3

CATCH UP

"So, talk to me, Kate. What's happening with you these days? I feel like I hardly see you anymore." Mom kept her eyes on the winding road and adjusted the visor to shield from the blinding morning sun.

"I know what you mean." Kate took a sip from her travel mug. "We used to have a lot more time to hang out."

"Right. I don't know anything about your new friends on the swim team, about your coach. . .if there are any boys you think are cute. . ."

"Mom!" Kate loved to confide in her mom, but every girl had her limit.

"Well, okay, aside from the boy talk, let's catch up after church today, okay? We'll go to lunch, just you and me." She glanced at Kate.

"Sounds great, Mom." Kate slid down in her seat, hoping to nap for the rest of the twenty-minute drive through the mountains to their church.

Kept awake by the caffeine, she just watched the beautiful scenery pass by her window. Her mind wandered to the events of the past few weeks. Much had changed for her, but she hadn't considered how those changes had affected her mom. Of course Mom was even more lonely now than she had been—why hadn't Kate seen that?

There were no more hot dinners waiting for her after work that they could linger over while they talked about the day. Now they just rushed into the house, threw something together, and ate in a hurry so Kate could disappear to do her homework. She had morning and Saturday practices, too—so no puttering around the kitchen on a lazy Saturday morning, no stopping for a bagel on the way to drop Kate off at school, no more late Friday-night movie rentals with a big bowl of popcorn.

The image of her mom walking around the house alone haunted Kate's imagination. She promised herself that she'd make an effort to spend more time with her mom—time like they used to spend together. While Dad had been sick, they'd grown especially close and bonded over his care. Then he left. Gone. Kate only hoped that one day she could find the kind of love her mom and dad had—even though it hurt so much when it was stripped away.

She smiled and shook her head at her predictable mom, gripping the steering wheel and leaning forward toward it, bouncing to the beat of the song on the radio. How could Mom be so happy when the greatest love of her life had been taken from her? She went from having it all to being alone. Yet she seemed happy.

Once at the entrance to the church, they waited in line just to enter the crowded parking lot. Mom groaned. "It's getting more and more difficult to find a space on Sundays if you're not here an hour before service." She shook her head and turned down one of the last rows of parking spaces. "They're going to have to expand the parking lot again—they'll need a shuttle service like they have at the airport." She went up one row and down the next with no luck. She threw her hands up in the air in exasperation and shrugged her shoulders toward Kate. Finally, she gave up her search and pulled the car into the grass at the far end of the lot. As soon as she did, other cars filed into the grass behind them.

As they made the long walk toward the church, Kate twirled in a circle and gestured at all the parked cars. "Who'd have thought this many people would be beating down the doors to get into church? I guess that's a good thing, though."

"That's true." Mom nodded. "Good way to put it into perspective, Kate. I guess I shouldn't complain."

They reached the side door where a waiting usher handed them a program and took them to a pair of open seats against a side wall. Sometimes the enormity of her church felt impersonal to Kate. But when they visited other churches, none of them felt like home.

The purple curtain began its slow, billowy ascent to the thirty-foot ceiling just as the band started playing soft music. As the drape lifted, revealing more of the stage, the music got louder. A massive choir, in their amethyst robes with gold braiding, stood across the back of the stage on risers, swaying to the music. They opened the service with a rousing medley of familiar, old hymns rewritten in a contemporary style.

When the people stood to their feet, the theater-style seating made quite a racket as the seats popped into place. Kate jumped right in, singing along and clapping to the music, her rich alto harmonies blending in with the choir. In moments like these, she missed singing with them—after having been a member for five years. But, she reminded herself, there would be time for that later. She couldn't do everything at once, and a one-year break would fly by.

After the worship time ended, Kate stooped back to push down her seat and then reached over to help her mom—she never could seem to get the hang of them. While the pastor walked across the long stage, the white-haired couple in front of her turned to compliment Kate's singing and asked why she wasn't in the choir.

"Thanks." Kate beamed. "I have been in the choir before. I'm just taking a break for this year." Her voice dropped to a whisper as the pastor began to speak. "I'm still planning to sing in the Christmas musical, though." Even as she said the words, she wished she could take them back. She would love to add that to her time off. But she promised Mom that she'd participate.

"Shh, Kate. He's starting."

Pastor Rick opened his sermon with a thought-provoking statement. "The trial may be inevitable, but the misery is optional."

Kate shifted in her seat, thinking about what

he'd just said. *The trial may be inevitable, but the misery is optional.*

"Sometimes life's twists and turns aren't always what we want, but we can't avoid them. We have to go through trials and pain in life. It's inevitable. But in the midst of those trials, it's up to us how miserable we become. We can choose to become bogged down in the mire of disappointment, fear, anger, bitterness. . .or we can remain hopeful and joyful."

Kate nodded involuntarily.

"Think of Paul and Silas," the pastor continued as he walked across the stage from one side to the other, involving the listeners in every crevice of the large auditorium and even looking into the cameras now and then to involve the at-home viewers. "Paul and Silas were imprisoned for their faith. They were stripped of every comfort of life and were in physical danger every minute of every day. What did they do? They sang. They praised God. They were filled with so much joy. Not because of their circumstances, of course—their joy came from the Holy Spirit, from within them."

He seemed to look into the eyes of every person seated in that room. His eyes bore through to Kate's soul.

"Joy is a gift from God that we can open in our lives. Joy has nothing to do with our circumstance. Nothing."

He let that sink in.

"Jesus promises that trials and tribulations will befall you. He also promises that He won't let you face anything so difficult that you and He can't get through it together."

He paused again and moved to the side of his podium. He leaned one elbow on it, resting conversationally. "Now, I have a question for you. Could it be that He might allow something to happen in your life in order to force your attention back to Him?"

Screeech! Kate stopped short on those words. *Could it be? Did He strip me of my best friend, my sister, and my dad so I'd turn to Him?* She couldn't accept that God would cause such pain and upheaval just to get her attention. How could He work that way? That's not the kind of God she wanted to follow. No way. Kate could believe He would help her *through* a trial, but she'd never accept that He *caused* it or even just allowed it as a way to turn her focus to Him. *No way.*

Kate forced herself out of her pensive reverie

to hear the final chords of the last worship song as the choir closed up the service. She'd missed the last few minutes, so lost in her thoughts that she hadn't even stood for prayer. She gathered her things and hoped Mom wouldn't question her lack of focus.

Before she had time to look at her mom, though, Kate felt two cold hands over her eyes. "Guess who!"

"Hmm, the Easter Bunny," she teased, unfazed, turning to look.

In feigned horror, Mark grabbed his heart, pulled out an invisible stake, and fell back against the faux plaster wall. He slid to the floor and to his certain death.

"Drama anyone?" Kate rolled her eyes. *That Mark. Funny, charming, and always entertaining.*

"Ha-ha. So, what are you doing right now? A bunch of us are going to go for pizza after church and then hang out at the mall until tryouts at three o'clock."

"Tryouts? For the Christmas musical? Oh no! I totally didn't know they were today." She glanced to see if her mom had heard. Lowering her voice, she said, "Mom and I have plans."

Mom interrupted. "You should go, Kate. That sounds like fun."

"Mom, you and I were going to hang out today. I can skip tryouts. I'll just sing in the choir for this year's musical and not audition for a special part. I wouldn't mind that at all." Kate pleaded for a reprieve.

"No way, Kate." Mom shook her head. "This is much more important than whatever non-plans we had. You'd have wound up being bored all afternoon after we had lunch together anyway. This is much better than sitting home alone all day."

Kate shot her a look. How could her mother not realize that she wouldn't want Mark to think she'd just sit home alone, bored? *Mothers. . .* Kate shook her head and smirked.

"Will you have a ride home, or should I pick you up?" Mom, oblivious to her recent blunder, pushed Kate ahead with the plans.

Mark cleared his throat. "I'll be happy to see that she gets home, Mrs. Walker."

"That'll be fine. Thanks, Mark." She gave Kate a quick kiss good-bye, squelching any protest, and slipped ten dollars into her palm before she made the trek back to the car, alone.

Kate sat on the tile floor of the entryway and leaned her back against the wooden door of the vestibule to watch the cars go by outside. What was taking Mark and his buddies so long? *Ah, footsteps, at last.* But they stopped on the other side of the door. She leaned forward to grab her bag and started to zip it closed when she heard her name. She paused in mid-zip and didn't move a muscle. They had no idea she sat on the other side of the door.

"Did you guys see Kate Walker sing? Does she have any idea how great she is?" Mark asked.

Steve chuckled. "You've got it bad, man. Does she even know?"

"I don't know what you're talking about, Steve. Kate's just a good friend. But that girl's got chops, that's for sure."

Steve and P.J. both laughed. Kate heard a slap—she pictured them high-fiving each other. "You owe me five bucks," Steve said.

Kate panicked. Frantic, she looked all around her with no idea how to get out of her current situation. She didn't want them to think she'd been spying now that she'd heard them talking about her. She could feel the heat rising to her face—sure that her neck had turned a bright shade of pink.

"Yeah, right. They have to go out on a date first," P.J. protested.

"Oh, they will. I guarantee it," Steve assured him.

"You guys have a bet?" Before they could answer Mark said, "Oh, never mind, I really don't want to know. Look, I've known Kate for over ten years. She's like a sister to me. I just think she's very talented. Have you guys seen her swim? She's amazing."

In the momentary silence, Kate imagined that Steve and P.J. raised their eyebrows while they waited for Mark to dig himself out of that last statement. Even she could tell he was deflecting. She patted her flaming cheeks and wondered how she would get out of this predicament. She would be mortified if Mark found out she'd overheard.

Now or never. With the stealth of a leopard, she leaned over to the glass door that led outside and pushed it open. Just as it closed with a loud clunk, she stood to her feet as though she had just come through the door. Then, with her head held high, she opened the interior wooden door that separated them and approached the boys as though she hadn't heard them. But she had. . .she'd have to sort through all of that later.

Chapter 4

JUST TRY IT

She didn't dare look back. She lost more of her lead with every single stroke. Had the water turned to mud? Kate's arms had never felt so heavy before. Rather than glide across the surface, her hands landed with a resounding thud on the water like when she swung the mallet at one of those amusement park games.

The unthinkable happened. She felt a flutter on her calf—the dreaded touch of the swimmer behind her. Her stomach sank to the bottom of the pool. First she saw a pair of hands pulling through the water near her face. She tried to speed up—not a chance. She just couldn't do it. The hands gave way to arms and then the top of a head. Who could be passing her? *Ugh!* It was Pam—a very smug-looking Pam. Kate knew she swam better than Pam—or did she? Maybe everyone had been wrong about her.

Kate had failed. She didn't want to talk to anyone or even show her face. She hurried through her shower and then rushed to her locker to try to get out of there before the other girls finished with theirs. She just wanted to go hide out in her classes until the afternoon practice. Maybe she'd even go home sick. She clipped her wet hair back without even combing it and shoved her things into her locker, but she didn't make it out in time.

Pam and Brittany, wrapped in towels, turned the corner down the row they shared with Kate. They got dressed in deafening silence while Kate shoved things in her bag and slammed her locker door. Pam sighed and looked up at the ceiling for a moment. Then, she stared into Kate's eyes and said, "Hey, Kate. It's no big deal. We all have bad days. Don't let it get you down."

"Yeah, I have bad days all the time." Brittany rubbed her hair with her towel.

"Listen. . ." Pam put her foot up on the bench and rubbed lotion on her leg while she talked. "I had a really hard time my second year on the team. I started to take my swimming more seriously, so I worked really hard. I was tired all the time and my schoolwork started to suffer." She grimaced at the memory. "My parents almost made me quit the team because I just trudged around, barely making it through the day." She put her leg down and started on the other one. "Eventually, I just had to find a way to get the energy I needed to get through everything and still perform well."

"Me, too," Brittany said. "I had my issues when I first started, too. Over time, after you find out what works for you, you settle into a routine and everything gets a little easier. You'll figure it out."

"That's the thing. I don't know what to do." Kate plopped onto the bench, put her head in her hands, and blinked back the tears. "I feel so much pressure. My mom is pressuring me not to let anything slip. Coach is pressuring me to be the best. I'm pressuring myself to earn a scholarship." She took a tissue from Pam and blew her nose. "All of those are good things, but sometimes it's just too much when you put them all together—especially when I'm so tired."

"Tell me about it! We all feel those stresses . . .or at least some of them." Brittany slipped her arm around Kate's shoulder as they left the locker room to head to their first-period classes. "I tell you what, meet us out here before practice this afternoon. We'll share one of our secrets with you."

"I'll be here," Kate promised. Maybe they did have the perfect solution—only one way to find out.

"Here." Brittany shoved a shiny blue metal can, about half the size of a soda can, toward Kate. Kate's backpack slid from her shoulder to the floor with a thud as she took the can, inspecting the label.

"What is a Red Dragon? I've never heard of it."

"Oh, it's just an energy drink. It's totally legal, and it's sold in every gas station. You'll see, though, it's way better than just coffee because it has other stuff in it that makes the energy stick with you a lot longer," Brittany assured her.

"I don't swim without one." Pam looked around her on all sides and then lowered her voice. "It's the only thing that gets me through a grueling workout and still leaves me with enough energy to do my homework later."

"Hmm. . .really?" Kate wasn't sure she

wanted to resort to such drastic measures.
"You're sure it's legal?"

"Oh yeah. I mean, there's no way they'd sell
it to me at the gas station if it wasn't, right?"

Kate narrowed her eyes, skeptical. "True. . .
but then why do you have to keep it a secret?"
What would Mom say?

Pam shook her head. "It's not that it's a
secret. We just don't want it thrown in Coach's
face that we use this stuff. She probably knows,
anyway. It's just not the natural approach she'd
like us to take."

"Yeah, you know Coach. She preaches about
all that good stuff—diet, plenty of sleep, herbal
tea. . .health." Brittany snorted. "But believe me,
she's happy with the results even if she doesn't
know it."

Pam narrowed her eyes. "And, Kate, there
are others on the team who drink this stuff.
We're not the only ones. Pay attention. You'll
start to notice cans in their swim bags and on
the bus. Just don't make a big deal out of it. . .
'cause it isn't one. Okay?"

"Okay. If you're sure, I'll give it a try. What
do I owe you for this one?"

"Oh, don't worry about it. Go ahead and
have it. I'm sure you'll be buying your own after

this." Pam reached into her gym bag and pulled out a can for herself and one for Brittany. At the same time, they popped the tops and tapped the rims in a mock toast. "It's best to drink it fast, because it doesn't taste all that great," Pam warned.

"Thanks for the warning." Kate took a sniff and wrinkled her nose. "Here we go." She tipped back her head and sucked down the tangy fizz. *Eww.* They were right. She gagged a bit on the first drink but kept choking it down. She shuddered as she swallowed the last little bit in the can. They turned to the locker room and dropped their cans on top of the other three that were already in the trash. Almost late for practice, they hurried to change and get out to the water.

Within fifteen minutes, much to her surprise, Kate buzzed through the pool, even a little giddy. Her fingers tingled and her head felt lighter. She pictured herself swimming to Alaska—she might actually make it that far. Could it all be in her head, though? No matter, she was back. She sailed through the water with her usual ease, and no one got close enough to even think about touching her leg—what a relief that that had only happened to her once.

"Hey, Kate!" Coach beckoned her over to the side of the pool toward the end of practice. "Come on over here. You're doing really well this afternoon. Let's work on some speed drills. How about a race?"

"Race? Um. . .okay." Kate gave a nervous chuckle. She couldn't think of a better day to test her limits. Coach called for Sandy to race the 100-meter freestyle—Kate's favorite race—against her.

"Swimmers, take your mark. . . ." Coach readied her whistle while the girls pulled forward into their starting positions. "Get set. . . ." They tightened up their stance, perched to spring into the pool. "Go!" The whistle blew and off they went. Kate had the best start of her life. A thing of beauty. How was Sandy's start? She couldn't tell.

Kate swam with all of her might. She breathed on every third stroke and sailed into her first turn in what seemed like record time. The water cascaded over her head and through her body. She had never felt so alive and in her element as she did in those moments. As she continued out of her turn, she realized Sandy hadn't even arrived to the end of the lane yet. She had almost half a pool length advance on her. How had that happened? Instead of relaxing in her clear victory, Kate pushed harder.

Nearing the end of the swim of her life, Kate gave it all she had. With as much extra thrust and power in her strokes as she could muster, she sailed to the end and touched the pad in record time.

She ripped off her goggles and looked at the timer. She had beaten the school record for the one hundred by a little over two seconds. Kate and her coach looked back and forth at each other and at the clock, stunned, as they waited for Sandy to finish her race.

She floated out from the wall, trying to cool her body down. At least two dozen swimmers hanging on the lane lines had witnessed the momentous occasion.

"Good swim!" Sandy said.

Kate tried not to make a big deal of it. "Thanks a lot. You, too."

She heard her coach's voice from behind her. "Kate, can you come into my office before you leave the pool area? For now, though, go ahead and cool down. I'm sure you need it."

Chest heaving, Kate swam two easy laps on her back to cool her body down. She hoped her rush wasn't just because of that energy drink. She felt like she had been under her own power, her own skill. . .but how could she be sure? By the end of her cool-down, Kate decided that she had just found a way to tap into the strength she already possessed. Ready to talk to Coach, she hoisted herself out of the pool and made her way to the office.

"Well, well, well, Miss Kate. Nice swim, to say the least." Coach shook her head in disbelief. "Something tells me you've got a lot of surprises in you." She put down the papers she had been shuffling through and turned her chair to face Kate. "I want to know how serious you are about swimming. You're a first-year swimmer, a sophomore, and you've beaten our school record in a practice. Unfortunately, the time doesn't get recorded because it's not a formally timed event, but things look really bright in your near future."

Coach leaned her elbows on her thighs and clasped her hands together. "Then, there's the long-term future to think of. Kate, you have an amazing talent and you just keep getting better and better. What do you think of all this?"

"I don't know. I mean, I love to swim; and I want to push myself. I'd like to earn a scholarship and swim through college, if you still think that's a possibility."

"A possibility? Do you understand that the record you beat today is eight years old?" Coach shook her head, as if hoping she could get Kate to grasp the significance of what had just happened. "If you can swim like that in an impromptu race after you already swam a full practice, just imagine what you're capable of doing at the Regional invitational on Saturday. If you come even close to a time like that, you'll definitely get some attention and the powers-that-be will start watching you.

"Here's what I want to do." Coach picked up her clipboard, and Kate leaned forward in her chair. "I want to have you swim several events on Saturday. Let's get in there and make some waves. You can swim the 100-meter and 200-meter freestyle races, as well as the freestyle leg of the IM relay, and the anchor leg of the free relay."

Kate panicked. "Um, Coach. . .Sandy swims the IM relay."

"Not anymore, Kate, not anymore."

Kate left the office buoyed by the possibility of her future but concerned over the pressure she'd face from the other swimmers. Not only would they be counting on her to swim at least as fast as Sandy, but they'd expect her to prove why she was a worthy replacement. She hoped her coach wasn't making a horrible mistake. No matter how it turned out, Sandy would hate her for sure.

I'm going to need more energy drinks.

"Liv! We need to talk!" Kate shut the door to her room and sprawled out on her stomach across her bed, her cell phone in hand. "I have so much to tell you, and I need your advice."

"Okay. I'm all ears."

Kate took a moment to soak in the image of her friend closing her bedroom door before settling down into her beloved purple banana seat. Once the sounds of settling stopped, Kate launched into a monologue about her life. She left nothing out: Julia's baby, the tryouts at church, the energy drink that helped her win a proverbial gold medal at practice that day, a shot at a scholarship, and then finished it off with Mark.

". . .He said I'm amazing. Well, I guess he said I sounded amazing, or something like that . . .oh, now I can't remember his exact words."

"I don't need the exact words. I already know you're amazing. And I already knew he thought so, too. You two have been destined to get together. It was only a matter of time."

"So, you think I should let it happen? I mean, if he wants it to, of course. He hasn't asked me out on a date or anything."

"Yes!" Olivia laughed. "I do think you should 'let it happen,' and he will ask you out on a date for crying out loud. I guarantee it."

Kate remembered that Steve had said the exact same thing. "Okay. I believe you. But we'll have to see. I still feel weird about it, though. He's such an old and good friend. Maybe it will feel like dating a brother."

"Perfect first-date material, if you ask me," Olivia assured her. "There's nothing to worry about. It's all part of your life's inevitability. Just live it."

Kate laughed at Olivia's cosmic approach to life. "That's true. Okay, enough about Mark. What do you think about the other stuff?"

"It all sounds so incredible. You're living a dream. Are you able to do it all, or are you falling apart?"

"I did have a hard time for a little while, but I'm fine now. I think I'm getting my second wind." Kate thought of something. "Oh, Liv. I wish you could be here for the invitational on Saturday. It's going to be so exciting—a lot of pressure, though. Coach says this is going to be the moment that everyone sits up and takes notice of this new swimmer at Sandusky High School. What if I crumble?"

"Yeah, you'll crumble under the pressure because that's your style, right?"

"Ha-ha, funny. But seriously."

"I'm sure it's unnerving. But you deal with stuff like that well—look at what happened today. Just do the same thing on Saturday. Boy, I wish I could be there, too. I assume your mom is going?"

They talked for almost two full hours while Kate watched the sun go down outside her window. She ached for her friend.

Chapter 5

ON THE ROAD

Reclining sideways against the window, Kate ducked to miss the balled-up towel that flew by. A sigh escaped her lips as she gave up and shut her geometry book. No use trying to study with all the racket. Slipping her book back into her bag, she pulled out a Red Dragon to sip. Turning in her seat, she drew her knees up and pressed her shins against the vinyl seat back so she could join the chaos in the back of the bus for the rest of the two-hour ride to the swim meet.

She popped the top on her energy drink. *Thunk.* The vacuum released. Only two more rolled around at the bottom of her bag for later, so she took small sips to make it last. Was it just her imagination, or did she have to drink more to get the same effect now?

"Gross! I have to chug mine when I drink them. They taste terrible!" Amber, a senior, shot Kate a disgusted scowl from across the aisle.

"I used to think they were gross, but the taste has kind of grown on me. I like to drink them slowly so I can feel the energy building in me." She waved her hands in billowing motions in front of her body.

"Do you really think it has that much of an effect, though?" Amber asked Kate, looking doubtful. She took a sip from a bottle of orange juice.

"Absolutely. I even like to mix in some coffee sometimes."

"Hmm, I just don't think I get that big a benefit from them, so I rarely spend the money."

"Oh, believe me, I hear you on the cost." Kate rolled her eyes. "I have to use half of my lunch money in order to buy enough for the week." *Mom better never find out.*

"That's what we do, too." Pam spoke up from the seat right behind Kate, pointing with her thumb to include Brittany who shared her seat.

"Who needs to eat, anyway?" Brittany laughed, patting her midsection.

"That's what I'm saying." Kate joined in the laughter, feeling the buzz already.

The bus brakes squealed in the parking lot of a gas station. When it came to a stop and the driver opened the door, Kate stood up and raised her arms high in the air to stretch. The three girls ambled toward the door past a few rows of sleepy swimmers who were just rousing themselves.

"Come on, everyone!" Pam shouted and clapped her hands. "Up and at 'em! Let's see some excitement around here!" A few girls moaned, one covered her head with a pillow, and another lobbed a wadded napkin at her.

In the gas station, Kate hurried past the rows of candy bars and chips, straight to the coffee machine. She poured a large steaming cup of coffee and slid it into a sleeve before the others caught up with her. She flicked three packs of sugar against the countertop then ripped off the tops of all three packets at once and shook them into the coffee, spraying granules of sugar all over the place.

"Hey! You're making a mess," Brittany complained. "Simmer down." She laughed.

Adding three tubs of cream, Kate did her best to make her coffee palatable. Blowing away the steam, she took a tiny sip. She wrinkled her nose and added another packet of sugar and one more cream to her cup.

After another sip, Kate said, "Ahhh. Now that's what I'm talking about."

About an hour later, almost to their destination, Coach stood in the center aisle to address the girls. "Team, this is an exciting day. For you new swimmers, as you're probably tired of hearing me say, this is our first event on our way to Sectionals and then State."

Kate moved to the edge of her seat.

"You'll be making a name for yourself and setting a standard for your personal season as well as for the team. Today's times count as records for the season. And"—she looked around the bus and made eye contact with each of the faster swimmers—"there's a chance that some records will be set today." She shifted her position as the bus swayed on the mountain turns.

"Some of you may feel that your contribution isn't as exciting as some of the other swimmers', but that's just not true. Take everything seriously and do your very best. Even if you come in last place for a swim, the seconds you shave off can make a huge difference for the team's morale.

"And for those of you who have your sights set on some big personal accomplishments today, relax, go easy on yourself." She pushed her glasses up. "I want you to do your very best, but more than anything, I want you to have fun."

They pulled into the parking lot of the Oregon State Aquatic Center and the bus squealed to a stop. Kate stumbled getting off the bus, unable to tear her eyes off the massive building in front of her. Was this where she'd swim? *Wow!* Old news to the seasoned swimmers, they looked away, unimpressed.

The instant they walked through the turnstiles at the entrance, Kate breathed deeply, filling her lungs with her new favorite scent: chlorine. She could hear the sound of rhythmic splashing as teams had already taken their places in the water, warming up for the day's events.

They walked as a team, maroon and gold duffle bags over each shoulder. Nerves set in and no one spoke as they headed toward the locker room. Kate paused at the trophy case. Did she dare dream that her name would be affixed to one of those shiny gold trophies one day? *Someday—but now I just have to get through today.* Her stomach flip-flopped, and her hands shook. She lifted her head, pulled back her shoulders, and took a deep breath.

Steamy air and the riotous clamor of voices

knocked Kate back a step as she opened the locker room door.

"Where've you been?" Pam wondered, tucking her hair into her cap. "We're almost ready to go out to the deck."

"I just needed a minute. Wait for me, okay? I'll hurry." She didn't want to step out onto the pool deck alone, so she put her things in a locker and changed into her racing suit in record time. She hurried around the corner, hoping they hadn't left her. But there stood four of her teammates, leaning against the shower wall, waiting for her. As a united front, they linked arms and walked out together.

The bleachers couldn't hold one more spectator. They came decked out in team colors, their conversations blended into one cavernous roar. Standing to the left of the bleachers, Kate scanned the crowd for signs of her mom's red hair. She looked up and down each row at the families—children with their books and computer games settled in next to their parents, grandparents with their cameras on straps around their necks, aunts, uncles, friends, loved ones all there to cheer for someone special.

After several anxious moments, she spotted her mom's bright red hair in the middle of the third row. As usual, her mom had gotten into a deep conversation with a stranger. Her ability to draw people out amazed Kate. *Wait!* That stranger sure looked familiar. *Could it be? No way!* It was Olivia! "Olivia? Mom? Over here!" She jumped up and down, trying to get their attention.

Olivia flashed a huge grin. "Ta-da!" She stood up and spread her arms as wide as she could, one toward the ceiling and the other pointed toward the floor.

"What are you doing here?" Kate mouthed, astonished to see her best friend.

"I wanted to surprise you!" The noise almost drowned out Olivia's shouted response, so she cupped her hands around her mouth.

"Come here!" Kate demanded with a big grin and pointed to the pool deck at her feet.

Olivia scrambled over legs and bags as she made her way to Kate.

Kate wrapped her best friend in a bear hug. "I can't believe you're here!" She looked her friend up and down. "You look exactly the same."

"Well, you don't," Olivia said. She held Kate back at arm's length. "You're all toned and muscular, like you're ready for the Olympics. I can't wait to see what all the fuss is about." Her eyes twinkled.

"Well, I'll try to make your trip worthwhile."
Kate laughed. "Hey, speaking of that—how did
you get here?"

"Oh, my dad had to come to town on
business, so he let me use some of his frequent-
flier miles. I'm staying at your house until
Tuesday."

"Perfect! We're off school on Monday."

"I know, silly. I arranged this trip, remember?"
Olivia poked Kate in her side just as the warning
bell sounded the start of the meet.

"I'm so excited you're here." She turned, in a
hurry to get to her team. "I've gotta go now. But
meet me in the hallway outside the locker room
after it's over. I hope you don't get too bored."
Kate gave a teasing smile.

"I'll be fine," Olivia assured. "You just swim
your heart out. I'm rooting for you."

"Swimmers take your mark. . . ."

Kate shook her arms to keep them loose for
her favorite swim, the 100-meter freestyle. An
hour before, she swam with her relay team to
take first place. She could still feel the adrenaline
coursing through her veins—the Red Dragon
surely helped with that, too.

"Get set. . . ," the announcer continued.

She bent down and grabbed the starting block, poised to pounce. In those last seconds before the starting gun went off, she made a mental list of what she needed to do to make this a record race and looked ahead at the serene water. Even though the pressure was on, the water beckoned, and she couldn't wait to swim.

Bang!

Kate sailed off the starting block and flew through the air toward the water. She sliced through the surface with ease. Already off to an amazing start, she swam with all her might, reaching like a little girl with her sights set on a cookie jar—just a little more. . .a little more. . . And she pulled through the water with strength even she hadn't known she possessed.

It came time for the flip turn. It still wasn't her strongest skill, and her foot slipped just a little, which limited the force she had for the push-off. But she pressed on. Relieved that the length of the Olympic-sized pool meant that a 100-meter swim only had one flip turn, she'd sailed through the hardest part. *Home free.*

One more length of the fifty-meter pool left to swim. She looked at the lanes to her left and, with the next breath, to her right—the water rested, undisturbed. No one came close. Still buzzing from her second energy drink of the day, she pulled from all the mental, physical, and spiritual energy she had. The buzz plus her adrenaline and determination—a record-breaking combination.

Lord, please help me.

She swam for her life. Her lungs seared and her shoulders screamed.

Stroke. Stroke. Stroke.

She felt the speed coming out of her finger-tips like lightning and heard the crowd cheering. She absorbed their energy and stroked even harder toward the end of the lane. One last big pull, she tucked her head and reached out for the timer pad and glided into it.

She looked at the clock—52.33! She did it. She broke the record.

Triumphant, she pulled off her goggles and her swim cap and floated on her back for a few seconds to cool down, still basking in the cheers. One by one the other swimmers finished their races. They took off their goggles and stared at the race results, panting to catch their breath.

"Congratulations, Kate," another swimmer offered before getting out of the pool.

"Congratulations. . ."

"Good swim. . ." People milled around,

and Kate lost track of who said what while she reveled in the praise that flew at her from all sides.

"Amazing."

"Congrats."

Kate exhaled, still trying to catch her breath, and smiled as she responded, "Thanks, same to you."

She hopped out of the pool to get some water and wind down in preparation for her next swim—she didn't have long. She dug through her gym bag to find the banana and granola bar she'd tucked in there for that purpose. Her hand brushed against something cold—her last Red Dragon. She wanted it badly but didn't want to show weakness by drinking it right there in front of the other teams and the spectators, and she had to swim again in less than a half hour. So it would have to wait.

Immediately after she finished taking second place in her third swim of the day, she picked up her duffle bag, slipped the strap onto her shoulder, and walked to the locker room where she laid back on the bench to gather her thoughts. Towel covering her face, she tried to focus by reliving every moment of the race so she could harness it and do it all over again in a little less than an hour.

"Hey! There you are. Everyone's looking for you. What are you doing hiding out in here alone? You should be celebrating!" Pam shouted.

"Oh, hey. I just needed some time alone to think." She noticed that Pam's maroon suit dripped water. "You just swim? How'd you do?"

"Oh, who cares? You're the star these days," Pam teased. Her voice didn't hold a hint of malice, but her eyes looked just a little envious. Kate knew she'd probably feel the same way—or worse.

"I'm sorry I missed your swim. I'm just trying to stay in the zone for my last race. I don't want to lose any steam." Kate popped the top on her Red Dragon.

"Oh, believe me, I can understand that. Everyone's talking about you."

"Ugh. Just what I needed to hear," Kate groaned, taking a big swig of her drink.

"There's no need to be nervous. You're doing all the right things. You're staying focused. And you've already finished three races. Three down, two to go. Easy. But, hey, if you need a little extra confidence boost, take one of these." Pam held out a little pack of white pills. "They're just caffeine pills. They'll sure give you a zing."

Kate narrowed her eyes. "Oh, man. I don't know. Are they even legal?"

Pam assured her, "Oh yeah. Definitely. You can buy them anywhere without a prescription. Totally legal."

Kate recognized the pills as the ones her mom took that first year after her dad died. After being awake all night, she had needed some help functioning at work. Kate turned the sheet of pills over and read the back. If her mom had taken them and they helped her a lot, why not? She couldn't get mad if she'd done it herself. . .right?

"Perfect." Kate peeled back the silver foil backing of the sheet of pills and popped one out into her hand. "Down the hatch."

After her last race, Kate sat on the bench in the locker room. She held three blue ribbons and one red ribbon for the IM relay in one hand and a card with her record-setting time in the other. Her eyes flitted back and forth between her winnings. Which to look at first?

She shook her head to clear it and tucked her memorabilia safely away in her swim bag. She pulled on her track suit and tied her hair back into a ponytail and escaped the chaos of the locker room to go find her mom and Olivia.

"Kate!" Olivia came running down the hallway when Kate first poked her head out. "You were incredible! I can't believe how great you were!" She jumped up and down and squealed. "Four races. . .three first places and a new record!"

Kate and her mom just laughed while they waited for Olivia to get it out of her system.

"You're going to the Olympics!" Olivia grabbed her hands and squeezed them. "You could seriously be the best swimmer ever!"

"Whoa, whoa, whoa. I'm going to have to stop you there." Kate held up her hand and shook her head. "Incredible? Maybe. Great? Sure. Best swimmer ever. . .nah. . .you don't think?" But she couldn't keep the big grin off her face.

"Kate, you really were beautiful out there, sweetie. I'm so proud of you." Kate's mom beamed and hugged her. "All that hard work is paying off."

If only it was all because of my hard work.

Chapter 6

→

FIRST DATE

Kate and her mom stumbled through the door with their arms full of packages. Kate let her school bag and purse slide to the floor. She reached to help as Mom heaved the two grocery bags, the carton of fried chicken, and her turquoise leather purse to the countertop. Kate lifted her mom's purse and waved it in front of her face. She wrinkled her nose in disgust and raised her eyebrows at her mom before she lowered the purse to the floor.

"You're a funny one, Kate," Mom said sarcastically—usually she harped on Kate for that. She turned to put the frozen mashed potatoes in the microwave. "You're right, though. The bottoms of purses carry more germs than—"

"Hello, Walker residence."

"Did the phone even ring?" Mom interrupted.

"Shh," Kate whispered with her hand on the receiver.

"Hi there. It's Mark Hansen."

"Oh. Hi, Mark. How's it going?" Kate tried to keep her voice from shaking and turned her back.

"I was just calling to see if you wanted to go out on a real date with your ol' buddy Mark."

Kate laughed. When did he not make her laugh? "Ol' buddy, huh? How nice of you to ask. When were you thinking?" She picked up a pen to doodle on the pad of paper near the phone.

"Friday night is as good a night as any, don't you think?"

"That sounds great. . . . I'll have to clear it with my mom, but it should be okay. I'll talk to her, and then I'll let you know in school tomorrow. Sound good?" She smiled and flipped her fully doodled paper over to the clean side. Mom tried to step in her line of sight, but Kate wouldn't look at her.

"Perfect. I'll talk to you then."

"Thanks for calling, Mark. Talk to you tomorrow. . . . Bye." The cap of her pen flew off when she slammed it down on the counter. She groaned. "Mom! This is exactly why I need a phone in my room or at least a cordless phone that will work in my room." She had an afterthought. "Or a cell phone package that I can use to talk to more people than just you, Julia, and Olivia."

Mom laughed and put the tomatoes in the produce bin. "No. Calls from boys are exactly why you don't need a phone in your room. What are you so upset about, anyway?"

"I'd just like a little privacy when I'm having a conversation instead of you distracting me by making gestures and comments to confuse me while I'm trying to sound intelligent." She slumped onto a stool and put her face down on her crossed forearms that rested on the cold granite.

"You don't need to *try* to sound intelligent, Kate. Besides, it was Mark Hansen, right?"

Kate nodded without lifting her head.

"I mean, come on. You've talked to that boy in person every week of your life for years and years. Why all of a sudden is a phone call something special?"

"Well, that's just it. He's never called before," Kate whined.

"Come on, Kate. Be respectful." She narrowed her eyes.

"Sorry." Kate sat up a little straighter.

"What did he want, anyway?"

"He asked me out on a date." The microwave beeped an exclamation point as Kate stared at her mom, waiting for her reaction.

Mom stepped toward Kate without closing the refrigerator. "What? A date? Really?"

"What, Mom?" Kate challenged her with one brow lifted. "Is it so difficult to believe that someone might want to go out on a date with me?" She gestured up and down her body.

"Of course that's not what I mean, Kate, and you know it." Mom sounded frustrated and tired. "I just wasn't expecting this so soon."

"What do you mean, so soon? I'm going to be sixteen in three weeks. Most kids my age have been dating for a long time."

"I understand that, but you're not—"

"—most kids my age." Kate had heard it all before. She jumped off her stool, and it screeched backward against the tile floor.

"I've said that a time or two, huh?"

"Yeah, Mom. You really need to get some new lines." Kate rolled her eyes and smiled, beginning to calm down. She picked through the chicken to find a breast, peeled the fried skin off with two fingers, and left it in the box. "The thing is, I want to go out with Mark. I think he's great and if anyone should be my first date, it should be him."

"Maybe no one should be your first date." Mom took a seat on the stool next to Kate at the island.

Kate ignored those words. "I know you've always said that I had to be sixteen to date, but are you seriously going to hold me to a matter of days?"

"No. Of course not, Kate." She sighed. "I'm not unreasonable, you know." Mom took a deep breath. She pushed her untouched plate away with one hand and rubbed her eyes with the other. "You know, your attitude has changed lately—more agitated and irritable. You've been using a tone with me that I don't like. Let's get a handle on that. Okay?"

Oops. She'd gone too far. "Okay, Mom. I'm really sorry."

Mom nodded. "Now, if you want to go out with Mark, under certain conditions, it's okay with me."

Kate stopped chewing. "What conditions?" She tipped her head to the side and slumped her shoulders, sure she'd hate the answer.

"I want you home by eleven. I want to know everywhere you are, even if plans change." She pointed at her fingers like checking off a list. "I don't want you to be alone in someone's home without an adult. Always wear your seat belt— and all the other rules that you already know."

"Okay, Mom. That's all pretty reasonable." Relieved, she came back with a cheeky comment and a twinkle in her eye. "For now."

"Boy, you sure are a funny one, aren't you." Mom swatted her on the behind as Kate squeezed past her with their garbage.

"How did this happen so fast? You're not ready for this," Mom mumbled as she left the kitchen. "Come to think of it, neither am I."

❊

"So, where are we going?" Kate asked Mark as he looked in the rearview mirror.

"It's a surprise." He wiggled his eyebrows up and down and grinned. "You look really nice, by the way."

"Thanks." Kate ran a shaky hand down the leg of her best jeans—a pair of comfy sweats was more her style. Whoever thought denim was a good idea, anyway? She crossed her legs at the knee then uncrossed them and fluffed her hair which she had worked on for almost an hour. She took a deep, steadying breath—she didn't have to be nervous with Mark, so why couldn't she calm her racing heart? "So, come on, where are we going? What could be the big surprise? And Mom made you tell her. So, let's have it. . .out with it."

"It's not that big a deal. I just don't think you've ever been there before, and I think you'll really like it." Mark grinned with secrecy. "And . . .we're here." He pulled into the parking lot of a small, plain brick building with no window or signs.

"It looks like an abandoned warehouse." Kate knitted her eyebrows and squinted to peer closer.

"Well, it used to be a warehouse, but it certainly isn't abandoned." He turned the car off and winked at Kate. "Let's go. You're going to love this."

The car doors slammed shut, and Mark set the lock. Kate counted six other cars in the parking lot, but no people in sight.

He started to walk toward the building but must have noticed her hesitation. "It's okay, Kate. Trust me. Really."

Her shoulders relaxed, and Kate laughed off her trepidation. "Oh, I'm fine. Just trying to figure this place out."

Mark opened the door for her to enter ahead

of him. She stepped around him and walked through the doorway, pausing to allow her eyes to grow accustomed to the darkness. The heady smell of rich coffee beans wafted through the air—she took a deep breath, inhaling the aroma. The bottoms of her feet tingled from the thump of the steady drumbeat and bass rhythm that traveled through the floorboards. She patted her hip in time with the music, warming up to the place as Mark guided her past the restrooms, through the carpeted vestibule, and past a red velvet curtain into what appeared to be a bar of some sort.

Her eyes finally adjusting to the dark, Kate could make out little round tables in the center with their chairs positioned so their occupants could see the stage. Each table had three votive candles in the center and a menu with PERKIES on the front. Around the outside edges of the main floor sat clustered groups of overstuffed chairs and love seats where people could relax in a more comfortable and intimate setting. She scoured the room but didn't see a bar anywhere. Loud music already blared out of the huge speakers as though they expected a huge crowd, but only five of the tables had occupants.

"Let's sit over here, okay?" Mark put his hand

on her elbow and steered her across the room.

Kate pointed to one of the stuffed-chair clusters away from the giant speakers where they'd still be able to talk.

"What a neat little place! How did you find this?" Kate asked as they sank into their chairs. "How cool to have live music at a place that isn't actually a bar. I never would have thought something like this existed."

"I don't think you've actually figured out just how neat it is just yet. It'll hit you in a minute." Mark smiled, his eyes twinkling.

A waitress approached their table and opened the little menus for them. "Can I get you two anything?"

"Sure. . .I'll have a. . ." Kate looked the menu up and down. "A café mocha sounds great."

"There's hope for the hopeless, rest for the weary. . . ," came the deep, raspy voice from the speakers.

Kate's ears perked up at the words to the song. She leaned in and listened, sure they sounded familiar to her.

"Cry out to Jesus. . . ."

Confused, Kate furrowed her eyebrows and looked at Mark. "This is one of my favorite songs. . . . It's Christian music?"

"Yep, it's a Christian coffeehouse. It's all

Christian music."

"How cool! How is it I've never heard of this place?" She picked up the menu and read the name.

"It's pretty new. They just converted it over from an old warehouse, and word is just now getting around. I'm helping them with their marketing a little bit by going to some of the area churches and passing out flyers to the youth ministers and pastors. I really hope that people will come out and support this place so it can stay in business."

"What a great idea for a hangout. I'm so glad you brought me here."

He sat back in his chair and tapped his foot to the music, a pleased smile spread across his face.

"So how do they pick the bands?" Kate asked him after they listened for a little while.

"Funny you should ask. . ."

Uh-oh! She'd seen that glint in his eyes before. He had something up his sleeve. "Oh boy, here it comes." Kate laughed good-naturedly and shook her head, used to his dramatic ways.

"The bands here don't get paid, and there aren't a whole lot of good Christian bands in the area, so they will pretty much let anyone who wants to get involved just take an evening and run the entertainment. When they don't have a band, there's recorded music, but you can imagine that the place loses its cool vibe when that happens."

"You're right. The live music really makes a big difference." She tipped her coffee cup to drain the last drops.

"So, I was thinking,"—Mark gave her one of his drop-dead smiles—"what if we put together a little group and played here once a month or so?"

Kate sat up straighter, intrigued. "I don't know. . . . What did you have in mind?"

"Well, you would sing, obviously. I'd play rhythm guitar. We'd have to get Ty to play drums and Gabe on bass. Maybe we could even get P.J. on keyboard, but we could do it even if we didn't have a keyboard."

"Hmm. Well, it sure sounds interesting. It could be a lot of fun. We'd have to get together and practice to see if we'd sound okay."

"With that lineup, we couldn't help but sound great." Mark exuded complete confidence without a hint of boasting. "But you're right. So, what are you doing Sunday after church?"

Kate laughed and waggled a finger at him. "You have this set up already, don't you?"

Mark hung his head in mock shame then chuckled.

"Knowing how bad you are at taking 'no' for an answer, I guess I'm practicing with you guys after church. But. . ." Kate hesitated as she thought of her schedule. "I won't be able to get too involved in anything like that until December. My swim schedule is about to get really intense over the next month up through the State competition—assuming I qualify, of course."

Mark rolled his eyes at her humbleness. "Of course you will. But whatever works for you is what we'll do."

"So maybe we should look at starting to practice in December but not try to play here until after the New Year."

"That sounds reasonable. But let's see how it goes on Sunday. We'll just have some fun for an hour or two—no pressure—and then I can drive you home."

It did sound fun. But she tried to imagine squeezing another thing into her already-full schedule. She would go to practice with them on Sunday, but that didn't mean she'd do it for sure. *I can say no. It's easy.*

When the waitress came back to see if they wanted something else, Kate said, "Sure, that's enough mocha for me, though. I'll have a regular coffee this time."

"Oh, not me." Mark shook his head. "I'd be up all night long. Decaf for me, please."

The rest of the evening passed much like the first part had. They laughed, teased, and enjoyed the music like old friends. Surprised, Kate felt comfortable with Mark and laughed more in that evening than she had in a year. . .or more. Kate felt very lucky to have been around through Mark's transformation from goof-off to growing-up. She couldn't wait to see more. . . *much* more.

Chapter 7

TRICK OR TREAT

"Trick or treat...trick or treat...trick or treat...," Kate chanted to the waves at practice the afternoon of Halloween. A distance practice, no sprints. So Kate got settled into a comfortable pace and had plenty of time to think.

If I do well at Sectionals, I'll qualify to swim at State, Kate reminded herself every five minutes. For the next two weeks, she planned to put everything else on hold. She would skip practice for the Christmas musical—they wouldn't be too happy with her, but it couldn't be helped. She intended to turn down dates with Mark, too—if he asked her out again. No shopping trips with her sister—not that Kate had called to invite her. *Swim. School. Eat. Sleep. Swim.* Sometimes the pressure felt like a crushing weight on her chest.

But she wouldn't trade it for anything.

*Trick or treat. . .trick or treat. . .trick or treat. . .*She continued her strong strokes and stayed in her easy rhythm for the long swim. It felt very much like her swims at the lake. No whistles, no timers, no shouts from the pool deck, no starting blocks or flip turns. No one else.

Just me and my thoughts.

Olivia. It had been a full two weeks since she'd talked to her best friend. She hadn't even had a chance to tell Olivia about her first date. Olivia would be so disappointed when she found out. They had promised each other they wouldn't let distance come between them, and they'd still share all those special things. But the first important thing happened, and Kate didn't even call her. How would Kate tell her best friend that she had been too busy to pick up the phone to include her in one of her most important milestones? Olivia would be hurt— Kate could only imagine how she would feel if Liv did that to her. How could she make it up to her? She'd have to find a way.

Stroke. . .stroke. . .stroke. . .

Julia. Her baby belly had started to show, so Kate had heard. She hadn't seen her since the night Julia surprised them with the news about

the baby. *It's not my fault, though.* Julia just didn't
come around very much, and she didn't come
to church with them like she used to. Come
to think of it, she'd never even been to a swim
meet. But Kate knew she needed to do her part,
too. She'd have to call her sister later.

Stroke. . .stroke. . .stroke. . . The soothing
water washed over her head.

Mom. Time had served her well. Kate could
remember when every single night, her mom
would get ready for bed, close the door to her
room, then break down. She must have thought
Kate couldn't hear her. But Kate fell asleep to
the sounds of her mom weeping more nights
than Kate cared to count. Over the years, the
crying jags quieted and slowed, and now they
only happened once in a while. *It's been weeks.
Mom's making her peace.*

Mark. Hmm. Kate picked up some speed
when she thought of him and had to remind
herself to slow down. She had a long way to
swim and wouldn't be able to finish if she didn't
pace herself. *Mark.* He really liked her—she had
no doubt—and she liked him. But she feared
that she didn't have the time to dedicate herself
to the expectations of a new relationship when
she barely had time for her old ones. She knew

Mark understood her schedule, but did he really support her commitment to it? Time would tell.

Trick or treat. . .Trick or treat. . .Trick or treat. . . Kate cleared her mind of the heavy thoughts and slipped back into the rhythm fueled by her mindless mantra.

Dong! The broken doorbell chimed only the last half of its announcement. Kate's knees popped as she unfolded from the couch. She put her biology book face down and hurried to the door.

"Trick or treat!"

"Oh boy! What do we have here? Let's see, a princess, a cheerleader, a scary monster." A terrifying roar pierced her ears. "Oh my, how scaaary!" Kate shuddered, playing along with the kids. "And a ballerina, a dinosaur, and a pirate. What a great bunch of costumes, you guys!"

Propping the screen door open with her knee, she held out the candy bowl for them to help themselves. Chubby little hands reached out from their costumes and dug in the bowl for the perfect piece of candy. Each child only took one, so she whispered, "Go ahead, take two, just for being so cute and polite."

"Thank you!" They hopped off the porch step and ran to their waiting parents. "She gave us two, Mom," she heard several say.

One after another, the parade of children continued through the evening. By nine o'clock, the steady flow of kids had slowed to a trickle.

When the phone rang, Kate checked the caller ID. "Hey, Mom. I need to take this. Can you man the door?"

Mom put her magazine down on the arm of the recliner and gave a mock salute. "I'm on it."

Stepping into the kitchen for privacy, Kate answered the phone. "Hey, Mark. What's going on?"

"Nothing much here. How about you?"

"Oh, we're just having fun with the little trick-or-treaters. Have you had many?" Kate peeked out into the family room to make sure Mom couldn't hear her and then sat on one of the kitchen stools.

"Well, my parents don't want to support Halloween because of its pagan roots and all that. So we just keep our front lights off, and the kids don't come here."

"Oh man, I would hate that. I love seeing their cute little costumes. And they don't mean anything bad by it." Kate reached for the doodle pad and pen.

"Oh, I know they don't, and they definitely are cute. I'm not really sure how I feel about the whole thing. But I guess I can agree with my parents that it's best not to further any darkness when it's something you can avoid."

"So are you saying that if you had kids, you wouldn't let them wear a costume to school?" She doodled a jack-o'-lantern with question marks for eyes.

"Hmm, I hadn't thought of that." He paused for a second. "You know, I don't think I'd go that far. But I sure wouldn't let them dress up as anything evil like witches or ghosts. You know?"

"Sure, I think that's gross when kids do that anyway. They're little kids. They should be princesses and superheroes."

"Right." For several moments Kate listened to the dead air, wondering if Mark was going to speak. Should she say something?

"Well, now that we've got that settled. . ." Mark broke the awkward silence, and they both laughed.

"You mean that's not why you called?" Kate teased.

"Um. . .no. . .although it was interesting. The real reason I'm calling is to see what you're doing this weekend. Want to go out to a movie on Friday night?"

Kate groaned. "Oh, you're tempting me. I promised myself I wouldn't do anything but swim, eat, sleep, and go to school until after the State championships." She made a quick decision. "But I suppose a movie won't set me back much."

"Good! You've still got to have a life. I promise I'll have you home early."

"Well, this is my life right now." Kate chuckled. *Take it or leave it.*

"Score!" Mark hooked the empty popcorn carton into the trash.

"That was a decent movie." Kate said as she stepped through the movie theater door that Mark held open for her.

"I'll go with decent, but probably not much more than that. Definitely not a re-watcher." He put his hand on the small of her back as they walked through the parking lot.

A nervous shiver ran through Kate's body as she felt his touch.

"You cold?" He pulled her closer.

How do I let him know that this is not a first-kiss night? Or is it?

"Want to go to Perkies for a cup of decaf and to check out the band?"

Kate looked at her watch. *Plenty of time.* "Sure, I'm up for that."

Once they had settled into their favorite

overstuffed chairs, Mark ordered a decaf mocha.

Kate said, "I'll have a large, no foam, extra whip, sugar-free vanilla latte with an extra shot." She laughed at Mark's chin that had fallen into his lap. "What? You never heard someone order coffee before?"

"Well, Kate, come on. You didn't just order coffee." He shook his head and chuckled. "You ordered a four-course meal complete with soup and dessert. In fact, you even told the chef how to make it." He laughed and then stopped short. "Wait a second. Did I hear you right? Did you ask for extra whip, sugar-free? Don't they kind of cancel each other out?"

The waitress arrived with their drinks before Kate had a chance to answer. She took a sip and said, "Ah. . .perfection." She sat back with a satisfied smile.

"Nothing wrong with perfection, I guess." Mark looked deeply into her eyes.

Kate broke eye contact by looking away. "I'll be right back." She grabbed her purse and went into the restroom. She didn't need to use it, but she needed to gather her thoughts. *I like him— how could I not?* She stared at her reflection in the mirror. *But. . .* Nerves nagged at her—it was happening too fast. *One thing at a time, Kate.*

But she knew she could trust Mark, so, if need be, she could slow him down. For now, she decided she could handle the way things were going. Probably.

Chapter 8

REALITY STRIKES

After a hot shower, Kate padded barefoot down the hall toward her room, tightening her robe on the way. She hesitated, surprised to see her bedroom door open. Hadn't she closed it? She brushed off her concern and smiled when she saw that she had a visitor—Mom sat waiting on her bed. Kate's smile wavered a bit when she noticed her mom's somber expression and the swim bag on her lap.

"What's up, Mom? You packing me up and sending me away?" Her voice quivered as she joked. She bent at her waist and flipped her hair over to comb through her thick curls, trying to figure out what could be going on. Why did Mom have her swim bag? *Uh-oh.*

"We need to talk."

Hearing the seriousness in her mom's tone, Kate flipped her hair back over and sat down on the edge of the bed beside her. "What's going on?"

Mom fingered the zipper on the maroon and gold duffle bag. She took a deep breath. "Kate, I don't search through your things, you know that. I just wanted to put a few granola bars in your bag because I've been concerned that you're not eating enough. You're getting too skinny, honey."

Kate opened her mouth, but Mom held up her hand to stop the protest. "But that's not what we need to talk about right now."

Kate closed her mouth and waited.

"I found these." Mom reached into the bag and pulled out a small pile of caffeine pill packets, little bottles of single-serving energy serum, and four cans of Red Dragon—two full, two empty. She just stared at Kate.

She had to answer this just right if she had any hope of convincing her mom that she didn't have a problem. *But I can't lie to her.* She rose from the bed and went to the mirror where she picked up her comb and pulled it through her hair. *Be calm—stay casual.* "Mom, I don't understand. What's the problem?"

"Kate, these are addictive substances, like speed."

She shook her head. "No, they aren't speed at all; and they're no more addictive than coffee. Most people drink coffee every day. You can't start your day without half a pot, yourself. And this stuff won't discolor your teeth," Kate said, trying to brush it off.

"Kate, this is far more serious than coffee." Mom took several moments before she spoke again. "I have some questions, and I expect honest answers. . . . First of all, where did you get this stuff?"

"Oh, they sell it at every gas station, drug-store, grocery store—everywhere. I'm not sure where I picked up each item." Kate kept her tone casual, knowing the wrong answer would seal her fate. "Most of it came from the gas station by school, though. It's all perfectly legal, Mom. As legal as buying a cup of coffee." Still trying to diffuse her mom's concern. "By the way, I checked; there's really no more caffeine in these drinks than there is in a good cup of coffee. So, what's the difference?"

"First of all, comparing it to coffee isn't a great move, Kate. Coffee has three times the amount of caffeine that a soda does—it's not good for you regardless of how many people drink it. Including me. And caffeine is only one of the ingredients in these products. Here, look." Mom tossed a can to Kate as she read off the one in her hands. "Guarana, ginseng. . .do you know what those are and the effects they can have on your body? How about the other unpronounceable words on there? Do you know what they are? I sure don't."

"No. I don't know." *What does she want from me?*

"Do you have any idea what your heart rate is before and after you drink these?"

Kate shook her head and crossed her arms.

"Well, isn't it possible that the 'energy boost' involves an increase to your heart rate, which you wouldn't want to add on top of what an intense swim workout does to your heart? Right?"

Kate nodded. *Busted.*

"Do you know that kids have died from drinking these drinks?"

That did it. Kate held up a hand. "Mom, come on. Kids have died crossing the street or from choking on gum. That's not my fault, and it doesn't mean I shouldn't cross the street or chew gum, right?"

"But this is completely different, Kate, and

you know it." Mom looked up at the ceiling as though collecting her thoughts. "Let me ask you, Kate. Do you only take one pill *or* one energy drink *or* one cup of coffee?"

"At a time, sure," Kate reassured her mom.

"Kate, I want you to level with me. You know I can tell when you're not being honest. I want to know how much of this stuff you take in a day. I know you drink coffee in the morning on the way to swimming. Then what?"

"I usually take a caffeine pill at school." Kate hesitated. Could she get away without telling her the rest?

"And. . . ? Then what?"

"Oh, I don't know. I don't keep track, really." Judging by the look on her face, Mom wouldn't let it go at that. And if she didn't give her mom the information she wanted, it would make the whole thing appear a lot worse. How could she say this without lying? "I take a caffeine pill at the start of every practice and then drink an energy drink midway through if I feel like I need it—you know, if it's a hard practice or I'm unusually tired." She almost added "That's it" to the end of her sentence, but that would have been a lie.

"That plus the half-a-pot of coffee you have

in the morning equals. . ."—Mom did the math in the air with her finger—". . .anywhere from one thousand to twelve hundred milligrams of caffeine a day, not to mention the other stuff in that can. And that's if you're telling me the truth about how much you use." She stared hard at Kate. "But I'm concerned that you're understating the truth." She paused for a moment, rubbing the creases in her forehead. "Tell me this, Kate. Where do you get the money to buy this stuff?" She gestured in disgust at the stash of promised energy that lay in a heap on Kate's bed.

"Oh, it's just a few bucks here and a few bucks there. I don't know—my allowance, I guess."

"Tell me what you've had for lunch this week. And I'll be able to check the school cafeteria menu to see if it was on the menu that day." She shook her head and held up her hand, reconsidering. "No. That's not necessary. We have an honest relationship, so I think I can just ask you what I need to know and believe that you'll tell me."

Kate nodded, grateful. At least her mom still trusted her enough not to check up on her.

"So, here's what I want to know." She

paused, staring into Kate's eyes as though willing the truth from them. "How many times last week did you skip lunch so you could buy energy supplements?"

"Twice." *Liar!* But she couldn't tell her mom that she only ate lunch once. Not only would she have a fit about the misuse of her lunch money, but she'd start in on Kate about her health again.

Mom pursed her lips and shook her head. "Well, Kate, that's going to stop right now. If I have to, I'll put your lunch money in an account at the school so you have no choice but to use it for lunch. I hope I won't have to do that, though—I'd rather trust you. And if you keep losing weight, I'll come to your school on my own lunch hour and sit with you while you eat."

"Okay, Mom. I promise. I'll eat a good lunch every day." She meant it but had already started doing mental calculations to find a way to have enough money to buy her energy drinks anyway. *Babysit? Sell some stuff? Borrow?*

"This has to stop, Kate. No more energy supplements, okay?"

Figures. But Kate wouldn't give up without a fight. "Mom, I promise that I won't ever touch that stuff again once the swim season is over.

I have State coming up, and I really need the boost."

The light dawned on Mom's face, and she asked, "I hope your coach doesn't push this stuff on you. . .does she?"

"Oh no! She has no idea. She wouldn't like it, either."

"Good." She sounded relieved. "It's decided. You're done. State or no State, I'm not having my daughter pouring this garbage down her throat every day. If you're under so much pressure that you can't swim without this stuff, I'm happy to let you quit the team." She stared hard into Kate's eyes. "I hope you don't feel that kind of pressure from me."

"No, Mom, of course not. I just really want to do well." She pondered her situation and paced across her beige shag carpet. "I tell you what. I'll stop completely except for the day of Sectionals and the day of the State competition. Okay?" By clearing out her system before then, the supplements would have more of an effect on those days, anyway.

"No way. I want to go and watch you swim knowing that you're doing the very best job you can without hurting yourself. I can't support the need to win at all costs. What kind of mother would I be if I did that?" She stood to leave, bending to scoop up the pile of contraband. "Kate, don't forget that you have power through Christ to not get sucked into the trappings of the world. You don't need this stuff." She gestured to the substances. "You can pray for strength, power, energy. He'll give you what you need if it's His will for you to have it."

"I'll try that, I guess."

"Prayer isn't something you 'try.' You're either committed to God's will for you, and then you surrender to it through prayer. . .or you don't trust Him, and you look to outside things. That's something you need to work out."

Mom stood at the door. "I know that teenagers use this stuff, and I know it's legal, Kate. But it's not healthy, and I won't allow it. I care about you too much."

Frustrated, Kate looked out the window in the dark backyard, watching her mom in the reflection on the window. *Mom won't be in the locker room,* Kate told herself. If she really needed help, Pam would get her what she needed.

Mom put her hand on the door frame and turned to add, "You're done with this stuff. I'm going to trust you not to go against my wishes

on this. Don't sneak around, Kate. Our trust
is strong, but it can easily be eroded." She left
without another word.

Kate looked at her reflection in the window.
How had Mom read her mind? *Oh, she was a
teenager once, too. She probably knows you better
than you know yourself. She's right, though. I
haven't prayed about this at all—not for real. But I
can't. I wonder why I can't.*

The next day, when Pam and Brittany
went to the locker room for a quick shot of
Red Dragon, Kate stayed in the pool to avoid
the inevitable questions. She felt proud, even
glad she'd quit. At the end of the workout, she
had to admit that she hadn't craved an energy
supplement at all. She had plenty of zip without
them—maybe she didn't need them after all.
The day after that, though—another story
completely.

"Come on, let's go get you a boost of
energy." Pam nudged Kate, who sat slumped on
a bench, and motioned toward the locker room.

"I'm fine," Kate snipped, not even lifting her
head off the concrete wall where it rested with
the crook of her arm covering her eyes. She
lifted her arm just enough to look at Pam with
one eye. "I'll let you know if I need something,

not the other way around. Okay?"

"Fine. Sheesh, Kate. What's gotten into you?" Pam looked like she'd been stung. "Are you getting nervous about Sectionals next week?"

"I'm sorry. I don't mean to be cranky. I don't know what my problem is," Kate lied and squinted through her blinding headache.

"You seriously need some pep in your step. Let's go get a drink." Pam turned toward the locker room but realized that Kate hadn't moved at all. "You coming?"

"I can't." Kate shook her head and told Pam the whole story with her eyes closed while she rubbed her temples.

"Oh, no problem." Pam waved in the air. "We can fix that. I've got stuff in my bag. I'll share."

"No. I can't." Kate sighed and looked up at the ceiling, trying to think of a way to explain. "First of all, I can't afford it. And. . .well. . .my mom and I have a trust thing. I don't want to break that."

"Well, don't worry about the money. I have all of my birthday money. I'll get you through the next couple of weeks, and you can pay me back a dollar a week if that's all you can do."

Pam shrugged. "But as for the trust thing, come on, Kate. No one ever does everything the way their parents want them to. It's no big deal. She'll never even find out."

"Seriously, Pam, I can't—the money is only a small part of my reasons. The real issue is that ever since my dad died, I've tried to make things easier on my mom. Then my sister got married and moved out this summer. So it's just me and Mom." Kate shook her head. *No backing down.* "If I disappoint her or break her trust in me, it'll hurt me more than it'll hurt her, I think. I just can't do it." She looked away, teary eyed. "She's been hurt enough."

For a moment, Pam looked like she had more to say. Instead, she just shrugged her shoulders. "Well, it's your call. The offer stands if you change your mind. I'll be right back."

Even though she had a headache, Kate finished the rest of the practice as best she could. She felt like she lost even more steam about halfway through, but she didn't give up. When the day ended, at least she could say that she'd remained true to her mom's wishes.

She got dressed in silence, trying to formulate a plan. She'd just have to really buckle down even more and get plenty of sleep. She'd shoot for nine hours a night for the next couple of weeks and hope that the added recovery time would make up for her lack of energy support. But would it be enough?

Chapter 9

──────────────→

THE CHAMPIONSHIPS

Coach Thompson balanced in the aisle of the moving bus as she looked up and down the seats. "Team, this is a momentous occasion. But we'll talk swim stuff tomorrow morning. Tonight, just rest your minds and your bodies. Have fun, girls. Soak this in. This is the experience of a lifetime—for some of you, this is only a stepping-stone." She made eye contact with Kate. Kate nodded almost imperceptibly.

"Now, here's what's going to happen. We should arrive at the hotel in about five minutes. We'll get checked in and then head right over to the pool. Tonight is the diving competition. We'll all go together to support our divers."

A cheer erupted at the front of the bus as

the divers and their coach waved back to the swimmers.

"Then, it's early to bed. There will be no movies, staying up late, hanging out, or chatting. This is the very last night that you can do anything to affect your performance. Please, don't throw it away because you want to party. Let's stay focused—for your own sake, for the sake of your team. Deal?"

Everyone nodded in agreement, their faces somber.

"Okay then, here we are. Let's get to it, girls."

❀

"Let's see." Kate checked the list Coach gave them. "We're supposed to have oatmeal, fruit, and an egg-white omelet." She, Pam, and Brittany ordered the same breakfast and topped it off with coffee—not on Coach's list. They gobbled their food, in a hurry to get to the pool.

They jogged across the parking lot of their hotel to the sports arena across the street. The bowl of oatmeal sat like a heavy lump in Kate's belly, and the egg-white omelet didn't agree with her at all. Hopefully, the nervous rumbling in her stomach would pass soon. She took the last swig of her coffee and dumped the cup into the trash outside the women's locker room.

"Here we are, girls." Coach looked around the circle of teammates. "I can't believe the season is almost over. This is it. What a way to end it!" She made eye contact with each swimmer and then blinked her eyes several times.

Holding back tears? Really, just an old softy. Kate smiled.

"This is the first time we've ever had this many swimmers who qualified for the State competition."

Kate's cell phone rang in her bag and Pam, Brittany, and Sandy snickered. Without changing expression, she used her feet to shove the bag farther under her seat so Coach wouldn't hear it.

"Not only does this reflect well on me, your coach, but it reflects on each one of you. It shows the support and encouragement that you've all given to each other. I'm so proud of you girls." She gestured with open arms. "This is a very special group, and each one of you is very dear to my heart."

Kate's phone uttered one last lonely beep to signal a voice mail message.

"Girls, you know your stuff. I'm not going to spend a bunch of time telling you how to swim. If you didn't know how to work your meet already, you wouldn't be here. Just go out there, do your thing, and have fun!" The girls stood and cheered. Their energy sizzled with electricity. "Kate and Sandy, I'd like to see you two, if you don't mind."

"Whoops! We're in trouble, Kate." Sandy laughed.

When the others had cleared out, Kate said, "What's up, Coach?"

"Girls, you're both scheduled to swim four events. Unfortunately, Kate, two of yours are merely separated by three heats—maybe twenty minutes. That's going to be tough. Your other two races should be fine, though." She pointed at the schedule.

"I'll be fine, Coach. The two hundred is first—that worked well for me at Sectionals. And there's over an hour between the IM relay and the one hundred. I'll just have to get some rest in there. I'm ready for this." Kate nodded with confidence. Could they hear the butterflies fluttering in her stomach?

"Me, too." Sandy put up her hand for a high five, and Kate's hand met hers with a satisfying *slap*.

"I know. I can't wait to see how things go today. You two have really made this an exciting year. You and my new ulcer." They all laughed.

Right before she went out to the pool, Kate checked her phone to see who had called. *Olivia.* Kate groaned. She'd missed two other calls from Olivia in the past week. She probably just wanted to wish Kate good luck. It would have to wait.

She walked out onto the deck and stopped. People had to walk around her while she stood transfixed, unable to move. The sight of the crystal clear water, the echoing sounds of the preparations going on all around her, and the smell of the chlorine spelled home to Kate. The packed bleachers looked like a faceless sea of people, yet she felt like she knew each one of the spectators. Even the extra seating in the upper deck behind the glass windows overflowed.

Snapping out of her daze, Kate glanced up and down a few rows of bleachers, looking for her mom, but gave up her search and hurried to the starting block to squeeze in a warm-up. She spit into her goggles to prevent them from fogging and then pulled them over her eyes. She swam a few brisk laps in the Olympic-sized pool and gave herself a pep talk.

You can do this.

This is no different than any other meet.
This is swimming. It's what you do better than anyone here.
You're most at home in the pool.
Just swim like you've been swimming.
You can do this, Kate.
This is no different than. . .

The whistle blew its warning, and the swimmers cleared the pool. Kate toweled off and stood with her team during the National Anthem. She put her right hand over her heart, but she hopped and moved around on her feet to keep her muscles warm and shook her left arm to keep it limber. When the last bars faded, the sounds of the crowd, the water, and the swimmers erupted into an instant roar. She shook her right arm out and readjusted her goggles on her forehead. *It's time.*

By some miracle, she happened to look to the right, straight at her mom. Mom sat beside an empty space—the only one in the whole place, Kate thought. She imagined her dad sitting there, holding his wife's hand, cheering for his daughter.

Kate begged her mom for encouragement with her eyes. She smiled, nodded, and then put her hands together in a symbol of promised prayer. Kate squeezed her eyes shut for a brief moment and nodded her thanks as she climbed onto the block.

"Swimmers, take your mark. . . ." Kate closed her eyes. *Lord, help me.* When the gun blasted its call to action, she sprang off the block. She sailed through the water with the ease of a dolphin. Kate pictured her mom watching with tears in her eyes. By the turn on her last of four laps, Kate glanced to the sides and saw no disturbance to the water on either side of her—not even one swimmer competed for the win.

Reinvigorated by the taste of impending victory, Kate pulled from deep within her and gathered everything she had to finish the last length of the race. Fifteen meters, ten meters, final pull, glide, touch. The race ended as quickly as it started. She, a first-year swimmer, had just won her first race at State. *Could it be enough for a new record?* Kate lifted her head and peeled off her goggles to check her time.

As soon as the water cleared her ears, she heard the riotous cheers. One by one, the other swimmers glided into the timer pad. She had won the race with a huge margin—but no new record. Over the PA system, Kate heard, "Kate Walker has taken first place in the 200-meter free."

She floated on her back for a moment, allowing her body to cool down. *I won!* She couldn't let her victory become clouded with disappointment over not setting the record. *I won!*

Cooled down, she hoisted herself onto the pool deck, and Coach Thompson ran to hug her.

"Congratulations, hon. You deserve this."

"Congratulations, Kate." People she didn't know were shaking her hand.

"Congrats, girlfriend." Pam patted her on the back as she walked by.

Kate stumbled toward the locker room, still in a fog, unable to really wrap her mind around what had happened. *I did it,* Kate said to herself. *I did it.* She looked up to the stands where she had found her mom before the race and saw her wipe away the tears. She gave Kate a big thumbs-up and nodded her head, grinning from ear to ear.

With at least an hour before her next race, Kate rummaged through her bag for a protein bar and a big bottle of water and headed for the locker room. The cheers and congratulations rang in her ears. *Come on, hold it together—just one more minute.*

Once inside the locker room, she ran to a bathroom stall. As soon as the door swung shut, she pressed her forehead against the cool metal door and collapsed into sobs. She couldn't hold it back any longer. She watched as the tears ran down and dripped onto the floor. She took a raggedy breath and sat back, rubbing her eyes. *Too much pent–up emotion.*

About forty-five minutes later, Kate's team took third place in the IM relay and second place in the free relay. Coach had told Kate not to push too hard. She really wanted her to save as much energy as possible for her last and most important—hopefully, record-setting—race.

Kate needed a break. In ninety minutes, she'd be swimming her last race. She moved around the pool deck and gave herself little pep talks the whole time, trying to keep her mind focused and her muscles warm. *Yawn.* She stretched and hopped side to side. *Come on, wake up.*

"Hey, Kate." Coach came up behind her. "You seem to be fading. Why don't you go eat a granola bar or a banana?" She put her hands on each side of Kate's face and looked into her eyes. "You really need to perk up, kiddo. It's crunch time. This is the most important race of the year. I didn't want to tell you this, but do you see that lady over there?" Coach pointed to a pretty woman in a sage green dress on the sidelines with a clipboard in her lap. When Kate nodded, she continued, "She's the head coach of the OSU team. She asked about you."

Kate was stunned. "She did? What did she say?"

"She asked me to keep you going and to point you in her direction when it got to be picking time. She said that she imagined she'd have a full ride for you if you keep it up."

"Oh, wow! Talk about pressure! I'm so glad you told me, though. It really gives me something to swim for right now." She yawned again. Why was she so tired?

Coach eyed her. "Kate, I'm not kidding. You need to go get some fuel in your body. But it's getting close, so don't eat too much." She put her hands on Kate's shoulders and steered her toward the locker room.

Pam and Brittany followed her in. "Hey, we heard what Coach said. That's so cool!" Pam patted her on the back.

Kate collapsed onto the bench in front of her locker. "Yeah, it sure is, but I'm so nervous. I'm just not feeling it. What if I bomb?" Her knuckles were white as she squeezed the seat beside her legs.

"You'll be fine, Kate. You can do this in your sleep." Brittany waved her hand in the air. "No problem."

What am I going to do? I can't do this without help—but I promised Mom. Kate shook her head to clear her doubts. She made a quick decision. "You guys, I need a Red Dragon. Please tell me you have an extra." Kate looked up at them with puppy eyes.

"Oh man, I was worried you were going to say that. We each just drank one, and I gave one to Sandy. We don't have any more. I'm really sorry." Pam knitted her eyebrows, looking concerned.

"Oh no. And there's no time to go out for one. Do you know anyone else who might have some?"

They both shook their heads with regret. "Not anyone who's here."

Kate plopped on the bench in despair. "Okay, I'm going to have to put any hopes of an energy supplement out of my mind and find my energy from within, right?" She peeled a banana and took a bite. She practically swallowed without chewing and then threw half of it away. She paced the floor. "There's nothing left for me to do."

"Not necessarily, Kate." Pam and Brittany eyed each other, and Kate saw Brittany shake her head. Pam nodded and opened her locker.

"Kate, I just need you to trust me. Take one of these." She held out the palm of her hand. In it lay a tiny blue pill.

Speed. With wide eyes and an open mouth, she looked from the pill to Pam and then over to Brittany and back to the pill. She could tell by the way they were acting that Pam held the real thing.

"Pam. . .I. . .um. . .I. . .don't know what to say." Kate stalled, trying to think. "Where on earth did you get that?"

"Now, Kate. We're in the big leagues. Everyone takes these. It's pretty much expected." She talked fast while Brittany just nodded. "In fact, when you walked off to the locker room, Coach motioned for us to follow you because she knows, without being able to come right out and say it, that this is what you need right now. I promise you, you'll sail through this race. You'll thank me for this."

Kate shook her head. No way Coach Thompson was involved. But she couldn't worry about that right now—no time. "My mom would kill me if she knew I even considered it. And I'd probably be yanked off the team for even thinking about it, let alone actually doing it. What are you guys thinking? No way." Kate swung her head side to side the whole time she talked—*Olivia, why couldn't it be you standing here with me right now?*

"Don't get all preachy and whiny on me. You've got to get a backbone and do what it takes to get through this race with a bang. It's not the time to be a prissy mama's girl."

Someone came in to use the bathroom, so Pam lowered her voice to a whisper. "Kate, you're running out of time. This is it. You have no more time to prepare yourself. Are you ready to get on the block and swim in the state you're in right now?"

Kate shook her head and looked down, twisting her swim cap in her fists.

"I didn't think so," Pam rushed, almost out of time. "Look, I can promise you that your mom would never tell you to take this little pill, but I can also promise you that her trust on an issue as minor as this"—she held out the pill again—"is far less important than a college scholarship. You *will not* get caught, and you *will* swim the race of your life. Kate, there's really no decision here."

The time has come for Kate to make a very difficult decision. Think long and hard about what you would do if you encountered the exact same circumstances that Kate is facing. It's easy to say that you'd make the right choice. But are you sure that you could say no and risk a college scholarship? What if your mom struggled with only one income and didn't have the money to send you to college? What if you truly believed you wouldn't get caught and promised yourself that you'd never ever take another drug or energy supplement again? Would you consider doing it? Would you be tempted? Are you sure?

Once you make your decision, turn to the corresponding page to see how it turns out for Kate—and for you.

Turn to page 315 if Kate is able to stay strong and refuses to take the drug.

Turn to page 350 if Kate decides to take the pill—just this once.

The next three chapters tell the story of what happened to Kate when she decided to do what she knew was right.

Chapter 10

DIFFERENT STROKES

The clock ticked on the locker room wall while Kate stared at the little blue pill in Pam's hand. Her thoughts spilled over each other; and every time she opened her mouth, the words just stuck to her dry tongue. Finally, she looked at Pam and then at Brittany. "I'm not taking speed," she sputtered. "I can't believe you even thought I might." She shook her head. "We'll talk about this after I swim. I have to go now."

"Well. . .I. . .I mean. . ." Pam's face reddened like she'd been slapped.

Kate spun on her heels and bustled out of the locker room. She held her head up high and her shoulders back, confident she'd done the right thing. But right or not, she still had to find a way to swim her race, even though she

315

wanted to just collapse on a bench. A new level of nervousness assailed her senses—one she never imagined.

For once, Kate couldn't hear the sounds on the pool deck because of the drone in her ears. She couldn't smell her beloved chlorine because her chest ached and she couldn't take a deep breath. And now, facing her most important swim ever, she'd thrown it all away—any chance at a record and a college scholarship—by not preparing mentally and physically.

Kate squared her shoulders, took a deep breath, and set off to find a secluded corner of the deck to collect herself in the minutes before the race. She passed a few people who called out her name, but she ignored them. She'd given too much time to external things. Right now she needed to focus within herself, to take a moment to pray.

After a few jumping jacks, Kate shook her arms, trying to loosen them up. She rotated her head from side to side in half circles, and stared at her hands, willing them to stop shaking.

"You okay?" Coach approached her with concern in her eyes.

"I don't know, Coach." She shook her head and looked down at her still-shaking hands. "I can't focus. I'm not ready to get in the water. I wish I had another hour."

"Well, kiddo, you don't." Coach put her hands on each of Kate's shoulders and made solid contact with her stormy sea-green eyes. "Whatever it is, Kate, whatever happened. . ."

Kate opened her mouth to speak.

"No, don't tell me, we don't have time to let your mind go there now. Whatever went on in that locker room, it just doesn't matter."

"But. . . ," Kate protested.

"Listen to me." Coach squeezed her shoulders a little bit tighter.

Kate looked away, but Coach moved into her line of vision, forcing her to maintain eye contact. "Even if it matters more than anything, nothing can change it over the next few minutes. Five minutes from this very second, you'll be done swimming, and you can think about whatever it is that's troubling you for as long as you want to think about it."

She tightened her grip on Kate's shoulders. "Right now, though, you need to focus. You'll regret it if you don't take control of yourself, Kate. Look at me. You can do this. You know how to swim this race instinctively better than any swimmer I've ever had the pleasure of coaching. You have a very long future in swimming still ahead of you."

Kate shook her head, hopeless. "But what if. . . ?"

Coach brushed her off. "Your swimming future—no matter how much you've told yourself it does—does not ride on this one swim. Take some pressure off yourself. Lighten your load, and get out there and do what you love to do. Let the water wash away your cares. Listen to the sounds of the rushing water, not the voices in your head. Shut them off." Coach waited, searching her eyes. "Are you doing it?"

She gave a weak nod.

"Come on, kiddo." Coach released her grip. "You. Can. Do. It. Do it. Do it." She whispered, pounding her fists in the air in front of Kate's face.

Kate offered her coach a shaky smile, second by second taking more control of herself. She looked from her coach to the pool and then back to her coach and nodded. "I'm good."

Satisfied, Coach didn't say another word and steered Kate toward the starting blocks.

"Swimmers take your mark. . . . Get set. . . ."

The gun went off, and Kate flew off the block. Awesome start, maybe her best ever! She swam with all of her might and talked to herself the whole way. *Come on, Kate. You can do it, Kate. Don't think about it, Kate. Don't...*

But no matter how hard she tried to prevent it, her mind wandered back to the little pill. She couldn't believe that she'd allowed herself to come so close to taking drugs. How had that happened? She pictured a bent radar antenna coming from her brain. Apparently, she'd been clouded and blinded by the glamour of being the best. So clouded that she almost risked everything for success.

Having trouble clearing her mind, Kate forgot to watch the lanes next to her as each stroke brought faces to her mind: *Mom, Julia, Olivia, Pastor Rick, Mark, Olivia, Mom, Dad... Oh, Dad, did you see me today? Did I scare you? I'm so sorry, Dad.*

What is that scripture? There's no temptation that I might face that isn't common to everyone? Something like that. Okay, I was tempted. I passed the test. Right? Right. Now swim, Kate. Swim! Kate snapped back to attention as she realized that she only had about half a pool length to swim in her first State competition. She glanced to the right. Clear. To the left—a swimmer almost neck and neck with her! Panic set in— she could still win it, or she could give up. Kate knew what she had to do.

She tucked her head down, reached a little
farther, and pulled a little harder. She turned
to breathe every fifth stroke instead of every
third—her lungs on fire.

Fifteen meters—

Ten meters—

PULL!

Five meters—

Stretch!

She gave it all she had and touched the
timer pad with the very tips of her fingers
before she slammed the full force of her body
into it. The swimmer beside her plowed into her
timer mere milliseconds later. But that was all
Kate needed to place first.

Kate pulled off her goggles and patted her
closest competitor on the back. "Nice swim."

But she didn't have to look at the timer
to know she hadn't set a record. She'd swum
a good race, some would say great, but not a
record-breaking swim. It didn't matter, though.
She had won a different kind of race today—
one that she knew would impact her life in even
bigger ways. Definitely cause for celebration.

She climbed out of the pool, breathless and
shaky. The team ran over to her and jumped

up and down, suffocating her with hugs. *Smile, Kate.* Their hands slapped on her wet back, and her hand got pumped by numerous, faceless people. She couldn't see out of the crowd that encircled her, so she had no idea if Pam and Brittany stood among the cheering crowd. But it didn't matter. This was her moment—no one could take it away from her.

After the fervor died down, Kate looked up to the bleachers where her mom still sat. Kate held up one open hand, asking for five minutes. Mom nodded and beamed at her, clearly proud, and reached into her purse. Kate smiled when her mom pulled out a tissue to wipe tears from her eyes.

In the locker room, Kate looked up and down the aisles hoping to find Pam and Brittany so they could talk. She heard the zip of duffle bags, the flushing of toilets, someone with headphones on sang off-key—but no Pam and no Brittany. Kate sighed. She really didn't want to have this conversation by phone. It would probably have to wait until school on Monday. Oh well, she'd have some time to think things through and work out what she wanted to say to them.

"So, what's going on, Kate?" Mom didn't waste a single second when the car finally turned on to the expressway and they started on their trip home through the mountain pass. "You should be much happier, but you seem so solemn. What happened? Did your coach get mad at you for not breaking the record?" Mom's eyes flared like a struck match at the possibility.

"Oh no! Not at all, Mom. In fact, before the race she even told me to take some pressure off and to just do it because I love it."

"Oh, okay then." Mom sighed in relief. "I don't want you put under a lot of pressure. . . . So. . ."

"There is something wrong." Kate hesitated. "I'll tell you all about it. I need to." She spilled the whole story out onto the dashboard. At least she didn't have to start from the very beginning—Mom already knew that part. "You were right. It was leading down a dangerous road, one I almost traveled."

"Yes." Mom squeezed her eyes shut for a brief moment, and her lips moved as if in prayer. "I'm so relieved that you see that. So, what now?"

"I don't know, Mom. I just don't know."

"Well, let me ask it this way, then." She bit her lip. "What is it about all that's happened exactly, that's upsetting you the most?"

"I guess I'm upset that Pam and Brittany are doing drugs." She contemplated her answer for a moment and then added, "And I'm upset they offered them to me."

"Is that all?"

"Yeah. I. . .um. . .I think so. I'm not sure. I just feel unsettled," Kate said, feeling confused but still not sure why. "That's why I didn't want to ride back with the team."

"Do you want to know what I think, sweetie?" When Kate nodded, she continued. "I think those are two of the reasons, but I don't think they're the main ones."

Kate scrunched the corners of her eyes and peered through her lashes at her mom, perplexed. "What do you mean? What other reasons would I have?"

"I think more than anything, you're mad at yourself. I think you realize you were spiritually unaware of the danger you were in. You risked some big trouble over some issues you've always prided yourself on being able to avoid. You found yourself right in the middle of temptation, and it scares you. I think you're also mad at yourself because you came close to doing it. Thank God you didn't"—Mom blinked her eyes, moisture coating her lashes—"but you came close, didn't you?" She spoke in a casual tone, but white knuckles gripped the steering wheel.

"Well. . .I wouldn't exactly say 'close.' But I definitely considered it. I felt the weight of all that was riding on my performance, and I thought maybe I could do it just once and never again."

"There would have always been a next time, Kate. Once you take one step, it's far too easy to take the next step because there are fewer unknowns with the second step and even fewer inhibitions with the third and the fourth. It's a slippery slope."

Kate nodded. Looked like Mom had been right. "Yeah, that makes sense. I am mad at myself, I guess. I mean, how could I have let that happen? Even worse, how did I not see it coming? What if I had taken that pill?"

"Whoa, one question at a time." Mom laughed. "How could you let that happen? Because you're human, Kate. You didn't want to see that your dependency was misplaced on energy sources other than the true Lifegiver.

But thankfully, God doesn't expect you to be perfect. He just expects you to get back on the right path when you realize you've veered off it."

Kate flipped the zipper of her duffel bag back and forth while she listened.

"How did you not see it coming? Because you wanted to be a part of the elite group. You wanted to be in control of your body and make it do what you wanted to do. You didn't want to see that what you were doing was wrong." She loosened her grip on the steering wheel and shook out her right hand. "As to your last question, what if you had taken that pill? I'll tell you, Kate, it could have been bad. If you guys had been caught somehow, you'd have had trouble with the police. Or worse, you could have had some kind of physical reaction to it and had trouble in the pool. But even if none of that happened, it would have continued. That wouldn't have been the end of the drugs."

"No, probably not." Kate looked out the window at her beloved mountains zooming by. "What now?"

"I think you need to pray about what to do, sweetie. You're going to have to figure this one out for yourself. In the end, though, Pam's and Brittany's parents are going to have to know.

You realize that, right?"

"Yeah, I guess. I'm not quite sure how to deal with that, though."

"I could tell you what to do. But I'm not going to this time." Mom shook her head. "You need to think about things and pray for a solution. I'll support whatever you come up with."

Lord, help me know what to do now.

Sunday morning dawned bright. Sunshine shed hope and clarity on the previous night's darkness. Before leaving for church, Kate decided to call Pam—she had to get it over with. "I hate to say this on the phone, Pam, because I'm afraid you won't understand my intent from the tone of my voice. I'm not angry; I'm scared. I don't want you to hate me, but I have to take that chance. I can't go on and pretend I don't know what's going on. What if something happened to you or to Brittany, or whoever else is involved, and I had done nothing to stop it? I could never live with myself."

Pam's silence was deafening.

"So. . ." Kate could feel her nerve stuttering and weakening, threatening to abandon her completely, but she pressed on. "I. . .I have no choice but to bring it all into the light. I'll give you guys until school starts tomorrow to talk to Coach Thompson or to your parents. But someone's going to have to know what's going on."

"You wouldn't." Pam's shaky voice belied her bravado.

Kate winced as she bit her fingernail too low. Everyone would hate her. "I—I—I have to, Pam. I wish this wasn't even going on, but I can't pretend. Not only is it wrong, it's dangerous." Kate had to fight to keep from whining. She didn't have to convince Pam of the right thing. She just had to do it.

"Wrong? Who are you to decide what's wrong? We are held to such high standards as swimmers that we can't possibly live up to them without help of some kind. Wrong? What's 'wrong' anyway?" She snorted in disgust.

Kate sat down on a stool, choosing her next words very carefully. "Pam, God decides what's wrong. He tells us to follow the law and to honor our parents. It's wrong to take drugs because it's illegal, dangerous, and disobedient."

"Oh, you're kidding me? You're one of *those*?" She snorted. "I had no idea you were a religious nut."

"I told you a bunch of times that I went to

church, Pam. It's not like it was a secret."

"A lot of people go to church, Kate. I even go to church. But that doesn't mean anything. So what? You go to church. But how does that make you the judge and jury?"

Anger spewed from Pam's mouth, and Kate didn't blame her—she probably felt betrayed. Shame washed over Kate. How could she have spent so much time with these girls but never shared her faith? "Well, I'm sorry. I guess I didn't let you see that part of me well enough. I'm really sorry about that. But the facts are the facts." This wasn't going anywhere—no point in arguing more. "Look, I'm going to let you go. We're leaving for church now. Think about what I said. I'm not backing down from it."

On the drive to church, one of Pastor Rick's famous lines kept running through her mind. "Going to church doesn't make you a Christian any more than going to McDonalds makes you a hamburger."

Chapter 11
DE-CELEBRATIONS

Hesitantly peering around the door frame to the office, Kate whispered, "Coach, do you have a few minutes?"

"Kate, come on in! I'm so glad to see you. . . but why aren't you at lunch?" She slid her desk chair back and gestured toward the guest chair.

"I'm really not hungry. I wanted to talk to you."

"Okay, well, have a seat. First, how is your day going? You're a big celebrity around here!" Coach grinned.

"Oh, it's great, Coach." Kate tried to sound as excited as she knew Coach wanted her to be. It had been a victory for them both, and Kate knew she owed it to her to let her enjoy the moment. "Everyone is so excited and supportive. I can't wait until next season."

"You're going to be swimming with the boys'
team practices, right? They start next week."
Coach peered over her glasses. "You need to
keep your skills up in the off-season."

"Oh, definitely. I just meant that I couldn't
wait for next year's competition. I'll be in the pool
every day until then. It'll be fun to swim with the
boys' team, too. I'll get to see how their workouts
are different than ours. . . ." Her voice trailed off
as she picked at a loose thread on her jeans.

"Okay, kiddo, what's going on?" Coach got
serious. "I assume this is about whatever was
bothering you before your last race."

Kate nodded, unable to speak through her
quivering lips and pounding heart.

"Did someone give you a hard time?" Coach
leaned forward, eyes intent.

"N–n–no. It isn't that. Not really." She took
a deep breath. "Something happened, Coach.
Something's been happening, actually." She
launched into the whole story. Told Coach
about the energy supplements and the caffeine
pills. Explained about how Mom found her
stash and made her stop and how pulling
back from all those things had affected her
swimming for a few days.

Coach nodded. "Ahh. That explains it."

While she finished the story, Coach looked down at her desk, clicking her pen open and closed, open and closed, open and closed.

"Then, at State. . .well. . . ," Kate stammered, not wanting to continue. Her friends would hate her.

"It's okay. Whatever it is, you can tell me." Coach put down her pen and gave Kate her full attention.

"They offered me speed. The real thing."

Coach Thompson peered at Kate over her glasses with her mouth wide open.

The ticking of the clock on the wall filled the room like a ticking time bomb.

"Are you sure, Kate?"

Kate nodded. "Not only that, but Pam said that it was partly your idea. . .that you wanted her to offer the pill to me so I'd swim better." She hung her head, knowing that last part would hurt.

"Wow. I can't think of anything that would have surprised me more. I thought I knew this team better than that." She rubbed her temples and squeezed her eyes shut. "I mean, I knew you guys fooled around with those goofy energy drinks. But even though I didn't really like it, I thought they were harmless."

Kate gave her a minute to process all she'd

just heard and then continued. "I told Pam
that I would give her and Brittany until school
started today to come forward on their own.
They chose not to, so I had to do it. I'm sure
they thought I was just bluffing. But this is too
important to just ignore."

When Kate ran out of words, she just sat
there, silent. The bell for her next class rang—she
wouldn't be going. She gazed sympathetically at
the coach she'd come to love, sure that Coach
had no idea what to do next. What could she do
to help?

"Kate, it's times like these that I wonder
if I'm in the right profession. I guess I would
have thought that I was doing a good enough
job of making everyone feel valued for who
they are and not for what I wanted out of them.
No one on this team should ever feel so much
pressure that they become capable of something
like this." She shook her head and rubbed her
forehead so hard it turned red.

"Coach, I don't see it that way. We all create
our own pressure. You actually detract from it by
talking us down and telling us to have fun. Any
pressure we feel is our own doing."

Knock, knock. Both of them jumped. Coach
opened the office door then stuck her head out

into the hallway. "Come on in. I think I know why you're here." She sat back down in her seat and waited for Pam, Brittany, and Sandy to squeeze past her into the tiny office.

Pam glared at Kate, who occupied the only other chair in the room, and slumped onto the floor in defeat. Brittany and Sandy didn't look at her as they took a place on the floor beside Pam.

Looking from one girl to the next Coach said, "I am so disappointed, girls." She shook her head from side to side, over and over. Finally, she put both hands on her thighs and heaved her small body out of the chair as though a weight pressed down on her. "I'm going to have to bring your parents and Principal Coleman into this. So, why don't you hang on before you say anything? I'll give you each a chance to speak, but let's save it until the principal gets down here. I'll be just outside the door using the phone." Coach left them alone.

Squirming, Kate looked at everything in the room but the other girls.

"Why couldn't you just leave it alone, Kate?" Sandy broke the silence. "We wouldn't have pushed you. You could have kept doing your thing, and we'd have left you alone. Why?"

Kate shook her head, her lip trembling again.

"I mean, do you realize that we'll all be off the team?" Sandy's voice was laced with venom. "You crippled the team by what you did, Kate. How can you live with that?"

Kate had enough. She sat up straight and slammed her fists on her armrests. "How can I live with that? *Me?* I crippled this team? *Me?* Sandy, you guys made the choices you did, and you involved me in them." Kate looked down at her hands. "I'll admit to my own weaknesses and that I used substances as a crutch, too. But it crossed the line for me when it became illegal. I can't go that far. I have to do what's right. I have no choice."

"When did you get all high and mighty, anyway? It's not like you've been a goody-goody this whole time." Sandy put her head back against the wall.

"You know,"—Kate looked at each of the girls—"that's my one big regret in all of this. I am so sorry that I hid my faith from you guys. It wasn't a conscious choice. I don't even know why it happened like that, actually. I should have let you guys in to that part of my life. Who knows, maybe you'd have made a different choice about offering me drugs, or even taking them yourselves, if you'd seen Christ in me. But

whether you believe me or not, my faith is a
very important part of my life."

Pam snorted in disgust—the first sound
Kate had heard from her in over twenty-four
hours.

"Pam, I know you feel the most betrayed,
and you don't believe I'm a Christian like I say
I am. That's okay. I have to live with that. I've
learned a lot about why it's very important to
make people aware of where my priorities are."

"That still doesn't tell me why you couldn't
just walk away and leave it alone, Kate. Maybe
you just want us off the team so you don't have
to compete against us." Sandy crossed her arms
and glared.

Her snide remark twisted in Kate's gut. "It's
not that at all, Sandy. What you said doesn't
even make sense. This whole thing was a big
mess and. . .well. . .I had to try to fix it." She
shrugged her shoulders. "Plus, it was the only
way to get you guys to stop using drugs. Think
about it. Not only did you risk yourself every
time you got into the pool on drugs, but you
were also risking our team."

All three girls rolled their eyes, but Kate
continued, undaunted. "If you had gotten
caught, it would have been made public and the

whole team would have been under scrutiny, not to mention our titles, wins, records, and even Coach and the school would have been called into question."

Kate shook her head. "But that's not even the most important thing, which is you guys. I couldn't sit by and watch this happen right in front of me and do nothing." She opened her mouth and took a breath, not quite finished but unsure of how to go on. "What if we had to scrape one of you off the pool bottom one day after you had a heart attack because your heart rate got too high? How would I have felt, knowing I could have prevented it?" She shuddered at the thought.

"And. . .well, I feel like I've done a disservice to my faith by not being a Christian example to you guys. I want to be that now, even if it means some of you get hurt for the short term. I wish it had unfolded differently, but that's the way it is now." Finished, Kate hung her head in the silent room. She wished someone would speak, but the silence remained unbroken until Coach Thompson and Principal Coleman walked into the room carrying an extra chair.

The principal sat in the chair and crossed her legs, her high-heeled shoe falling to the floor.

"Okay, who wants to start? What happened?"

After a long silence, Kate opened her mouth to speak.

Principal Coleman shook her head and held up her finger. "I think I'd like to hear the story from one of the others."

Chapter 12

➜   TRUE FRIENDSHIP

Oh, Olivia. Why haven't I been a better friend?

With Christmas break drawing to a close,
Kate feared that she'd let too much time pass
and there would be no way to fix things with
Olivia. But she couldn't put it off any longer.
Kate took a deep breath, pressed the speed-
dial button, and closed her bedroom door.
She walked to the corner of the room, pressed
her back into the wall, and slid to the floor.
When she heard Olivia's voice, she started the
conversation with the plaintive plea of a kitten.
"Can you ever forgive me?"

Olivia answered with a clipped and aloof
tone. "Forgive you for what? I'm kind of busy.
Can we talk another time?"

Ouch. Kate deserved that. "Liv, I screwed up.

I know I've been a selfish, terrible friend. I hope you can forgive me and let me make it up to you." Her voice caught. "Don't shut me out. . . ."

"You're the one who shut me out, Kate," Olivia reminded her. "You have no need for me anymore. I'm of no use to you." Kate had never heard Olivia sound so sad.

"No, Liv, that's where you're wrong. I have no explanation; I'm not even going to try to convince you. I'm hoping we can just start over, though. If you can forgive me and we just erase the past few weeks, we'll be back to normal."

Silence.

"What do you say, Liv? Please?"

"Well, I don't know. . . ," she teased, sounding like her old self.

Kate's shoulders relaxed, and she breathed a deep sigh of relief. She could tell that Olivia's heart had softened. She'd never let life get in the way of making time for her best friend ever again.

The doorbell rang at the same instant as she hung up the phone.

Mark! Kate scurried to change her clothes. She couldn't believe she'd forgotten their plans to go for a walk in the snow. Hurrying down the stairs, she pulled on her mittens and then went into the night.

They walked in silence under the stars as the snow fell.

How can I say this? Kate knew she needed to be honest. "This vacation has been an incredible two weeks. We've had so much time to spend together, and I've enjoyed every single second of it." She bit her lip.

"But?" he prodded.

"But I'm afraid that by rushing into a relationship that I'm not ready for, it will be the death of a wonderful friendship. . . . I don't want to risk our friendship, Mark."

"I know what you mean." He looked up into the sky and let the snowflakes hit his windburned cheeks. "It just sort of felt like this was supposed to be our next step, and I didn't want to let the opportunity get away from us. Because you're important to me—you always have been."

Kate nodded and blew steam from her mouth. "You know what?"

"No, what?" Mark answered and laughed, tweaking her on the chin.

"If we're really meant to be more than friends, a couple of years wouldn't make a difference, right?"

"No, I suppose it wouldn't."

"But if we're not meant to have that kind of

relationship, then by rushing into it, it will cost us a great friendship."

"Hmm, that's a good way to look at it." He slipped a casual arm around her shoulders as they walked.

"So, let's just step back to what we know we can handle and put the rest on hold. I mean, we'll still be together all the time, so nothing will change. We have band practice and our gigs, plus we can hang out anytime without the pressure of a relationship."

"I'm all for that, Kate." He actually looked relieved. "Will you promise me one thing, though?" He had a twinkle in his eye.

"Sure, what?"

"Don't let anyone else have your first kiss. Okay? It's all mine." He winked and gave her a gorgeous grin.

Her stomach flipped. Friends could still be handsome, right?

"Deal!" They shook hands and laughed.

How could Christmas break be over already? Kate couldn't believe how fast it had gone. She groaned, rolled over, and pulled the covers over her head. Her body clock still beat to the rhythm of vacation.

When she finally pulled herself from her

bed, she had to rush to get out of the house for her first swim practice with the boys' team. It would be strange without Pam and Sandy to swim with—and no other girls had been invited to swim off-season. So she'd be the only girl in the pool with twenty boys.

Ugh! The boys might not like having me there. I'm a nark, after all. Kate's thoughts ran wild as she hurried to get out of the house. The drive to the school ended way too fast.

"Hi, Kate," the boys' team called out in one voice when Coach Thompson introduced her.

"She'll be the only one from the girls' team joining us for now. I hope you'll all make her feel welcome." Coach narrowed her focus to include each boy. "This is your season. Kate won't get in the way of your practices. She's just here to swim and stay in shape."

"Well, that shouldn't be hard for her."

Kate turned beet red but had no idea which boy said that. Several others snickered.

"Okay, let's not be childish, boys," Coach scolded. "Come on now, go swim." She sent them off to find their lane assignments and workout schedule.

"Hey, Kate."

She turned from the bleachers to find two

popular seniors waiting to say something to her.

"Yeah?" She braced herself.

The tallest one said, "We just wanted you to know that we're glad you turned in the girls for using speed. Junk like that gives sports a bad name." He looked shy. "So. . .good for you."

He left before she had a chance to thank him. Smiling, she eased herself into the cold water and adjusted her goggles. *Ahhh. Home.* She started her swim at a steady pace, warming up her muscles that had been on a two-week hiatus. She eased her speed up to a clip that would tax her, but not force her to crawl from the pool in agony.

How could water be so healing? She let its purity wash away all of her worries and cares. It cleansed her soul and comforted her heart. Nothing mattered in the pool.

Sitting at a desk, Kate looked out the window, lost in her thoughts of walking with Mark the night before. She chewed the end of her pencil, knowing she'd done the right thing.

"Hey, Kate."

She dropped her pencil as a voice at her left shoulder snapped her back from her snowy memories. *Sandy.*

"Hey." Kate looked down.

"We don't have much time before class. But I wanted to tell you that I did a lot of thinking over the holiday." The bell cut her off. "I'll have to talk to you later, okay?" She left before Kate could respond.

A little later, after the third-period bell rang, Kate and Mark walked into the bustling lunchroom. As always, students climbed over benches, bags were tossed from one table to the next, and smells had mingled into an unidentifiable biohazard. While they waited in line, she took a quick look around and immediately noticed Pam and Brittany on one of the benches right outside the commons. They saw Kate and looked the other way, whispering. Kate sighed, hopes of forgiveness and the restoration of their friendships. . .impossible.

"Hey, what did you expect?" Mark read her mind as they slid onto a seat with one of the red plastic lunch trays that always smelled of mildew. "They weren't really your friends, anyway. They didn't even know the real you."

"I know." She poked at her food. "I just hoped they'd have figured some things out in the time away."

"Just pray for them. Keep praying for them.

Someone outside of the situation will have to show them what's what before they're ever going to be able to come around and forgive you."

"That's probably very true." She played with her food. "I'll have to just pray that the Lord sends someone their way who can help them see the truth."

"Kate, can I talk to you for a minute?" Sandy asked in a soft voice near Kate's shoulder.

Kate coughed, choking on her drink.

"Hi, Sandy. Sure you can. Have a seat." Mark grabbed his apple off the tray and waved good-bye as he headed to his class while Sandy sat in his spot.

Kate looked at the clock. "We've only got about ten minutes."

"Probably. If I were you, I wouldn't even want to listen that long." She took a deep breath and looked into Kate's eyes. "I'm really sorry. You were so right about everything and. . .well. . .I have a secret to tell you."

Kate leaned forward.

"Well, I take that back; it's not going to be a secret anymore. It's something I've kept hidden at school but shouldn't have." She took another deep breath and looked down at the table. "I'm a Christian, too. There, I said it." She exhaled and looked Kate in the eye. "Why is it so hard for me to tell people? It shouldn't be, but it just is."

Kate smiled. "Sandy, I'm so glad you told me. You're right, it shouldn't be. But I understand. It's like Peter. . ." Kate shared with Sandy the same story that Mark had reminded her of a few weeks ago. "So, you see, even Peter failed when it came time to share his faith in Jesus. None of us are perfect, but the question is how are you going to change now that you know? No more secrets, right?"

Sandy nodded then lowered her big brown eyes. "I'm afraid, though."

"Sure you are. It's okay to be afraid. It's only not okay if you let it cripple you into doing nothing." Kate looked up and rubbed her chin. "Hey, I've been thinking about starting something, and I think that now might be the perfect time."

Sandy eyes lit up, and she took a bite of Kate's uneaten brownie.

Kate waved her hand, offering her the whole thing. "I think we should start a Bible study group before school. I know Mark would join and a few others. We could take turns leading the group. It would only be for about twenty minutes right before class. What do you think?"

Sandy's big eyes grew even larger. "Oh, wow. Talk about making waves." She took a deep breath. "Well, it's time for me to put up or shut up, I guess. Count me in." Sandy smiled and ate the rest of Kate's brownie.

Exactly two weeks later, Kate rushed to get dressed after her early morning swim so she could get to the first Bible study meeting on time. She jogged down the long hall from the locker room to the meeting room that Principal Coleman had offered for their use. Rushing in the door, almost late, she joined the eleven students who had arranged their seats in a large oval. Several even had Bibles with them. Panting to catch her breath, Kate slid in between Mark and Sandy and tucked her bag under her seat.

"Welcome to the first meeting of our new Bible study and prayer group." Mark smiled warmly. "First, I want you to know I've been so excited ever since Kate came to me with her idea about starting this group. That there are students in this school who will give up their time and risk having a reputation of being a religious fanatic"—several students giggled at

the term— "because of their passion for Christ
. . .well. . .I'm at a loss for words. It sure lit a fire
in me."

He nodded as he looked around the room.
"This group right here,"—Mark spread his arms
out to include all the students—"this is our
core group. We are called by God to be leaders
in this school, to share the gospel, and to be
examples of Christ." He looked right at several
of them. "You want to know how I know He's
called you for that?"

They all nodded, transfixed.

"Two reasons. One, because He's called me,
too. We're all called to be ambassadors for the
cause of Christ—every single one of us. And
two, because you're willing—you're here. That's
it. That's all it takes to be used by God."

Mark opened up his Bible. "This is what
I want for us to be to each other here in this
group. . .it's the same thing that Paul asked of
his friends as recorded in Ephesians, chapter
six. Paul asked them to 'Pray also for me, that
whenever I open my mouth, words may be
given me so that I will fearlessly make known
the mystery of the gospel, for which I am an
ambassador in chains. Pray that I may declare it
fearlessly, as I should.' "

Kate stared at Mark, humbled by his words and impressed by his clear thoughts. He'd make a great preacher one day.

Mark closed his Bible and looked around the circle. "So, let's commit to each other to be here each week. We'll have a prayer time, a short devotion which we can take turns leading, and then time to share concerns." He smiled at the group. "Eventually, people will want what we have, and this room will be overflowing."

At that very precise moment, the door slowly creaked open.

Kate and Sandy stared with open mouths as Pam and Brittany peeked into the room. After a brief hesitation, Pam timidly asked, "Is it too late to join you guys?"

Kate smiled and scooted her chair over to make room in the circle. "It's never too late."

The next three chapters tell the story of what happened to Kate when she chose to take the pill Pam offered her.

Chapter 10

NO ONE WILL KNOW

Before she could change her mind, Kate grabbed the little pill out of Pam's hand and gulped it down without water. Starving for confidence and desperate for success, it seemed her only option.

She waited.

No fireworks went off inside her—just yet. After about five minutes, she felt the warmth traveling through her body. It started with her fingers and toes and moved up her arms and legs until she felt like an electric current. *Is that it? That's not so bad.*

"Now, try not to be overexcited or too chatty." Pam steered her out to the pool deck. "You don't want to give yourself away."

Giddy, Kate clapped her hands together and said, "Well, let's get this thing going! Time to swim!" Was she being too loud? How could she turn it down? Her blood pumped, and her adrenaline flowed. The swim of her life lay just ahead. *And then I'll never take drugs again.* Her mind raced. *What have I done? Nope, don't go there. No regrets.*

Off the block like she'd been shot from a cannon, Kate gave it all she had. Her heart raced; her limbs tingled. The water felt even colder than usual on her flushed skin. She swam the whole race only taking a breath every five strokes, something she'd never done before.

After she made her turn and started on the last length of the race, she passed the other swimmers who hadn't made it to their turns yet. She would win for sure, and it looked good for setting the record—*but at what cost?*

She cleared any dark clouds from her mind and focused on the race. *Push, pull, stretch. Bam.* The race ended as fast as it began. The roar of the crowd pretty much confirmed that she'd set a new record. She ripped off her goggles and looked at the clock.

48.35! She would forever be a record-breaking swimmer. Her teammates, who had been standing at the end of the lane cheering her on, reached down into the pool and pulled her out. They hugged Kate and clapped her on the back. Everyone danced around her.

Coach Thompson came to offer her congratulations, tissue in hand. She pulled Kate into a tight embrace, too choked up to speak.

Her mom came down from the bleachers to hug her. "Mom! Did you see that? I broke the record." Kate jumped up and down. "I did it, Mom! I did it! Do you think Dad saw?"

"Slow down, sweetheart. I can hardly understand you!" She laughed, shaking her head. "I'm so proud of you. That was amazing! And, yes, I'm sure your dad saw you." She choked on those last words.

Oops. Kate wished she hadn't asked about her dad at that moment—it made Mom sad. But Kate was sure glad to know that Mom believed that he had been watching. *But that means he probably saw me in the locker room.* She quickly dismissed that thought—nothing would cloud her beautiful day.

Still, bubbling with excitement, Kate wanted to be with her team. "Mom, I know you drove a long way to see me swim, and I normally ride home with you. You probably won't want to drive home alone, but would you mind if I went back with the team? It's going to be tough to pull myself away from the celebration right now.

I kind of want to hang out and celebrate. . . ." Kate screamed at her brain to slow down, but it just wouldn't.

"Okay, just relax." Mom laughed. "It's fine with me if you want to ride home on the bus. I think I would, too, if I were you." She hugged her daughter and looked deeply into her eyes. "I love you, Kate, and I'm so proud of you. I'll pick you up from school, and we'll celebrate together at home later."

"Thanks. Bye, Mom!" Kate kissed her and then skipped as she entered the locker room.

"There she is! The star of the show!" The whole team turned and clapped as Kate approached.

Grinning, she took a theatrical bow and said, "First I want to thank. . ."

"One. . .two. . .three. . . Hip, hip, hooray! Hip, hip, hooray! Hip, hip, hooray!" they cheered again for Kate as she climbed onto the bus. Her face reddened, not used to having all eyes on her—but she could get used to it.

Kate found an empty seat toward the back by Pam, Brittany, and Sandy. She got up, sat back down, got up again. After three times, Sandy pretended to pull her down and hold her there. "I'm not going to let you up until we get to the school."

"You might have to sit on her." Brittany laughed.

About ninety minutes later, amid the raucous laughter and chatter that had been going on for the whole drive, Kate noticed that Pam had gone strangely quiet. Catching Pam's eye, Kate mouthed, "What's wrong?"

Pam shook her head and pointed down at her open bag on the floor—the bag where Pam had hidden the bottle of pills.

Instantly, Kate feared the worst—*please don't let them be missing*. She questioned Pam with her eyes.

Pam just shook her head again and mouthed one word: *Gone.*

Where could they be? What could she do? *If we get caught.* . .but she couldn't think about that. They had to solve the problem before the coach found the pills. They had to find them first. She stood to her feet to start her search, when she saw Coach Thompson standing there, waiting for everyone's attention.

"Kate, would you mind having a seat? I need to talk to you guys."

Kate slumped into her seat and looked out the window, imagining her dreams fading away like the mountains they passed. She braced herself.

"Girls, without any problems, I want a simple answer. Whose are these?" Coach held up Pam's bottle. "Just take responsibility for them and tell me whose they are. And then we'll figure out who used them."

Coach stood there and looked from girl to girl for three full minutes before Pam spoke up. "The bottle's mine, Coach."

Without expression, Coach replied, "Thank you, Pam. Now, who took the pills?" She looked at each girl again.

Kate's insides were torn to shreds. She looked at her friends—if only she could talk to them. What if they didn't want her to confess and ruin the day for the whole team? There was no way to know. If she didn't confess, they'd probably hate her for leaving them to face the consequences alone. *I don't know what to do!* She sucked on her finger, which had started to bleed where she had bitten her nail too low. She panted her breaths and her heart raced—panic or drug induced?

"Girls, I'm going to ask you one more time. Just once more. And if no one confesses, or if I don't believe that everyone who needs to has confessed, I'll just have to call the police. Who took these pills today? Raise your hand if you

355

took one or more of these pills today."

Kate looked around as three hands went slowly into the air. The moment of truth. Pam and Brittany had their hands up, and so did Sandy. *Do the honorable thing and join them, or try to fade into the background and avoid it? Now or never.* She didn't want to do it, but she didn't think she could live with herself if she didn't.

"Going once, going twice. . ."

Kate slipped her hand into the air.

Coach sighed and squeezed her eyes closed for a moment.

Kate wished she could shrink and disappear.

The bus pulled into the driveway of the school. "All right, you four who raised your hand, please stay on board the bus. Everyone else, you're free to go. But I'm going to give you all one more chance to join your teammates if you had any part in this. Don't let me find out later that you didn't come clean when you had this chance. Trust me, it would be much worse on you if I found out that way."

Everyone else filed off the bus. Coach shrank as she lumbered behind them toward the door of the bus—her shoulders slumped and her head hung low. Kate wiped the moisture off the window with her sleeve and peered out. The swimmers met up with their parents, hugged them, climbed into their cars, and sped away—free. When they all pulled away, Coach approached the remaining parents who were obviously confused.

Watching the coach's back, Kate assumed by her head movement that she was talking. The parents listened intently, their faces blank, until. . . *Shock.* There it was. They knew.

Mom! Oh, no. She looks so disappointed. The face she'd studied her whole life. *How could I have done this to her?*

After what seemed like a lifetime, the group broke up and the parents made their way onto the bus. Two moms looked as though they'd been crying. Kate's mom sat across from her but didn't look at her. Kate sat in silence and waited. Awkwardly, fearfully, very much alone.

Finally, Coach addressed the group. "Folks. . ." She looked at the grief-stricken parents, most of whom hadn't spoken to their girls yet. "I know how difficult this must be for each of you. I'm at a loss myself." She looked down at her feet and rubbed her temples. "At this point, I can't tell you exactly what will happen. I'm going to have to talk to the administration on Monday. I will probably find out that I should have called the police,"—she looked back up at them—"but I'm not going to." She made eye contact with a couple of dads, who nodded. "By the time the school gets involved on Monday, I'm guessing that it will be too late for that or that they'll decide not to involve the authorities. . . . At least I hope that's what will happen."

She paused before continuing. "I can promise you that any awards, trophies, records, or times from today will be removed from the record and from your possession. I'm also pretty confident in saying that you'll be asked to leave the team." She had been holding back tears while she spoke, but at that last part, she choked on a sob.

What have we done? Kate felt sick. Drugs or grief—she couldn't say for sure. Her hands shook, and her stomach threatened revolt.

Coach wiped her eyes and continued. "As you can see, this is very hard on me. I'm going to have to think long and hard about what I've done or said to contribute to the level of pressure it would take to drive you girls to this." Looking each girl in the eye, their coach said, "I'm just so glad you're all okay. I don't know what I'd have done if something happened to any one of you." Crying openly, she sat down.

Once they were sure that Coach had

nothing else to say, they gathered their belongings. One by one they filed off the bus. No one said a word.

Chapter 11

STRIPPED

On Monday morning, Kate's steps slowed as she approached the school—her heart pounded, and her stomach churned. It would be bad. But no matter how bad it got at school, it couldn't even come close to how difficult it had been at home over the weekend. Kate shuddered as she thought back over the past few days. Silence. Home had been like a funeral parlor, except worse. At least at a funeral, people hugged each other and offered support as they grieved their loss.

Kate sat quietly during her first-period class. When would the bomb explode? The door creaked open. She peeked up from her book—not really wanting to look. A student with an OFFICE badge pinned to her shirt handed a note to the teacher. *This is it.* Kate closed her book and reached for her bag.

"Kate." The teacher held the note out. "It's for you."

The walk from her desk to the front of the classroom seemed much longer than usual. She felt all eyes on her, their heat boring holes in her back. *Has word already gotten around?* When she got back to her seat, she unfolded the note.

Kate Walker, come to the office with your books at 11:00.

Her heart sank. Two hours to wait—she just wanted it over with.

The morning passed like slow drips from a faucet. *Plink. Plink. Tick. Tock.* Finally, Kate's watch said 10:55—*time to go.* She grabbed her bags and a few books that she might need later—in case the meeting ran long.

The secretary directed her to the conference room. Sunshine broke through the wall of windows at the back of the room. Kate looked down the long oak table and at everyone who sat around it. Pam and both of her parents, Brittany and her mom, Sandy and her dad, their coach, the principal, the school counselor and some silver-haired man in a navy blue suit and a yellow tie. *Uh-oh.* She took a seat next to her mom. Mom looked away.

The clock struck eleven o'clock, and Principal Coleman opened the meeting. She cleared her throat and tapped the edge of a stack of papers on the thick table. The noise made several people jump. "Well, I'm so sad we have to have this meeting, but we have no choice." She looked down and took a deep breath. Her eyes moved quickly down the sheet of handwritten notes that had been torn out of a spiral notebook and placed on top of her pile.

She pulled the second sheet out from her stack. "What I'm going to do first is read to you from this paper. It's a description of the events exactly as I understand they happened. I'd like you to listen and then, if the facts are straight, each student should sign the paper."

"Will we get copies of everything we sign?" Sandy's dad asked.

"Absolutely, Mr. Coble. Okay, here's what I have. . ."

Her words were lost on Kate—she couldn't hear through the roaring in her ears. The room buzzed just like the television did when the cable went out. She tried to focus on the words but couldn't. She watched the paper make its way around the table until it lay in front of her mom. Without moving her head, Mom covered it with her hand and slid it with a robotic motion toward Kate.

Kate scrawled her name on the page and then slipped lower in her seat.

"Okay, then. Mr. Stot, our district administrator, will take over from here." The principal dropped into her seat with a thud and exhaled, her part over.

"Thanks, Marsha." The man in the navy suit stood to address the group. "I'm going to keep this short because my job here is about the consequences. Parents, between yourselves, the counselor, and your kids' teachers, you'll have to deal with the moral issues." He pulled a padded brown-leather portfolio out of his briefcase and opened it on the table. Reading from a legal-sized sheet of paper, he said:

"Relating to the incidence of the possession of amphetamines and illegal drug use at a school-sponsored sporting event on November 29th, for the period of three days, Sandra Coble, Brittany Drummond, Pamela McSwain, and Kate Walker will be suspended from school. This suspension will be recorded on each student's permanent record. In addition, any medals won at the aforementioned event must be surrendered, and any times recorded will be void. Furthermore, participation on any sports team sanctioned by this school will be prohibited for a period of twelve months from this date."

Twelve months. Kate went weak at the thought of not swimming next season.

He cleared his throat and continued in his drone. "However, that twelve-month sports suspension can be reduced to six months by participation in a drug and alcohol abuse program. Information about such programs will be forthcoming, and participation will be monitored by Susan Moore, the school counselor."

It should take longer than fifteen minutes to lose her whole life—but that's exactly how long it took. She felt like this came out of nowhere—this stripping of everything important to her. What did she expect, though? Still, she just couldn't imagine how to move on from here—who would she be? What would it be like to return to school after a suspension? What would people at church say once word got around? *Mark!* Did he know already? She probably should have called him last night and told him herself, but she couldn't bring herself to do it.

"Are you coming?"

The first words her mom said to her all day. *Sigh*. Kate looked around in surprise to realize that the room had emptied. Her mom waited at the door, still not making eye contact. Grabbing her bag, Kate squeezed through the door past her, careful not to touch her.

They drove home in silence and then steered clear of each other for the afternoon. The tinkling of silverware at the dinner table grated on her like nails scratching a chalkboard. Kate opened her mouth to say something three different times, but her words just got stuck in her throat. After dinner, her mom just left the room without a word. Kate didn't know how to move on from this. What if they couldn't? What if her mom had finally cracked under the weight of grief?

No way. Kate slapped her hands on the kitchen table and stood up. Her wooden chair wobbled back and almost toppled.

She marched into the family room, determined to set things right. "Mom, we need to talk." Kate sat on the arm of the sofa, blocking the television.

Mom didn't look at Kate. Instead, she shifted six inches to the right and kept watching TV.

"Mom, we seriously need to get past this." Kate took in a slow breath and pulled from deep within her gut to find what she needed to say to reach her mom. "I'm—I'm—I'm so sorry, Mom." The words unleashed her tears. "I really screwed up. I don't even know what happened. Something came over me, and I made a spur-of-the-moment decision. I hardly even considered not doing it. I was just overcome with compulsion to just take the pill. I'd give anything to go back, Mom. . . ."

"Why, Kate? Because you got caught? Is that why you're sorry, why you wish you hadn't done it?" Mom's eyes narrowed in anger.

Kate tried to stop crying. She deserved her mom's rage. How could she convince her that she truly regretted what she'd done?

"You know, Kate. I tried to stop you. I told you something like this would happen. You didn't listen to me. You figured you knew best and your mom was just an old worrywart—out of touch." She finally turned to look at her daughter, making eye contact for the first time in days. "Well, I was right, Kate. Now you're in a whole heap of trouble, you've cost yourself a fun and exciting experience and probably a college scholarship. You've got a permanent school record with a suspension on it, and you can never say that you didn't take illegal drugs."

She stood and paced the room. "Illegal drugs,
Kate. I can't believe it. And now you have to go
to drug counseling, too—*you*, Kate. I don't get
how this happened to you. Why couldn't you
have listened to me?" She dropped to her knees
at the edge of the sofa like when she prayed at
the church altar.

"I did stop, Mom. . .when you told me no
more. . .I did stop." *Please believe me.*

"No, Kate. That's where you're wrong. You
stopped until it became too hard to keep your
word." She bit her lip and shook her head.
"Once things became too hard, you listened to
someone else. What, does Pam love you more
than me? Is she smarter than your simple old
mom? Or did she just give you a way to do what
you wanted to do all along?"

"I wish I could go back. . . ." Kate looked
away and sighed.

"Did your friends know you're a Christian?"

Kate hung her head in shame. "No, not really."

Mom made eye contact with Kate. "Is your
faith not as important to you as I thought it was?"

"No! Please don't think that. I screwed up.
This doesn't define me. I made a mistake. Please
don't make me out to be so bad." She walked
to the window and stared out into the snowy

night. "You know, Mom, I don't think I can ever really make you understand my motives and how I just got messed up. Everything you said is true. You're completely right. But there's nothing I can do now. I can't change anything about this situation. I can only change my thinking from now on."

"I'm sorry, Kate. You're right." Mom lifted her hands and shook her head. "We all make mistakes. You're going to have to give me some time to get over this. It's just so disappointing. And. . .and I miss your dad." Mom put her face in her hands and sobbed, her shoulders shaking with her grief. "He would have known what to do. No. . .this wouldn't have happened if he'd been around."

Unsure, Kate sat still for a moment. But even if Mom didn't want her comfort, Kate just couldn't sit by and watch her mom sob without going to her. She knelt on the floor next to her mom, their legs touching. Kate reached her arms out and pulled Mom to her.

Mom pressed her hands into her eyes, the tears leaking between her fingers like a breaking dam, and collapsed into Kate—months, years, of grief pouring out onto her daughter's shoulders.

The sun went down, but neither of them made a move to leave the now dark room. It had been years since they had held each other like this. Kate hadn't realized how much she hungered for the comfort of loving arms. Finally, they pulled apart and looked at each other. "I'm really sorry, Mom. I love you," Kate whispered.

"I love you, too, honey. I'm sorry, too."

Kate shook her head. "Why would you be sorry?"

"No, I really am sorry for making this so hard on you. You did the wrong thing. That's a fact. But I've done my share of wrong things." She blew her nose. "I guess, as a mom, I just want my little girl to avoid the hurt that comes from big mistakes. But it doesn't always work that way. I can't always protect you from everything. You're going to have to face the consequences of your decisions, Kate. But not alone. I'm here with you, for you. You, me, and Jesus—we make a pretty nice team." She smiled. "I love you."

Kate threw her arms around her mom's neck one more time. "Thank you, Mom. I love you, too."

"Can we pray together?" Mom looked hopeful.

"I'd like nothing more." Kate smiled.

One broken relationship fixed. How many more to go?

Chapter 12

GRACE—
A LEGAL DRUG

She dialed slowly, not quite ready to face the hurt she'd caused yet another loved one.

"Hello, Kate," Olivia answered with a short, clipped tone, enunciating the *t* so crisply that it felt like a slap.

Kate shrank away from the phone. She had messed everything up. Everything. "Liv. . ." She choked back the tears. "I'm. . .sorry. . . ." A sob welled in her throat and then overflowed. Her shoulders shook with her gut-wrenching sobs. She looked at the dripping phone and thought about just hanging it up, sure that Olivia wouldn't be on the other end when she got herself together anyway. But she just held on. And cried. *Jesus, please heal my friendship.*

371

When her tears slowed and her grief gave way to the promise of peace—at least inside— she took a few shuddering, cleansing breaths and placed the phone to her ear once again. "Liv?" she pleaded, desperate for acceptance.

"Kate? What on earth is going on? Talk to me." Her voice had softened, and she sounded just like the Olivia that she knew and loved— and needed.

"First, Liv, I need you to tell me you forgive me. Please. I've been a horrible fr–"

Olivia interrupted her. "It doesn't matter at all. You obviously went through something and got weird for whatever reason. I'm just glad you're back." She rushed her words. "But"—her tone grew more insistent—"you need to tell me what's going on."

Kate took a deep breath and grabbed her doodle pad. "Well it all started with a cup of coffee. . . ."

Olivia hardly said a word until Kate finished, and then she said the three words that Kate needed to hear more than anything: "I love you."

❀

Feeling like a felon in an old movie, she might as well have been wearing a black-and-white striped jumpsuit when she walked into the school the first day after her suspension. She kept her head down as she walked down the hallway to her locker, positive everyone was staring at her. *Just get through today. It will get easier.* Her head knew the truth, but her stomach didn't believe it.

What had she done? Everyone looked at her differently now.

Pam and Brittany saw her coming down the hall and immediately turned the other way.

"Don't mind them." Sandy came up behind her. "They aren't used to not getting their way. They don't have much use for you now that they know the real you. You're just finding out their true colors."

"Yeah, I guess so." Kate watched them walk away. "Maybe things will change in time."

"You never know." Sandy looked down and scuffed her shoe. "Hey, Kate. I was wondering . . .would it be okay if I went to church with you this Sunday?"

Kate's shoulders relaxed and she exhaled, relieved. "I would like nothing more. And I have another proposition for you. . . ."

❁

"You guys have room up there for a singer?" Kate walked down the aisle at the church. Mark and his buddies had arranged a practice for the band they decided to put together without Kate, if they had to. They hadn't talked to Kate about it since the "incident."

Mark beamed when he saw her coming toward them. "Room? As long as you check your big head at the door," he joked.

"Ha-ha, you're real funny, Mark." She looked at P.J., who had a cord wrapped around his hands, trying to set up the microphones, and Gabe, off to the side hooking up amplifiers. "How about you guys? Do you mind if I join you?" They stopped everything, shifted their weight, and didn't look at her. They certainly didn't look thrilled at the prospect of her joining the band. "Okay, let me have it, you guys. What's going on?"

"Well. . ." P.J. looked down at his shoe as he kicked at a piece of bright yellow tape on the stage. "It's just that we're concerned about you and aren't sure if it's a good time for you to do something like this. It's, well, it's a ministry. . . ," he trailed off and looked to Gabe.

"Kate, how are you doing with everything you have going on?" Gabe looked uncomfortable, too. "How do we know if you're. . .um. . .over everything?"

Ah, that's what they needed to know. "You're

asking me whether or not I'm back on the straight and narrow?"

"Pretty much. I mean, it's kind of important," P.J. said, now behind the drums.

"Sure it is. The best way I can explain myself is to tell you what a wise soul said to me yesterday on the phone." Kate winked at Mark. "I'm like Peter. I screwed up. I didn't stand up for my faith, I didn't share it with anyone, and then I made a really bad decision." Kate walked up onto the stage and looked at each of them. "But also like Peter, Jesus not only forgives me for it, but He knew it would happen. He has guided me through it, healed my relationships, and taught me a lot of things because of it. So, yes, He and I are cool."

"Works for me." Gabe turned back to the sound equipment, satisfied to drop the subject.

"That's all I wanted to know." P.J. smiled and let out a sigh of relief.

"So, in other news, Mark and I have a proposition for you guys." Kate baited them.

"What's going on?" Gabe looked confused.

"Well, we've been rustling up the Christians we know from school, and we already talked to Pastor Rick. We want to start a little Bible study/prayer group before school on Tuesday mornings." As usual, Kate's words tumbled over each other when she got excited.

Mark jumped in. "Yeah, we're feeling like we need a boost to our faith, kind of like an encouragement to live it at school. It's too easy to separate church and school."

"What a great idea." P.J. thumped the bass drum. "Count me in."

"Me, too. I'm all for it." Gabe looked excited. "Maybe we could take turns leading it or something."

"That's the spirit. I'm really excited, you guys." Kate beamed. "It starts this coming Tuesday at seven thirty."

"Now, if there's nothing else, we have some music to play." Mark hopped up onto the stage.

"Well," P.J. said, "there *is* one other thing I want to know. What's the deal with you two already?" He pointed at Mark and Kate.

They both laughed and gazed at each other with the deep love of friendship. "Should we tell them?" Kate asked, batting her eyelashes at Mark.

"Yeah, I think it's time to break their hearts. Let 'em down easy, Kate."

"P.J., Mark and I are great friends. We've decided that we're just going to keep it that way for a while."

P.J. pretended to pull a knife out of his heart.

"We just don't want to ruin a great friendship by rushing, and we don't want to find ourselves in another situation we aren't prepared for. . . . Everything in His time is better anyway, right?"

Mark didn't take his eyes off Kate and added, "All in *His* time."

My Decision

I, *(include your name here)*, have read the story of Kate Walker and have learned from the choices she made and the consequences she faced. I promise to think before I act and, in all things, to choose God's will over mine.

Additionally,

- I will never take any substance—even a legal one—that is offered to me by anyone other than a trusted adult.
- I will never take illegal drugs.
- I will guard my heart closely and not jump into a dating relationship before God says I'm ready.
- I will never be afraid to share my faith with others.

Please pray the following prayer:

Father God, I know that I am a blank slate. Please let the lessons that I learned as I read about Kate imprint on the slate of my heart.

Help me to honor my parents by making right choices and avoiding questionable situations. I want to commit to You now that I'll avoid any use of illegal drugs—please help me do that when the time comes and I'm feeling the pressure.

Also, please forgive me for the times when I haven't shared my faith with others. Help me to have the strength to do it even when it's difficult.

I know that You have everything under control, so I submit to Your will. Amen.

Congratulations on your decision! Please sign this contract signifying your commitment. Have someone you trust, like a parent or a pastor, witness your choice.

_____

Signed

_____

Witnessed by

CHECK IT OUT

For information on the latest
Scenarios books, great giveways, girl talk,
and more visit nicoleodell.com!

Also check out Teen Talk Radio at choicesradio.com—
where it's all about choices!

Find Scenarios author
Nicole O'Dell on the Web:

Web site and blog: www.nicoleodell.com/
Facebook: facebook.com/nicoleodell
Twitter: twitter.com/Nicole_Odell
Blog: nicoleodell.blogspot.com

SCENARIOS FOR GIRLS

DARE TO BE DIFFERENT

Lindsay Martin and her friends begin playing a game at sleepovers, and it all starts as harmless fun. . .until the dares become more and more risky. Drew Daniels wants to be as different from her twin sister as possible—new haircut, new clothes, new friends. . .and a boyfriend. What happens when Lindsay and Drew are faced with making difficult choices? Will they dare to be different?

SWEPT AWAY

Seniors and best friends, Amber and Brittany, are neck and neck in a good-natured competition for a car being given away by a local business. Sophomore Lilly Armstrong is always looking for ways to escape the confines of her unhappy home. What happens when Amber and Lilly are faced with making difficult choices?

Available wherever books are sold.